CLEAR SKIES

Suzanne Cass

Clear Skies

Storm Cloud Press, Perth Australia

Copyright © 2021 by Suzanne Cass

Edits by Tanya Saari

Cover by Vikncharlie

All rights reserved.

All rights reserved. No part of this publication may be reproduced, stored in a retrieval system, or transmitted in any form, or by any means, electronic, mechanical, photocopying, recording or otherwise, without permission in writing from the publisher.

This is a work of fiction. Names, characters, places and incidents are products of the authors imagination or are used fictitiously. Any resemblance to actual events, locales, organisations, or persons, living or dead, is entirely coincidental.

CHAPTER ONE

Dale Williams tipped his head to the sky and scowled at the low, gray clouds.

"Give it a break, will you?" Of course, the rain kept falling, large, fat drops landing on his already damp face. He lowered his head and let the drops create a small waterfall over the front brim of his hat. Warm, humid air swirled around him. Wet season in northern Queensland was exactly that. Wet and hot. His skin was clammy, sweat running down beneath his Drizabone. Bugger, he'd be better off without the raincoat. He shrugged out of the jacket and slung it over the handlebars of his motorcycle. Now he was getting soaked to the skin through his shirt, but at least the rain was fresh and slightly cooler.

It'd never rained this much in Montana. For the hundredth time since he'd returned to Australia a little over four months ago, he wished he was back at Stargazer Ranch. His mind drifted to the remembered image of the imposing peaks of the Bitterroot Mountains as they soared over the valley and pastures of the ranch. Snow-capped for most of the year, the clear mountain air had been crisp and cool. Unlike this humid air that was so heavy it felt like he was breathing through a wet dishcloth.

But there was no point in regrets and memories. He'd spent two years in Montana, learning the ropes from his Uncle Dean, and now he'd returned to help his mother run the Aussie equivalent. Stormcloud Station would be his one day, if he wanted it. And he did want the property. Didn't he? He'd spent most of his childhood and early adolescence working toward building this dream.

Why, then, couldn't he rid himself of this stupid ambivalence? His life was here. Not back on Stargazer. And certainly not with Violet. She'd barely even known he existed. It was stupid to be yearning for some unrequited love.

Enough of wallowing in regrets. The rain was still falling, and he needed to get across the creek before it became impassable. He pushed the button on his all-terrain motorcycle and it sputtered, but then died. Dale frowned. He pushed it again and this time it gave a few coughs, finally roaring into life. It needed a service. Which reminded him, their whole fleet of twenty ATVs needed to be serviced soon.

That thought made Dale's frown deepen. Because it also reminded him, he still hadn't installed the lockbox to house all the ATV keys back in the machinery shed. He should do that today. It'd been a suggestion from Senior Sergeant Robinson after one of their ATVs had gone missing a few weeks ago. They'd finally reported it stolen when it hadn't turned up after they checked all the usual places. It was just one more thing to add to a list of odd things that'd gone missing from the station in the past month. The senior sergeant had quietly mentioned that perhaps they should keep a better eye on the staff working at the station. But that was ridiculous, all their staff had been with them for years, and were completely trustworthy.

Dale brushed the worrying thoughts aside and hit the accelerator, letting the motorcycle weave through the sparse eucalyptus trees, the front wheel flattening the long tussock grass as he went. A large bottle tree loomed in his path and he had to veer around the enormous trunk. At least the cattle were safe, he'd pushed them through the gate into North Paddock, where they could find higher ground.

His 4WD Land Cruiser ute appeared as a white smudge through the rain, right where he'd left it, parked on the road verge. He tucked his chin onto his chest, to keep as much rain out of his eyes as possible, while he steered across the last paddock toward the fence.

The ramp was exactly how he'd left it, leading onto the tray bed of the 4WD. He lined the motorcycle up and drove the bike up in one easy, practiced move, hooking the front wheel into the custom-built stand. Motorcycle secure, he slid into the driver's seat, plonking his sodden Akubra hat and Drizabone down on the floor beside him.

Time to get back to the lodge where he could get out of his soaking wet clothes and dry off. He checked his watch. Almost smoko time. Perhaps Skylar would have some of her famous pumpkin-and-wattleseed scones ready to come out of the oven. They were meant for the paying guests, but he was good at wheedling a couple of the warm treats from his older sister. She had a soft spot for him, and he exploited that fact whenever he could—mostly over her baked goods.

The 4WD roared to life, and he flicked the wipers on as he did a U-turn in the road and headed toward Stormcloud. The only thing that stood between him and those scones was Corella Creek, the largest watercourse this side of the property, not counting Jimbu River farther to the east. At least he didn't need to cross that one today, or he might well have been left stranded. Moving the cattle had taken him little more than an hour, and while the rain had remained constant, the creek shouldn't have risen too far in that time. It might become impassable later, but with his truck it shouldn't be a problem now.

He hoped Steve's predictions were wrong. The last thing they needed was a flood, especially this early in the season. It was only mid-November, and they still had plenty of bookings at the lodge. They were used to lots of water around here; by the end of the season, the lower floodplains often resembled a large, inland sea. The main lodge was never affected by flooding, however, as it'd been built in the rocky hills and rises surrounding Mount Mulligan. January and February were usually the wettest, and considered low season for bookings. It was the primary reason they closed down over those months; it gave them time to rest and recuperate. He was already looking forward to those few weeks of peace.

Dale peered through the increasing sheets of rain. Cresting the last rise, he held his breath as the creek came into view. It didn't look too high.

What the hell…?

Dale stamped on the brake, bringing the truck to an abrupt halt.

The creek had risen a little since he'd crossed it earlier, but remained low enough for him to get home. That wasn't what had made him stop so suddenly, however.

It was the small, white car heading into the water on the other side of the crossing. What the hell did they think they were doing? That vehicle wouldn't make it through. The water was over two feet deep already; it'd be over the doors as quick as… Even as he had the thought, sure enough, the water swirled around the front of the car, rising up the sides and covering the doorsills as it drove deeper into the creek.

He honked the horn, trying to get the driver's attention, to stop this madness. But they kept plowing through the muddy water. The creek crossing was about a hundred yards wide. The station manager, Steve, had demanded they pay for a concrete base, so the waterway was always stable, no matter how high or torrential Corella Creek became. But even so, this was no place for a little hatchback to be attempting a crossing.

He watched in growing horror as the vehicle made it a third of the way across. The car was a Toyota Corolla, if he wasn't mistaken—the preferred compact car for a lot of young city women—and he knew the water would be covering the tailpipe, and already half-way up the engine mount by now. The car slowed, its forward motion reducing to a crawl, before it came to a juddering standstill. Just as he'd predicted, the water was too high, and the engine had stalled.

Stupid bloody tourists. Why couldn't they learn? This wasn't the bloody city. Not even close. They were all the same, totally unprepared for the conditions up here and completely clueless when it came to their own survival. This couldn't be guests staying at Stormcloud, they were usually flown in by helicopter, or ferried in one of the large, 4WD buses bought specifically for the job. Who the hell would be out here in the middle of nowhere in weather like this?

He had half a mind to leave them right where they were.

The only problem with that uncharitable thought was their vehicle sat right in the middle of the concrete floodway and was now blocking his access. If he was to get home, he'd need to help whoever was in that car to move it. Besides, he wouldn't really leave anyone stranded out here, it wasn't his style. There was an unwritten rule in the outback; leave no one abandoned by the side of the road. People could die out here. But it got his goat when individuals did stupid things without thinking.

Dale opened his door and stood on the runner, sheltering his face from the rain with his hand. "Oi, who's there?" he yelled.

After a second, the driver's side window slowly wound down, and a face appeared in the gap.

It was a young woman. Large, shadowed eyes regarded

him from a shapely face, long honey-colored hair pulled into a ponytail. She didn't answer.

"Are you alone?"

The woman hesitated, before giving one, quick nod.

Damn. He was hoping someone else was with her, preferably a large, beefy guy, then perhaps he could've asked him to help get a rope attached to the front of the car and tow it out with his 4WD. This woman looked so slight; the torrent might sweep her away if she even set one foot in it. He could do it on his own, he supposed. It really was a two-man job, however. As he stood in the door of his car considering his options, a surge of muddy water hit the Corolla. The vehicle moved sideways a fraction. Shit. That wasn't good. The water was still rising, and with all this continuous rain, the level was increasing quickly.

Her predicament got more precarious by the second. Not only was she driving a completely unsuitable car in terrible weather on roads she clearly knew nothing about, but she was doing it alone. And now she was about to be swept downriver at any second.

She was still staring at him warily out the window, probably unaware of how much danger she was in. She hadn't actually spoken yet, which intrigued him slightly. Most women would either be screaming hysterically, or at the very least begging him for help.

He decided.

"I want you to put your car into neutral. Can you do that for me?"

She gave him a quizzical glance, but he could see her look down and fiddle with the gearshift.

"Good. I'm going to use my truck to push you backward, out of the water. You're going to have to steer, to make sure your wheels don't drop off the floodway. Okay?" He had to yell to make himself heard over the heavy rain beating off the roof of his truck.

Did she even understand what he was asking her? Dale had never attempted this maneuver himself, but he'd seen Steve do it when he was younger. If he connected gently, the front bumper of the Corolla shouldn't suffer too much damage. The way that water kept rising, though, it wasn't going to matter for too much longer, anyway, because the car was going to be swept away. The big bull bar on his truck would protect it from harm.

"But I want to be on that side of the river." His head jerked up at the sound of her voice. She pointed to his truck. "I need to keep going that way." Her tone was cool and demanding, like she wouldn't take no for an answer.

He shook his head. Didn't she realize that even if he got her safely out of the water, her car would be undriveable?

"No can do," he yelled back at her. She looked like she was going to argue, but he ducked into the cab and closed the door.

Putting the truck into gear, he slowly edged forward. His 4WD easily cut through the water, and he was in the middle of the floodway within seconds.

There was a loud bang, and the little white car moved a couple of inches sideways. Shit, it must've been hit by floating debris. A dead log or heavy branch that'd fallen in the water. He needed to hurry. The girl didn't scream, however, and she went up a few notches in his estimation. But her face finally took on an edge of fear as she stared at him through the windshield. He didn't blame her; his heart was going a million miles an hour at the thought of what he was about to attempt.

Dale sucked in a fortifying breath and realigned his bull bar with the front of her car. Then, ever so gently, he drove forward until their vehicles were touching. He gave it a little gas, and they moved together a few inches. There was another loud bang and his truck shuddered under the impact of something heavy. Bugger. There was a ton of debris in the water. At least this one had hit his truck and not the Corolla. He needed to move her. Now.

He touched the gas pedal again, and the car was rolling in front of him, headed out of the water. Thank God, Steve's trick seemed to be working. He could see the girl over the bonnet of his truck through the windshield, she was so close now. Eyes wide, and mouth drawn back in a half-grimace of panic. Then, a flicker of determination crossed her features, and she turned her head to peer through the rear window, guiding the car up the steep incline toward the security of the gravel road.

It took less than twenty seconds to push the little car out of the flowing water and onto shore. He kept going, indicating for her to steer the car off the side of the road, so they could park it out of the way. He stopped his truck and turned off the ignition. She was safe. They were both safe.

The adrenaline left his body in a rush, and he tipped his head against the backrest of his seat. Wow, that'd been intense.

Now that he had them both out of danger on the other side, his anger at the stupidity of it all returned. This girl was going to get a piece of his mind. He'd possibly saved her life, and he was entitled to vent his exasperation.

He opened his door, rammed his Akubra on his head and marched over to the driver's side door, which was already opening. In that split second, he caught his first full look at the woman. Even with straggling, wet hair, and face flushed pink from the heat and danger of her situation, she was extremely beautiful. Her skin had a dusky hue, the color somewhere between polished copper and the espresso he liked to drink in the morning. And those eyes, wide and blue-green, reminding him of a fresh flush of young eucalyptus leaves in the summer.

He had to remind himself that whatever excuse she had, it wouldn't be good enough. He didn't want to hear it.

"Thank you, I don't…" Her gratitude died on her lips as he fixed her with a steely gaze.

"Of all the crazy, stupid things to do. If that water had been any deeper, you could've been swept away. Why would you cross a flooded creek in this little…?" He waved a hand in the car's direction, unable to communicate his complete astonishment that she could have tried something so foolhardy. He didn't wait for her to reply. "This car is completely inappropriate for this country, not suited to the rough, dirt roads at all. What if I hadn't come along when I did?"

He stood back, hoping his words had got through. Those olive-green eyes narrowed in his direction, and a red flush crept up her neck to replace the pretty pink hue as her beautiful face turned hard. A flicker of doubt crossed his mind. Perhaps he could've toned his admonition down a bit.

She put her hands on her hips. "Who the bloody hell do you think you are? Bloody Sir Lancelot, or something?"

He almost laughed. She had an attitude, that was for sure. Standing there in the pelting rain as if she owned the road. He gave her a quick, assessing look, before returning his gaze to meet her eyes. She was tall, almost came up to his chin, which would make her around five-foot eight or nine, perhaps. Long-limbed and willowy to the point of being thin. She wore denim shorts, sneakers and a light blue tank top with flowers all over it, her brown skin slick with rain.

"I've driven these roads in this car lots of times. I don't need some hick cowboy to tell me what to do," she said, ignoring the rivulets of water running down her face.

What the hell? "Even if that hick cowboy just rescued your ass?" he asked, anger giving way to incredulity. But even as he spoke, his mind was ticking over, trying to determine if her words were true. If she had been driving these roads, been in the area, like she claimed, why hadn't he seen her before?

"Which I was about to thank you for, if you hadn't been such a meathead about the whole thing. You men and your bloody egos. You're more trouble than you're worth most of the time."

Where had that come from? He was pretty sure he didn't deserve that. That sounded more like the woman had issues of her own going on.

He took a deep breath. Time to get this conversation back on an even keel. He was already soaked through, but he'd like to get out of this rain, if possible.

"Look, I'm sorry I yelled at you." He held out a hand. "I'm Dale Williams. I work over at Stormcloud Station."

She continued to stare at him, and he was just about to lower his hand in frustration, when she reached out and took it.

"I'm...Daisy." She pursed her full lips. Was it his imagination, or had she not wanted to tell him her name? "And if you'll let me finish what I started to say earlier, thank you for getting me out of there." Her hand was warm and wet in his. Slim fingers lay against his wrist. Her touch was like...like time had slowed to a crawl, and they were the only two people in the world.

He shook his head and let go of her hand. He had no idea where that addled notion had come from.

Daisy. Cute name, it suited her.

"Now, can you please help me get across the creek? I need to keep going that way." She pointed back the way he'd come.

"I'm not going anywhere but Stormcloud. That creek is too dangerous to cross now. You'll have to come with me."

Her gaze went from furious frustration to outright fear as she considered his words.

"I can't go with you. I need to get across the creek. You don't understand..." Her words faltered, and she stared at him. "I've got to get home to him."

"Who?" Dale asked.

CHAPTER TWO

The reality of what this man was saying finally hit Daisy. She was stuck here. On this side of Corella Creek. Her mind had refused to believe it might be true, even as he rescued her from the flood. The creek was swollen beyond anything she could've imagined. When she'd driven through it yesterday on her way into town, it'd been the normal sluggish trickle she'd been used to. Sure, she'd only been in the area for a month, and she'd probably used the crossing less than half a dozen times, but how could things have changed so drastically and so quickly? It was one more lesson this country was forcing her to learn.

She needed to get to the outstation. Back to her brother, River. He would be worried about her. She was supposed to have returned this morning, but had got caught up waiting for the motorcycle part River needed. The delivery truck was late bringing it into the mechanic shop. Daisy wasn't known for her patience, but she'd had no choice but to wait. River was determined to get the motorcycle working again. It was the only thing that afforded him any freedom; a way to get around the property. Then he wasn't completely reliant on her and her run-down Corolla. The motorcycle had broken down four days ago, and it'd taken River a day to figure out what was wrong and one more day to get the part ordered in. He'd been like a caged bear the whole time. Daisy needed to stock up on food anyway, so it was a no-brainer that she head into town to pick it up.

She wasn't going to tell this man standing in the rain next to her any of that, however. She'd made a rookie mistake of mentioning there was someone else, and now she needed to cover her tracks. At least she'd remembered to give him her nickname, instead of her actual name. Replaying her cover story in her mind, she glanced up at the man, who was still staring at her with incredulity written all over his face. Had he mentioned Stormcloud Station? It sounded like he was from there.

The panic was still there, clawing around the edges of her belly, trying to escape, but she tamped it down. There was no way she could contact River to let him know what was going on. She'd have to hope he used his common sense and stayed put, and wait for her to return.

"Who do you need to get back to?" the man asked again.

She glanced up at him through the rain. He'd lost that holier-than-though tone from before, when he'd given her a tongue-lashing about driving into the creek. But it didn't mean he'd gone up in her estimation. Most men were dicks. At least, they were in her world.

"Oh…it's only my work colleague." She waved a hand dismissively, forcing her face into a bland smile. "He'll be wondering where I am. But it's okay, he'll understand I got stuck in this storm. He'll be fine." Which was probably a lie. River would be anything but calm. He'd be fretting about her like there was no tomorrow. He hated to be alone. She crossed her fingers behind her back and prayed he wouldn't do anything stupid; like get it into his head to come looking for her. River was so…unreliable. Was that the right word? She could think of at least a dozen others that might also fit.

Irresponsible. Reckless. Clueless. With a chip on his shoulder. But he was her brother, and she had no option but to overlook all his faults and love him unconditionally. Because as his big sister, that was her job.

The man's—Dale, she had to remember to call him Dale—face changed. It lost that hard edge, his brow wrinkling in concern.

"I've got a sat phone in the car. Do you want to try and call him?"

Wouldn't that be the perfect solution? If only River had a satellite phone, or a cell phone, or even if there was a landline at the outstation. But she had their only means of communication on the front seat of the car, an old iPhone that was out of charge.

"He hasn't got a phone," she said, much more breezily than she felt. "But that's okay, he'll figure it out."

"What about you, then?"

"What?" She wasn't sure what he meant.

"Do you have anywhere you can go until the creek drops?"

Oh. He was right. River wasn't the only one in trouble. What the hell was she supposed to do now? She had nowhere to go.

"I…ah…hadn't really thought about it. I guess, I'll stay here in the car and wait til the creek goes down. Then I can drive across as soon as it's safe."

The incredulous look returned to Dale's face. He opened his mouth and shut it again, as if trying to decide what to say. "Apart from the fact it could take days for the creek to go down, you know your engine will have water damage, don't you? Even if you let it dry out, and even if it does actually start, you shouldn't drive it. You could harm the pistons or the head."

Sheesh, she didn't know that. Although common sense should've told her so. Why had she been so stupid? Why had she thought she could get through the creek? Now, not only was she stranded on the wrong side, but she may well have wrecked their only means of transport, as well. She should've known better; she had spent a few years up in the top end of the Northern Territory living with her extended family, so she was no stranger to tropical weather. Creeks and waterway were notoriously dangerous in these kinds of downpours. But her thoughts of getting back to River had overwhelmed any sense of logic. And now she was trapped.

Standing out in the pelting rain was really annoying her, she had to keep wiping the drops away from her face. She was soaked through, her car was a wreck, she was stuck in the middle of godforsaken nowhere, while River was at the outstation getting up to who-knew-what. And she had boxes of perishable food in the rear seat that would spoil, if they were left out in this humidity much longer. She'd spent most of her remaining money on those supplies, they were supposed to last for the next month, she couldn't lose it all now. Could her day get any worse?

"Sorry, I didn't know." She took a step backward and her foot nearly landed on one of those horrible, ugly cane toads that were absolutely everywhere up here. She stepped around it, screwing her face up in disgust. She was completely out of her element. Which was a tad ironic, if you took her indigenous heritage into account. Born and bred in the city of Perth, she had no idea how to survive in this rugged country. But then, if it hadn't been for River, she'd still be happy and safe back in Perth, probably on her way to a lecture at the uni, right about now. She'd put her whole life on hold for her brother. The urge to put her head in her hands and cry was strong. But she didn't do that. Cry in front of strangers. A heavy weight settled in her stomach, and a weary fatigue settled into her bones.

Dale stood silently beside her, but he seemed to debate

something internally as he pursed his lips and looked at her. She avoided his gaze. The last thing she wanted was his scorn. She had more than enough self-flagellation to go around for the both of them.

"It looks like you'll have to come to Stormcloud with me."

She flashed a look up at him. "You'd do that?" Kindness—decency—wasn't something she was used to. Daisy got away with a lot of things others from her culture didn't, because of her looks. She understood that being attractive had unlocked a lot of doors for her that'd normally stay shut. But she was also extremely aware of the insidious racism found everywhere. Had encountered it in every form. Which was why his simple compassion shocked her. Now, she felt a little ashamed of the way she'd attacked him earlier. Her sharp tongue was her self-defense mechanism, and she knew even some of her best friends considered her prickly. She was working on taming her temper, but it didn't always work. And this poor guy had only been trying to help.

"Of course." He gave her a look that said he thought she was crazy even to ask. "We look after each other out here. Besides, my mum would kill me if she found out I'd left you here."

Dale smiled for the first time that day, and Daisy was almost knocked backwards. Oh. Wow. He had the most gorgeous dimples. They brought his face to life. She was momentarily mesmerized. Now that she took the time to look, even with the hat pulled down to keep the rain off, he was not just good-looking; he was stunningly attractive. What was a bloke like this doing out here? In the middle of bloody nowhere. His wet jeans clung to impressive thighs and his equally sodden shirt lay flat against his skin, showing off plenty of hardened muscles underneath.

She stopped to consider how she might look. Bedraggled, was probably one way to describe herself. Her clothes were completely wet through, and her hair was coming down from its ponytail and hanging in wet strands around her face. There wasn't a trace of makeup on her face. But then again, that was nothing new. Since she'd been here, in North Queensland, there'd been no reason for her to wear makeup, let alone a pretty dress.

Could she do that? Go off with this gorgeous stranger to his station to take shelter? She probably didn't have too many other options.

Dale continued, "I'll get Steve to come and look at your car when the rain stops. He's not a licensed mechanic, but he knows his way around just about any engine. If it needs to be towed to town, we can organize that for you, too."

"Thank you, that would be great." She nodded her appreciation. "Who's Steve?"

"The station manager. And my stepdad," Dale added, with the slightest hint of hesitation. "He's a good bloke, you'll like him." Dale stopped speaking then and ducked his head, almost as if he'd said too much.

She used his silence to weigh up her options. Which weren't many. There was only one choice, really. That was to leave her car here, where she hoped it'd be safe, and join this man. She screwed up her face in resigned frustration.

"I've got food in my car that needs to go in a refrigerator. Is it okay if I bring it?"

"Sure, let me give you a hand." He already had the rear door open, and was pulling out one of the large boxes. Daisy took hold of the other box, also grabbing the bag with the motorcycle part, her small backpack containing her overnight stuff, and her phone from the front seat. She'd only been planning on one night away, so she had no change of clothes, but there was a toothbrush and a hairbrush in there, which would help.

Dale shoved his box onto the rear seat of his truck, and she did the same. Then he beckoned her into the dry cabin. It was a relief to be out of the rain. The seats were getting wet from the water cascading off their bodies, but Dale didn't seem to mind. He started the truck, and they were on their way toward the most famous station in far north Queensland.

Of course, she'd heard of Stormcloud Station. Everyone in the district knew of the luxury eco-resort hidden at the base of the Mulligan Escarpment, a part of the Atherton Tablelands. It catered to celebrities and rich people. Yindi, River's friend at the aboriginal community over at Koongarra Station where they were staying, had told her it cost over two-thousand dollars a night to stay there. Daisy could never afford to stay at a place like that. Why would she want to, anyway? It didn't mean she wasn't curious, however.

Silence surrounded them as Dale negotiated the deep puddles forming in the road. Silence was good. It meant she didn't need to censor every word that came out of her mouth.

But it wasn't meant to last.

"It's strange, I haven't seen you around at all. Out here, we're acquainted with all our neighbors," Dale said.

She didn't appreciate his probing tone, and even though she'd anticipated his question, she snapped out the first words that came to mind. "Yes, well, if I hadn't got stuck in that bloody creek, you probably still wouldn't know I even existed." Why the hell did country people think they had a God given right to interfere in everyone else's business?

It was only when Dale glanced her way that she realized she'd said the wrong thing. Something a lot like suspicion hovered in his brown eyes. Shit, she needed to backtrack, and fast, because the last thing she wanted was for him to think she was hiding something. That she'd been staying out of sight on purpose.

"Sorry, that was aimed more at me, than you." She added a dose of apology, and what she hoped was a hint of self-criticism. "I'm still mad at myself for trying to drive through that creek."

He raised an eyebrow, but didn't comment. Which she thought might've taken a whole lot of self-control on his part.

Trying to get the conversation back on track, she said, "Sorry, what were you saying?"

"I was going to ask, where did you say you were staying?" Yep, it looked like he had a knack for driving straight to the heart of the very topic she didn't want to talk about. She snuck a quick peek at him. The puzzled look was back, his brow wrinkling in that charming way he had. He reminded her of an adorable puppy, with those big, brown eyes.

"Oh, yeah." She gave what she hoped was a nonchalant shrug. "My colleague and I are staying out at Koongarra. You know it?"

"Sure, I know it." Did she just imagine the slight frown that crossed his features? But it was gone before she could be sure. When she didn't give him any more information, he asked, "Are you staying up at the homestead? Working for Bryan?"

"Sort of." She bit her lip. This was the first time she'd had to use their made-up story. Would it stand up to his scrutiny? She didn't want to mention they were staying at the Back Paddock Outstation on the edge of the property, if she didn't have to. The less he knew, the better. "The Kuku Community Group have asked my colleague and I to do a bit of consulting for them."

"Oh, yeah." Dale kept his eyes fixed on the wet road, but she could almost feel the tension rise in the cab. "That's... interesting. What kind of consulting?"

"They've asked for an environmental assessment of the property." She hid her small grimace. She was studying environmental law at uni—was in her fourth and final year. And while she knew a lot of the correct terms and language, could probably fool the locals pretty well, it was a fair stretch to go from understanding environmental law to being a proper ecologist bent on conservation, which was what she was purporting to be.

"They have?" The slight uptick in Dale's tone was his only giveaway. His interest had turned to anxiety. She knew her cover story might cause people around here to become nervous. Use of an *environmental consultant* by an Aboriginal group was sometimes code for the group getting ready to make land claims in the area. She needed to allay his fears.

"Yeah, they want to expand their interests. The cattle make them a good living, but they want something more sustainable, more environmentally friendly, to make the best use of the land." She hesitated, wracking her brain to come up with some options she'd looked up as part of her cover story. "You know there are plenty of avocado farms around here already?" Dale merely nodded as she continued, "So, starting their own orchard might be a good idea. Or Macadamia nuts, perhaps. There's a ballooning market for those overseas. Setting up their own beehives is another option. They're even talking about starting their own art community. We're going to look at all of those options, plus more and give them a plan."

The Kuku Group was a group of elders from the Koongarra Station Aboriginal Community who ran the cattle station. As part of the homeland movement, where indigenous people moved home to their traditional lands, the Djungan people had bought the run-down station with the help of government funding and then organized Bryan as the station manager to help bring it back to life. They then used their own people from their small but committed community as station hands to carry out the work required. They were doing a good job of turning the station into a profitable commodity. A great example for other groups around the county to look up to.

"Wow, that sounds…interesting. I didn't know they were considering expanding into other viable markets. I'll be interested to see what you recommend. Maybe we can get some tips, too," he said, smiling. His eyes crinkled up when he laughed. It was endearing, and Daisy found herself staring, not really concentrating on his words any longer.

"So, you and your work colleague are here for what…? A few months?"

"Yes, that's right. We need time to examine and document the country and then consider all the options. My work partner, Ri… Ryan, has a family link with the Djungan people." Had he noticed her stumble over his name? She plowed on, regardless. "Ryan's here to help me liaise with them." Which was only partly a lie. They did have a link to the Djungan people, only through a friend of their mother.

But this was also where their cover story fell down. River would never pass as any sort of professional. His spiked, blonde hair—naturally blond, although most people found it hard to believe when they saw the dark color of his skin— numerous facial piercings, and tattoos, were a dead giveaway. Never mind the attitude he projected. Like he was still in Perth with his gang, taking part in their petty crimes and blustering bravado.

Much good that'd do him, however, because that very same gang believed he'd betrayed them and they were now hunting him to exact their revenge.

But as long as Dale never met River face-to-face, then everything would be fine. Because if he happened to see River, their cover might well be blown. River's face was plastered all over the police wanted lists back in Western Australia. Which was the other reason they'd fled to North Queensland, hoping to escape detection.

The police wanted to arrest him as an accessory to murder.

His gang wanted to kill him to send a message to other's who might want to double-cross them.

They were being hunted by the law and the law-breakers alike.

But she'd be damned if she'd let either of them have him.

CHAPTER THREE

Dale let his gaze leave the road for a second, checking out Daisy's profile as she stared fixedly through the windshield. Was she avoiding his gaze? Something about her words didn't ring true. And why had she snapped at him like a rabid dog when he asked why he hadn't seen her around before? It'd been an innocent enough question. It was almost as if she was hiding something. When you lived in the country, you needed to know your neighbors because you often relied on them, especially in times of trouble. There was an implicit trust between neighbors; between all country people. Which was why vehicles and houses were left unlocked.

But it was also why one of their ATVs had gone missing.

He gave a small shrug and returned his attention to the dirt road, which was becoming more treacherous by the minute. This rain wasn't letting up. Which didn't bode well for Daisy getting across that creek anytime soon. The rain had brought out hundreds of those pesky cane toads and they were throwing themselves at his car tires. Oh well, a few more dead cane toads were never a bad thing.

The turnoff to the station appeared, and Dale pulled the truck to a halt. The worst thing about living on a luxury cattle station was that no matter how luxurious you made it, you nevertheless had to open the gates by hand. And this was no ordinary gate; it towered twice as high as the 4WD, and it was made of ornately curved wrought iron. He jumped out of the truck, jogged to the gate, unlatched it, and was back in the car in twenty seconds. Long enough to become soaked all over again, however.

"I could've done that for you," Daisy said, as he drove through the opening.

"It's all good, I'm still wet from before." He smiled and jumped out to close the gate again. When he returned, he said, "We use cattle grids on most of the rest of the property to keep the cows in their respective paddocks. Mum thought it'd look better, having some impressive monstrosity of a gate for the guests to arrive through."

Daisy laughed at that. The first time she'd really let go of her smile since he found her in the creek. It was a nice laugh; she had a deep voice for a woman, husky with a smoky edge to it.

The drive to the lodge took less than five minutes. Dale could just make out the shadow of the escarpment through the heavy rain, hovering high above the clearing where the resort nestled. His mother wouldn't be happy that he'd brought home a stray. The resort was at full capacity this week. But they'd find a bed for her somewhere. Daisy could probably stay in the staff quarters, there was a spare room, since Paula had left at the beginning of season. Now, Alek *would* be happy with that. The Polish man was renowned for appreciating the ladies, even if most of them turned him down.

Daisy sat up straighter as the trees opened up to reveal the lodge and all of its out buildings. Admittedly, it was a washed-out, smudged version of the true thing, seeing it through the driving rain, but Dale knew Daisy would be impressed. Everyone who saw the place couldn't fail to be impacted in some way. The billabong was the first thing to come into view. On a calm day, the billabong was a scene of tranquility. As large as a football oval and festooned with water lilies, lush, green growth surrounded it on three sides. The fourth side was a long, grassy slope, leading up to a huge wooden deck with an infinity pool and plenty of deck chairs and gazebos scattered around, right out the front of the main lodge.

"Wow, it's gorgeous," Daisy exclaimed, eyes bright.

He felt an absurd stab of pride, and he let out a breath. For some reason, he'd wanted Daisy to be impressed. Which was silly; she was a stranger he'd rescued from a flood, nothing more. It was the first feeling of connection he'd had to the station since he'd returned from Stargazer. Along with that connection came the realization that he should be proud. He'd had a hand in the original design of the place, in helping to build a lot of those huts and the main lodge. His mum and Steve took most of the credit, sure. But he'd poured the majority of his time into helping this station become what it was today—foregoing the chance to attend university so that he could stay on and help.

He watched her out of the corner of his eye as he drove past the set of eight individual huts strung out around the western edge of the billabong. Her head swiveled in every direction, as if she couldn't take it all in at once.

The road skirted the huts and then wound around to the rear of the main lodge. It was a bespoke building that his mum designed, made from locally sourced timber, with soaring windows that let you take in the stunning scenery from almost every spot inside the building. He bypassed the main rear parking lot, and stopped as close to the kitchen door as he could.

"Let's take your boxes in, first. We'll find a spot for them somewhere."

"Great, thank you." She jumped out of the passenger seat and crawled in the back seat to snag her backpack and one of the boxes. Which left him holding the door open and looking at her nicely shaped rear end wriggling around as she tried to juggle the box. He took a step backward and only just managed to divert his gaze in time as she stepped down onto the sodden, red earth. It wouldn't do to get caught ogling the rescued woman's butt. Even if it was one of the nicest he'd seen in a while. And those long, bronze legs. They were about damn near perfect.

He leaned in and grabbed the other box, then led the way as they ran the few steps to the door, and he held it open as she dashed through. He followed her in, and nearly slammed straight into the back of her when she stopped, mouth open, staring.

"Holy hell," she breathed. "I thought you said this was a kitchen?"

He stopped and looked around. The air conditioning was the first thing he noticed, cool air flowing past his face, wiping away the perspiration from the humidity outside.

"Yeah, well, Skylar is pretty particular when it comes to her food prep areas." Now he thought about it, the place was somewhat intimidating, with all the stainless-steel countertops, state-of-the-art appliances, and sharp-edged efficiency. It was a first-class chef's kitchen, and it showed. But then, the food Skylar prepared was also first class, and she kept even the fussiest of guests satisfied, so his mum was more than happy to spend the extra money to bring the kitchen up to Skylar's standards.

A petite woman, hair tied up in a severe bun, appeared through the door to the hallway.

"Hey, bro," she called.

"Hey, sis." Even as he spoke, he lifted his nose, trying to

see if he could discover the wonderful aroma of freshly baked scones. And there it was. That slightly sweet, warm, buttery smell. Fantastic, she'd made the pumpkin scones after all.

"Meet Daisy." He gestured belatedly to the woman standing beside him.

"Hi, Daisy," Skylar said, not hiding the question in her tone. "I'm Skylar, chef at this joint. And his sister." Her gaze flicked to the boxes they were carrying and their bedraggled appearance, then her blue eyes fixed on him, one eyebrow raised.

"Nice to meet you." Daisy nodded her head politely, but perhaps struck dumb by the size of place, said nothing more.

"Her car got stuck in the creek," Dale said hurriedly, heading his sister off at the pass, because he could already see her forming the wrong idea as to what was going on here. "I brought her here to wait out the storm, because she has nowhere else to go."

"Fair enough," Skylar replied, but the eyebrow remained raised, and he could read all sorts of unasked questions hovering behind her smile. "Welcome to Stormcloud. I'm guessing you need to store that food somewhere." She pointed to a large, steel door in the far corner. "There's plenty of space in the big cool room, drop them in there."

Daisy shot Dale an astonished look that said *you have a big cool room?* but she didn't voice her disbelief. He led the way, opening the door and finding a shelf at the back that'd fit both of her boxes of food. It was mainly fresh, healthy produce, he noted. Fruit and veg, cheese, bread, and packets of meat at the bottom. Enough to feed two people for a few weeks, at least. Those boxes told him a lot about her. That she definitely wasn't used to living out here in far north Queensland. There was no tinned food, no dried staples, such as flour or sugar, or even pasta. All the basic foods that people who lived a long way from a supermarket were used to surviving on. All the foods you relied on when the electricity was out, or the roads were impassable for weeks, sometimes months, at a time.

"Daniella's not happy." Skylar called to him as he shut the door to the cool room behind him. She always called their mother by her first name, had done so ever since they were teenagers. To this day, Dale couldn't figure out why. To him their mother was always just Mum. "We're flat out trying to find things for the guests to do in all this rain. Some of them are getting restless. She's got Alek all in a tizzy about organizing a games night." She leaned against the steel countertop, checking a timer on the shelf above.

"I can imagine," Dale muttered. Poor Alek. He was the activities manager for the resort, plus he helped fill in any gaps if they needed help around the station. When Skylar was feeling in a mood, she'd sometimes call him the local dog's body. Alek often liked to boast that he was the complete opposite of your typical Polish man. He was effervescent and friendly, could talk the hind leg off a donkey. Perfect for making the guests feel at home, and Dale got on well with the man. Dale sighed. It probably meant he'd be roped in to help with whatever games Alek had in mind tonight. But that might be good if Daisy joined in, as well. It'd keep her mind off being stuck here and stop her worrying about her work colleague so much. She seemed to be overly concerned about a mere workmate. But who was he to judge? Perhaps there was more to it than she was letting on. Perhaps they were sleeping together, having an office affair. The thought struck an unusual note inside his chest. A hot, heavy flame licked the inside of his ribcage. Something like jealousy. But of course, he couldn't be jealous, he barely even knew the woman.

The timer trilled suddenly, the shrill noise making Daisy jump beside him. Skylar bent down and retrieved a tray from the oven underneath the countertop, positioning it onto the steel counter.

"Mm, my favorite. I thought I could smell these." He reached greedy fingers toward the tray.

Skylar batted his hand away as he stretched out for one of the buttery, yellow scones. "These are for the guests," she said, with a mock frown.

"But you always bake extra, just for me. Right?" He took off his Akubra, so he could look her properly in the eye. She wouldn't refuse him, would she?

Daisy watched their sibling interplay silently, and he wondered what she thought of all this.

Skylar silently put two plates on the counter and then transferred two scones to each. "Don't tell Alek I let you have these." The frown was still settled between her brows. "Or Steve, for that matter. They'll think I'm playing favorites and then they'll hound me until I give them some, too."

Dale put his arm around her and kissed her on the top of the head. "You're the best, sis."

Skylar didn't reply, which was unusual, because she always had to have the last word. Instead, she glared at the cool room, as if she could burn a hole right through the metal door.

"What's up?" he asked, troubled by the look on her face.

"What?" She glanced up at him, almost as if she'd forgotten he was still there. "Oh, it's nothing…it's just…"

He waited patiently while she seemed to struggle with the question of whether to tell him what was bothering her.

"You're sure you put three packs of steaks in the cool room for me the other day?"

"Yes, I'm sure. I asked Pete to cut me thirty steaks, and I watched him wrap them up," Dale replied. Pete was their local butcher mate, who came out to the station once a month to help them slaughter and then butcher enough cattle to keep the resort well-stocked, so they could feed the guests home-grown beef.

"And I believe you, because I saw them in there two days ago. Well, I can only find two packs in the cool room, now," Skylar said, worrying her bottom lip between her teeth. "But I'm not blaming you," she added hurriedly when Dale stood up to his full height next to her.

She better not blame him, because he was sure he'd put three packs in there, ten steaks in each pack, enough to feed all the guests and the staff for one meal, with a few extra left over just in case. And while he had been known to play games with Skylar and move things or hide them just to mess with her mind, he wasn't responsible this time. But a pack of steaks couldn't grow legs and walk away. They had to be in there somewhere.

"Do you want me to go and take a look?" he offered, placing the plate of scones back on the countertop.

"No, no," she grumbled. "Never mind. It just means I'll have to get creative with dinner tonight."

"Are you sure?" he asked, trying, and failing, to keep the hopeful note out of his voice. The smell of those warm scones was driving him a little crazy.

"Yeah, yeah," she grumbled. "Get out of here and leave me in peace. I need to get these out while they're hot and then start prep for dinner." She pushed him away and glared at him, giving him her normal Skylar piercing stare. "And you're wet, aren't you going to change into something dry?" He'd almost forgotten how damp he was, although the air conditioning was cooling his wet clothes. He needed to change. Daisy could probably do with a change of clothes, too. He could see goosebumps rise on her forearms from the air con.

"I will. After I've eaten," he promised. "Is Bindi giving you a hand with dinner?" Cooking gourmet meals for upwards of twenty-five people took all of Skylar's time. Bindi was her sometimes-unreliable assistant cook. She helped with lunch and dinner prep, but also liked to spend as much time as she was able at the cattle yards, or up at the stables.

"Yes, she should be here in half an hour, now get going."

Dale grabbed a knife, a jar of strawberry jam and a tub of cream from the large double-door refrigerator at the end of the counter and beckoned to Daisy. "Come with me, I know a great spot we can eat these undisturbed." He handed her the cream and jam to carry and led the way, letting the slightly odd conversation of missing steaks fade from his mind. He could sort that problem out later.

Their wet shoes made a quiet slapping sound on the deep-red, slate tiles, also sourced from the local escarpment, as he led Daisy through the maze of hallways to the family apartments at the northern end of the building.

Balancing both plates in one hand, Dale opened the door to the private living room, and poked his head through to make sure no one was there. "All clear," he said, and ushered her into the room. Steve would be out at the yards, and his mother was probably ensconced in her office, frowning at the paperwork, or heckling Alek to organize something exciting for the guests to do in the rain.

Daisy stared, her mouth half open. "Sheesh, you guys live in an amazing place. Did you know that? Even this room is gorgeous."

For the second time that day, Dale stopped and looked at where he lived, trying to see the room through a stranger's eyes. Two large couches formed an L-shape; made of soft, light-brown leather, they were extremely comfortable. Four winged easy chairs, done up in ochre-toned fabric, sat in convenient spots around the room, and two woolen rugs with Indigenous designs graced the wooden floorboards. Everything led the eye to the enormous picture window that afforded a view of the rainy billabong at the bottom of the hill, and the escarpment behind it. The room felt warm and inviting, with the rain pouring down outside.

Maybe he had become a bit too blasé about the whole place. It was a good reminder how lucky he really was to be living here. He had to remember to appreciate Stormcloud for what it was. He needed to get over this attachment he'd formed with Stargazer. Forget about his thoughts to go back to America, and perhaps live with his uncle for good. When he'd first arrived in Montana, he'd been overwhelmed by how big everything was. And how luxurious the lodge and the rest of the resort was over there. He'd started to see Stormcloud as a bit basic, second-class almost. But now he understood it wasn't second-class. It was merely understated. In typical Aussie style, everything was simple, but elegant—not overstated and flamboyant, like Americans tended to be.

Glancing over at Daisy, he thought he might even be able to get over pining for Violet, too.

Daisy had already taken a seat on one of the leather lounges and was pulling open her scone with her bare fingers. He handed her the jar of jam. "Thanks, I'm starving." She grinned up at him, a cheeky smile, full of sudden mischief, and he glimpsed the true Daisy. The one she seemed to keep hidden behind her cool façade and her sharp tongue.

"Oh, my God, these are amazing," Daisy said, through a mouthful of scone.

"I know, aren't they good?" He took a seat next to her, and opened the tub of cream, offering her a dollop from his knife. "Skylar uses wattleseeds in them. She grinds them up herself. She says that's what gives them the lovely, nutty flavor." Dale took a large bite of scone, slathered in cream and jam and then had to wait until he finished his mouthful before adding, "I don't really care how she does it, all I know is they taste great."

Daisy's wide, eucalyptus-green eyes fixed on him. "It's good that she uses native bush seeds in these. Does she use any other native foods in her cooking?"

"Yes, she does. It's part of the ethos of this whole place. We try to make everything as sustainable as it can be. And as authentically Australian. Skylar sources as much food as possible from the local area. She cooks with things like kangaroo, barramundi, and redclaw crayfish right from our billabong—even crocodile. And, of course, there's the beef we raise right here on the station."

"Hm, that's great." Her tone turned thoughtful, and he wondered if she was perhaps storing away ideas to help the Kuku Group with their plans for expansion. Perhaps they could start growing some of the more well-known native foods, create a product, and sell them to the general public— even get them into supermarkets.

As he was about to put his thoughts into words, the door of the living room opened, and Steve strode in.

He stopped when he caught sight of Dale sitting on the lounge. Steve was taller than Dale, and broader across the shoulders, still wearing his Drizabone and Akubra. Water pooled on the wooden floorboards as it dripped from his coat, but he didn't seem to notice.

"Good, you're back." Steve came forward, then seemed to notice Daisy for the first time. "Who's this?"

"This is Daisy. And I was about to come and report to you. The cattle are safe. For now. Although if we get too much more rain..." Dale trailed off as he noticed Steve staring at Daisy strangely.

"You look familiar. Have I seen you somewhere before?" Steve asked.

Dale turned to look at Daisy. She sat like a frozen statue, staring at Steve.

CHAPTER FOUR

Daisy forced a smile onto her lips.

"Nice to meet you, sir." She stood up and extended her hand. *Act normal. Act completely normal.* Her heart was galloping a million miles an hour. Please don't let him feel the tension running through her hand. "But I don't recognize you." She arched an eyebrow and looked directly into his face, as if considering his features. "I'm pretty sure we haven't met before. This is my first time in North Queensland." She gave what she hoped was an unaffected laugh. "And now I'm kinda wishing I never came."

The man Dale had called Steve took her hand, studying her face intently as he shook it. After what seemed like days, he finally said, "No, I guess you're right, we haven't met."

"Maybe I have one of those faces. You know, a common face, that looks similar to others," Daisy said.

Dale gave a cynical snort. "You have one of the least common faces I've ever seen." Then he seemed to comprehend what he'd said, and turned away to face the window. But not before she noticed a red flush creeping up his neck.

"Anyway, nice to meet you." Steve dropped her hand and turned his attention to Dale. "So, you moved those cattle?"

When Dale inclined his head in reply, Steve launched into an in-depth inquiry as to the cattle's health, their feed rations and other technical questions Daisy didn't understand or care about.

She took a step away from the duo and breathed in quietly. Holy shit, Steve's comments had rattled her badly. Her mind was whirling with scenarios. Where could he possibly have seen her before?

When she and River first fled Perth, River's face had been splashed all over the media in Western Australia. He was a person of interest in the murder of Daniel Stephens, a gang member and well-known troublemaker, as well as a small-time drug dealer. Now, she was terrified that the police had gotten wind of her involvement and released a picture of her to the media as well, in a bid to track her down. Had her face been splattered all over the newspapers, too? Daisy's breathing became ragged at the thought. *Please, please, please let it not be true.* If the police had listed her as a wanted person, then her life was truly over. And if the police knew about her, then the gang members who were hunting River might also be looking for her, too.

But even if the media had run a story about River—and perhaps one about her—in Western Australia, it was unlikely to have reached Queensland. Or at least, that's how she understood it. The cops had no reason to suspect they were in Queensland, and while they may well have alerted the police in other states to be on the lookout for the runaways, they probably wouldn't have told the newspapers. She and River were insignificant in the grand scheme of things. Surely, everything would've died down over there?

With the police, at least. She wasn't sure if River's gang would ever stop hunting for him.

She needed to call her mother. It was risky, but Evana would be able to tell her what was going on. She and her brother had been in Queensland for a month, and she'd only talked to her mother once in that time. Daisy and River had purposefully kept contact with their family to the bare minimum. The less they knew, the better. Evana had been the one who encouraged Daisy to take River and run. She was the one who'd organized a place to stay at Koongarra Station; she had a friend who owed her a favor. She'd also been the one who helped come up with a rock-solid story to fool the rest of the family, that Daisy was in the Kimberly, visiting a sick relative. So when the police questioned her whereabouts, that's what her extended family told them. Daisy had done everything her mother urged her to do. Because it would destroy her mother if River ended up in jail. Her mother hadn't been told about the other, much more dire problems she and River were facing. She'd kept the information that River's life was in danger to herself. There was absolutely nothing her parents could do to help, so it would do no good to send them into a panic. Daisy did it all alone, because she was a good daughter and a good sister, who did what was required to keep the family safe.

If she called her mother, she'd have to be careful her father didn't answer. Evana had purposefully kept him in the dark. Because he would've turned them in. Scott Lewis was a good man. He'd played for the West Coast Eagles football team in his youth, and had even coached some of the state WAFL teams after his career as a player ended. He was respected in the community. A pillar of hope, and a champion for their culture. He'd believed the story that Evana told him about Daisy returning to the Kimberly. Partly because Aunty Sharia really was sick, and because communication was so unreliable up there, and because her father would never in a million years believe Daisy was capable of deceit. So, Scott believed Evana's story, and helped her convince the cops it was true. Daisy had spent nearly two years on country before she started uni and had forged strong connections with some of her closer family up there. Aunty Sharia had been one of those people Daisy was devoted to, and Scott easily believed that Daisy had hopped on a plane and flown up to the isolated community to help her out. He never even thought to question why she'd left right in the middle of a police investigation into her brother's whereabouts. He trusted she knew what she was doing, and in his eyes, Aunty was equally important as River and his antics. It'd kill her dad to find out what was really going on. Daisy hung her head. And it was killing her to do this to him. If only—

Dale's voice interrupted her thoughts. "Where did you say you were from again, Daisy?"

"What?" Daisy looked up. "Oh, sorry, I was a million miles away."

"I could see that." Dale's eyes were full of concern. And something else that Daisy couldn't quite put her finger on.

"I'm from Darwin." She'd chosen the location because she knew it well enough to fool most people. Her two-year sabbatical before she started uni was spent traveling and exploring the country where her dad had been born. Reconnecting with his people; her people. Darwin was also far enough away from Perth to hopefully deflect questions about who she really was. "But I've been working for the past year at Monash University in Melbourne." Again, she'd chosen this uni to throw anyone off the scent from her study at the University of Western Australia. As long as nobody dug too deep into her story, she'd be fine.

"Ah, well, the top-end wet season won't be completely foreign to you, then." Steve said. She noticed his Drizabone was dripping on the floor. Obviously, a man who was used to someone else cleaning up after him, or who was so focused on his job that he had no time for petty things such as wet floors. The older man had a friendly face, open and honest, with kind brown eyes. She thought she might like him, given the chance.

"No," she agreed. "But this is a whole other sphere of wilderness up here. I'm sorry I got caught out, and you had to end up hosting me because of my mistake." She tipped her head on the side and gave a vulnerable half smile.

"Not a problem." Steve waved her apology away. It looked like he'd fallen for her damsel-in-distress act. Dale, on the other hand, was staring at her through narrowed eyes. He'd seen her in action this afternoon at the creek and wasn't so easily fooled.

"I need your help stabling all the horses before this storm gets any worse. Wazza radioed in to say he found a hole in the fence in Portico's paddock when he was moving the cattle this morning. He's gone back to repair that. Karri is supposed to be helping me, but I can't find her. Damn girl has disappeared again. So, it'll have to be you, I'm afraid."

"Sure thing. I'll just show Daisy to the staff quarters; she can have Paula's old room. And I'll get her some dry clothes. Then I'll be straight up." Dale gathered up their empty plates and other utensils. "See you soon," he promised, as Steve went out the door. Daisy grabbed her backpack from the floor next to the lounge where she'd dropped it, and followed Dale.

"I hope you don't mind staying in here?" He held the door open for her and she went out into the hallway.

"Not at all. Any bed is better than sleeping in my car, thank you." Daisy stopped outside the door as a thought occurred to her. "Would I be able to borrow a phone? Mine's out of charge and I've lost my charger. I'd like to call my mother. She's a worrier. She'll hear about this storm and be thinking the worst. I'd like to put her mind at ease, if that's okay." Her request might seem a little odd, but it was true that her phone was out of charge, and stupidly she'd forgotten the charger at the hotel room in town. It was also true that the less she used her mobile, the better. She was pretty sure her phone wasn't being tracked by the police, but just in case it was, it'd be prudent to use another phone.

"Yep, here, use mine. I'll organize a charger for you, if you like." He handed her his cell from out of his back pocket, then seemed to consider his words for a second, then added, "I was thinking earlier. We could always try calling Bryan, the manager, up at Koongarra. If he's around, he might take a message up to the community, to your work colleague, for you."

Daisy was lost for words. "Oh, yes…that's actually a good idea. Perhaps I'll do that from your cell, if that's okay?" That wasn't an option, but Dale didn't need to know that.

Last time Dale had mentioned Bryan, Daisy had deflected the question. Bryan was the station manager, employed by the Kuku group, and as such, he knew most of everything that went on around the station. Dale probably assumed that because she was working for the community, she was either staying at the main residence with Bryan, or in the community itself. But she'd failed to mention that she and River—Ryan, she needed to remember to call him Ryan— were actually staying in the old Back Paddock Outstation, on the far edge of the property. The outstation had been a temporary measure, hastily built ten years ago as a place to stay while the main homestead was constructed on the other side of the station. It was on the original site picked out for the permanent residence, and sheds and water tanks had already been set up, before Bryan changed his mind. After advice from a consultant, he chose a site on higher ground, well away from the floodplains, and with plenty of room to build the large cattle yards he'd need. The outstation was nothing more than three shipping containers tacked together, with a false roof over the top and a couple of metal sheds scattered around a cleared area. It was nestled close to the river, as well as having its own water tanks, so there was access to a water supply. But it was incredibly basic, with small solar panels and a generator for electricity, furnished with sparse, second-hand furniture. At least there was a refrigerator and a gas stove for cooking. But that was about where the luxuries stopped.

Bryan knew they were staying at the old homestead, but she'd never met him. He'd been fed the same cover story as everyone else, that they were environmental consultants, here to confer with the elders of the indigenous community. He was more than happy to leave them alone; it seemed that Bryan was a traditionalist; he didn't go in for all these new-fangled ideas and farming methods. Which was fine with Daisy. If Bryan stayed away, he was one less person who might identify them.

Dale seemed like a decent guy. It was a shame she had to lie to him. She'd have to add him to the growing list of people she was consciously misleading. It was getting longer by the day, and the idea almost gave her hives. She hated people who lied. Which meant she was fast coming to hate herself. Daisy had been a strict rule-follower when she was a child. Even now, her mum liked to say that she had too much integrity for her own good.

"Good idea," Dale replied. "You can give my phone back at dinner."

She followed Dale through the maze of hallways, to the kitchen where he dropped the plates, jam, and cream on the counter with a cheeky wink in Skylar's direction, ignoring her glare. Then he led her down some more hallways until they emerged at the other end of the enormous lodge. Her eyes traced the line of his shoulders as she followed him, the way his jeans sat snug and low on his lean waist. How those same jeans moulded nicely to a muscular, taught butt. Mmm hmm, he was the full package. Even if he was completely off limits, she could look, couldn't she?

"Sorry, we've been meaning to get this walkway between the lodge and the staff quarters covered, but at the moment we're gonna get wet," Dale gave her an enigmatic smile.

Daisy poked her head out the door. Sheesh, it was still raining; the water coming down in sheets now, instead of droplets. Normally at this stage in the late afternoon, there'd be bright sunshine, the sun hovering well above the edge of the horizon. Instead, it was more like a heavy twilight out there. So dark that Dale flicked a switch, illuminating two outdoor spotlights to help her see across the flooded, muddy space in between. If this rain kept up, she was going to need waders just to get between the two buildings.

How would River be coping back at their little camp? She had to assume that they built the place on high enough ground that floods wouldn't affect it. It was going to be the main residence for a short while, so surely, they'd taken that into consideration.

They sprinted through the rain, then Daisy followed Dale into the building. Down a long hallway, passing doorways on the left and right that she could see led to single bedrooms when she peeked into one on the way past.

"We've got five full-time staff on right now, so this place is pretty full," Dale spoke to her over his shoulder. "Paula left a few months ago. She followed a man down to Brisbane." Dale gave a quiet snort, telling her exactly what he thought of that plan. "She left in a hurry and we haven't found anyone to replace her yet. This is her room." Dale paused outside the last door on the left, pushing the door ajar. "Paula left a few things in her closet; said she wouldn't need them in the big smoke. I'm hoping she was about the same size as you, but even if they're not quiet right, at least her clothes will be dry." His gaze flicked up her legs and over her waist, then rose to take in her breasts and she felt a lick of heat spread through her at his perusal. He might well have just been sizing her up to make sure that Paula's clothes would fit her, but it felt a lot like he was undressing her with his eyes.

Dale glanced down at his own clothes. "I may as well stay in these, I'm going to get soaked again, anyway." He gave a self-deprecating laugh. "The bathroom is at the end of the hallway. There are fresh towels on a shelf in there." Dale pointed to the door right at the end, and she forced her gaze away from his face to glance at where he was pointing.

"Thank you." She looked him in the eye as she spoke. "I mean it. I'm sorry if I didn't sound all that grateful when you rescued me out of the creek. I was…" She had no words to describe how she'd been feeling then.

"No probs." He gave a slight shrug, but then that smile was back, his dimples lighting up the dark hallway. It had her wishing he smiled like that all the time. "It's not every day I get to play Sir Lancelot." He locked his brown eyes with hers, and she winced as she remembered how she'd accused him of having a big ego. "I'd better skedaddle before Steve tries to move those horses all on his own. Dinner will be around seven. Do you want me to call past and get you when it's ready?"

"Yes, please."

He paused for a heartbeat. "Will you be okay here by yourself?"

"Perfectly fine," she replied. Privacy was exactly what she was craving right now.

"Cool. See you in an hour or so." Then he was gone, striding down the hallway onto the sodden earth beyond.

Daisy turned around to survey her room. The place was clean, with an air of simple elegance. It seemed as much care and thought had been put into the design of the staff quarters as had been into the lodge. A big, double bed took up one whole corner of the large room, flanked by a small side table and reading light, both made of local wood, by the looks of it. A cozy, winged chair was set next to the large window, and would make a delightful spot to sit and read—if she ever had the chance. Daisy opened the two double doors in the far wall to find a spacious closet. And just as Dale had promised, a pair of jeans, some shorts and a couple of button-up shirts hung on the rack.

She lowered herself slowly into the chair. Alone at last. Time to fret about River and what he was up to. Worry that he was safe.

And freak out over the comment Steve made about recognizing her.

She stared down at Dale's phone in her palm.

He'd handed it to her without hesitation. As if he trusted her implicity. That kind of thing didn't happen to her very often. Someone showing no hesitation, treating her as if she were an equal.

Daisy sat back and considered Dale. If she didn't know better, she could stereotype him as one of those rich, country kids. Entitled, sanguine, supremely confident in who and what they were, who would one day inherit the family farm and keep up the burgeoning family name. But scratch the surface and Dale wasn't any of those things. There was a shyness, a reserve about him, that spoke of how perhaps all of his cocky confidence might be a front. His smile, for one. He only brought that smile out when he was truly affected by something. That smile could be used as a lethal weapon, if he'd wanted to. But he hid it most of the time behind a more serious façade. Daisy wondered why. Was he unhappy here? Perhaps he'd been burned by a failed love affair. But no, he was too young to have been that affected. Wasn't he? If she were to guess, Dale was a couple of years younger than her. Which put him at around twenty-three or twenty-four. She pursed her lips. She'd never been with a younger man. Not that a few years made a huge difference.

Troy was older than her by three years. Although you wouldn't know it, the way he acted. She hadn't contacted Troy once, not since she'd left Perth in such a hurry. And to tell the truth, she didn't miss him one bit. Troy was a footy star, a key player for the West Coast Eagles. And didn't he love to rub it in whenever he got the chance. His constant revolving door of supposed friends coming and going to his place had become maddening. And then there were the drugs. Troy didn't even try to hide them anymore. Things between them had been on the downhill slide even before she left.

Troy had brown eyes, much like Dale. But Troy's gaze had a hard edge to it. Unlike Dale's, whose eyes had flecks of gold hiding in their depths, and seemed to glow with a compassion and kindness that Troy would never have. An image of Dale's liquid-brown gaze swam across the viewfinder of her mind. She could definitely get lost in their depths. And she could also get lost in those powerful arms; she hadn't failed to notice his tanned forearms, leading up to nicely bulging biceps.

She shook her head to rid it of all her silly fantasies.

Dale wasn't stupid. His family weren't stupid. She needed to put her game face on and keep her wits about her over the next twenty-four hours, or however long she was stuck here, if she were to keep her cover story in place. Keep River safe.

Thinking about her brother, a dart of doubt shot through her guts, but she squashed the uneasy feeling down. He was innocent, and she needed to protect him, that was her main aim in life right now.

In her mind, she flashed back to the conversation they'd had on the long, boring drive across the Nullarbor in the little white corolla after they'd fled Perth.

"I promise you, sis, I had nothing to do with the murder."

It was probably the sixth or seventh time he'd said these words, and Daisy had finally snapped. "So you keep saying, but up until now, you haven't told me anything else. It's time I knew the full story, River. I'm putting my life on hold here—putting my life on the line—and you need to tell me the truth." Daisy had taken her eyes off the endless stretch of tarmac in front and glared at her brother. "I deserve to know the whole truth," she'd declared.

"Yes, you do," he agreed, shifting around in the passenger seat as if he were uncomfortable.

Reading his mind, Daisy said, "Start at the beginning. Why were you in that alley in the first place? Who else was there?"

River cracked his knuckles—a most annoying habit—and stared out the window. She let him find the words in his own time. "I was over at Tommy's place, we were just playing Battlegrounds, you know? Just chillin and passing the time."

Daisy could imagine. She'd only been to Tommy's place once; the place was a dive, where River went to play Xbox games and smoke drugs. River still officially lived at home with their parents, but he spent most of his time crashing on friend's floors or couches, so they hardly ever saw him.

"Anyway, Ralphie and Kyron came around, looking all hyped up, you know?"

No, she didn't know, but she nodded for him to continue.

"They asked if we wanted to join in a bit of fun. There might even be some money in it."

Daisy wondered what Ralphie and Kyron considered *a bit of fun*. Daisy hadn't met these two—she was loath to call them thugs, but that seemed like the right word—but she'd heard about them from River. They had a loose connection to a street gang by the name of The Black Kings. River swore blind that he wasn't part of this gang, but Daisy had never been truly sure.

"Me and Tommy said why the hell not? And so we hopped in their car and they drove us into Northbridge."

A chill of premonition ran down Daisy's spine. Already, she didn't like the sound of this.

"It was only around nine o'clock, not late or anything. Ralphie said if we helped him get this job done, then he'd pay us a thousand large each." River's tone became animated as he recounted this part of the story. The thought of easy money always excited him.

"He parked the car around the back of some bar, I don't know which one, but they must've had a live band, I could hear the music pumping. We all went into some alley way behind the bar and stood around…just waiting. Then finally this guy appears. I recognized him straight away. It was Daniel. And all of a sudden, I knew what they'd come here for. I was scared."

River was right to be alarmed. A few weeks ago, he'd recounted a story where Daniel had reneged on a deal with The Black Kings, and owed them a lot of money. The Black Kings were mad; they didn't like to be double-crossed.

"They got him on the ground and began kicking him so hard. I swear, sis, I tried to stop them. I yelled at them and told them to get the hell outta there." River's voice broke into a sob. "But they wouldn't listen, and in the end I just ran away. I had to get away. You understand, don't you?"

"Of course, I do," she soothed. "You did the right thing. The only thing you could do."

River went on, almost as if she hadn't spoken. "Now I realize, they always meant to beat him up. Make an example of him. Tommy told me afterwards they lured him in by offering to sell him a KG of coke. That's how they got him to come to the alley in the first place. The sound of the live band covered any commotion we made. But I don't think they meant to kill him, things got out of control, that was all."

Daisy very much doubted that, but she kept her thoughts to herself.

"Did Tommy know where you were going?"

River merely shrugged.

Not that it mattered now, because Tommy was in custody, awaiting trial for murder. As was Kyron.

But Ralphie had gone to ground on the same night as the beating. Ralphie was smart. Smarter than the rest of them. But rumor had it that Ralphie was blaming River for turning them all in to the police.

And that was the main reason driving Daisy to protect her brother.

Because now, it wasn't just that the police who wanted to question him as a person of interest in the crime.

The Black Kings were coming for him because they thought he was a traitor. Someone had accused him of taking photos at the scene and they were scared he'd turn them over to the police. That he would betray them. River swore black and blue that he hadn't done that.

River told Daisy the cops would charge him with murder, or at the very least, accessory to murder. He knew he wouldn't survive in prison.

But that was the least of his worries, now. If The Black Kings caught up to him, he was as good as dead. And that was why she'd helped him to escape. Daisy was a good girl, she followed the rules and trusted in the justice system. She would've probably let River take his chances with the law; let them arrest him and have the trial by jury play out the way it should.

But when it came to gangland justice. Daisy couldn't let her brother be killed in cold blood.

So, she'd agreed to take him on the run.

CHAPTER FIVE

Dale watched Daisy over the rim of his glass. What did she think of all this? She was seated across the table from him, keeping her eyes directed at her plate, and her interactions with others to a minimum. At Stormcloud, the staff and family members ate with the guests, randomly scattered amongst the two long tables that practically filled the dining room.

He took a sip and rolled the liquid around in his mouth. The red wine Daniella had chosen to go with Skylar's meal of aged beef strips with wild mushroom jus and charred leeks was superb—Skylar had stretched the steaks by serving them in thick slices instead of whole, and then supplemented the meal with a larger serving of the entrée, local banana prawns in a rich, garlic sauce. The wine was smooth, heavy on the plummy flavors, just the way he liked it. This was something he'd missed while he'd been in Montana. The taste of a big, bold, Australian wine.

Daisy had changed into some of Paula's old clothes, and damn, they'd never looked half as good on Paula. A pair of faded denim shorts hugged her hips like they'd been made especially for her, and the pale-yellow, button-up shirt, rolled up to the elbows, brought out the soft honey gleam of her skin. She wore her hair loose tonight, and it fell in waves of dark-golden silk. Dale's gaze caught on her lips as she pouted down at something on her plate. Her mouth was full, with plump, pink lips that drew his gaze, as he watched, fascinated, while her tongue came out to lick a morsel of mushroom.

His mind jerked to the moment Daisy had handed him his phone this evening when he'd collected her for dinner. Their fingers had touched as he took the cell, and it'd been as if she'd shocked him with a hundred volts of electricity. He'd tried to hide his reaction by nonchalantly tucking his phone into his back pocket, but his hand buzzed for some minutes afterwards.

She fascinated him in a way few other women did. Even though he'd been madly attracted to Violet, it'd been more of a physical lust kind of thing. Violet was pretty and vivacious, the life of the party; it was hard not to be attracted to her. It was different with Daisy; she was serious and pensive, but there was something so…alluring about her. Something dark and mystical, but also familiar. Like something inside her was calling to him on a spiritual level.

He lurched back in surprise. God, never let Skylar hear him say those words, she'd think her shy, retiring, sensible brother had gone stark, raving bonkers. And she'd probably be right. What was he thinking? He'd only known the woman for a few hours, they'd shared a drive to the station and some pumpkin scones together, and that was it.

Daisy lifted her gaze and caught Dale's eye. She looked out of her element here, and he took pity on her, because he knew how she felt. He was very good at putting on a bold face when he had to, but give him a quiet corner in the kitchen where he could eat and drink in peace any day. Daisy didn't strike him as the shy introvert he was, however. She gave him another, long, cool look, before the man next to her—an IT consultant from Sydney with a double chin who'd brought his wife to Stormcloud *to experience the outback* which made Dale laugh—nudged her elbow and pointed out the window to the sky. Dale heard him say something like, "Thank God that blasted rain has stopped. It was ruining our holiday." Dale tuned out the rest of the florid man's words as he considered the weather. The rain had indeed finally stopped. Which was a good thing, but not merely for their guests. Any more rain and they may well have been cut off from Dimbulah, if the Jimbu River also flooded. As it was, the roads were going to be a nightmare to drive in the coming weeks, with huge puddles and large potholes opening up unexpectedly. He wasn't going to tell Daisy until he absolutely had to, but Corella Creek would be impassable for at least another day, probably two.

Steve came up behind Dale and lay a hand on his shoulder, breaking his train of thought. "I want to have a quick chat with everyone," Steve said quietly into Dale's ear. "In the kitchen in five. Okay?"

Dale nodded his understanding. It must be something work related, if Steve didn't want to talk in front of the guests. He watched as Steve went over and spoke quietly to his mother. She frowned, but also nodded in agreement. Daniella was the ultimate host. She'd hate to leave her guests unattended. Which was one more reason she was in charge of the accommodation and resort side of the station, while Steve looked after the working side. She had a knack for keeping the place running smoothly. Dale wondered if she even noticed that it often came at the expense of her family, who always seemed to come a distant second, nowadays.

Dale stood up and considered Daisy for a moment. He didn't want to leave her out here, at the mercies of Double-Chin Man, so he caught her eye and tilted his head in the direction of the kitchen. She nodded as she got his meaning and apologized to the IT specialist, who was now droning on about the advantages of driving a Mercedes over an Audi. Dickhead.

Dale picked up his empty plate and excused himself from the well-dressed lady sitting next to him. Patricia had brought her daughter on a mother-daughter holiday to try to *reconnect with her*. Going by the fact that the daughter, Brianna, was sitting clear across at the other table, Dale thought that might not be going so well.

Daisy took up her plate—which was still half-full—and followed him into the kitchen. "What are we doing?" she whispered as she watched the other family and staff pile their plates on the sink and then stand around, most of them leaning up against countertops.

"Steve wants a chat, that's all," he said quietly. "I thought you'd rather be with us, than stuck out there with the guests."

"You guessed correctly," she replied with a tight smile, crossing her arms over her chest and leaning her backside on the countertop next to him.

Skylar was already there, of course, and looked mildly surprised when everyone filed in but didn't stop scrubbing down the stovetop. So was Bindi, the assistant cook, who paused from stacking dishes in the dishwasher to stare at them all.

Wazza, their other full-time ranch hand, strolled in, hands buried deep in his pockets and Akubra tucked under one arm. That guy never went anywhere without his hat. Daniella didn't like hats being worn inside, and especially not at the dinner table, but Wazza lived in his every spare second of the day. He gave Daisy a rakish grin as he brushed past them both to take up a spot at the countertop right next to her. They'd all been introduced before dinner, so everyone knew the short version of why Daisy was here. Wazza leaned in and whispered something in Daisy's ear, and she gave him a smile in return. A flash of anger so sharp and so completely unexpected raced through Dale, surprising him with its ferocity. He had to consciously unclench his balled fists. Whoa. That'd never happened before. Dale liked Wazza, got on well with the man. But Wazza and he had very different tastes in women. Until this evening, it seemed.

Alek strolled in, staring at the clipboard in his hands, and Dale used his appearance to distract himself from Wazza, who was still leaning in way too close to Daisy for his liking. Poor Alek was probably still trying to come up with something to keep the guests entertained tonight. Often, they'd take the guests out stargazing, or spotlighting to show off the many nocturnal animals around the station. Or they'd light an enormous bonfire and sit around it, roasting marshmallows and making damper. This much rain meant they'd be stuck inside, and Dale had overheard Daniella say that she specifically didn't want something boring and old hat, such as Charades or Pictionary. Alek smoothed a hand abstractedly over his hair. He kept it long, shoulder length, but always stylishly sleek, either tied up in a ponytail, or tucked behind his ears. Alek thought it made him look more sophisticated and urbane, but Dale couldn't imagine trying to work in the scorching sun all day with that long hair. The guy was good looking, with his high cheekbones and long, straight nose.

Sally Tsun, their petite receptionist, slash waitress, slash sometimes cleaner, came in carrying an armful of dishes, which she handed over to Bindi. Sally was one of those ever-ready women who never stopped moving, almost as if she had no *off* button. She immediately grabbed a cloth and began wiping down the middle countertop, transferring dirty saucepans and utensils to the sink where they could also be loaded into the dishwasher. Sally's straight, black hair was pulled up, as always, into a tight bun at the nape of her neck and she flicked Dale a glance, curiosity in her dark eyes. He gave a light shrug.

Sally turned to Skylar and said, "Another one of those disgusting creatures was hopping around my feet again today."

Skylar looked up from her scrubbing, slightly confused. Then her furrowed brow cleared. "Oh, you mean a cane toad." She gave a light laugh and returned to washing her pot. It was no secret that Sally *hated* the toads with a vengeance.

"I had to get Alek to come and get it for me," Sally continued indignantly. "But he only shooed it out the door. I don't get why you don't kill them." Sally gave Alek a look that spoke daggers.

Dale knew it would've been a fruitless effort to kill the toad. There were far too many of the pests; killing one or two of them wouldn't even make a dent in their numbers. Besides, you had to be careful how you handled them because of the poison glands on the top of their heads. They were a particularly vile animal, especially as they weren't even native; some do-gooder had introduced them to kill insects in sugar cane and their populations had exploded to plague proportions. Everyone else had learned to ignore the animals. It was par for the course that the amphibians sometimes found their way inside, especially when they were frisky with all the rain. Sally just couldn't seem to come to terms with them.

"Do you know what this meeting is about?" Sally continued, her gaze darting to the door and back to Skylar. "I'm busy. Got lots to do. I don't have time—"

Skylar cut her off with a wave of her hand. "I have less information than you," she retorted. Sally had a way of rubbing Skylar up the wrong way sometimes, and Skylar didn't suffer fools easily. Sally glared at her, but said nothing more, going back to her wiping with more force than was necessary. Dale considered Sally for a second, watching the woman's angry moments. She'd seemed a little more stressed than usual. Over the past few weeks, she'd been snapping at everyone. And now Skylar was finally snapping back. He counted backward mentally in his head. It'd been a while since Sally had any time off. Perhaps he should mention that to his mother quietly later on. By the murderous look she shot in Skylar's direction, a break from the station—and the way they all worked in such close-quarters together—might be exactly what she needed.

Daniella came in, halting any further conversation. Steve followed closely behind her; almost as if he were herding her like a recalcitrant heifer into the kitchen. Dale could tell she was feeling harried by the tiny frown lines between her blue eyes, but not many other people would've picked up on her tension. Steve would have, and perhaps Skylar, but everyone else would see the stylish, completely in-charge woman that Daniella wanted them to see.

"Do we really need to do this now?" Daniella asked Steve over her shoulder. "I need to talk to Alek about the games for tonight. And then I need to get back to my office. I've got paperwork coming out of my ears. I've got about a dozen overdue bills that need to be paid. Those images for those new brochures we're having done need to be finalized." His mother gave a theatrical wave of her hand. "I've just had a previous guest on the phone saying we charged them double the fee for their accommodation, when they stayed with us last month. Which is ridiculous." Daniella snorted. "But now I have to go and pull out all their documents and go over them again."

Sally's head shot up. "Do you need a hand with that? I can find the invoices, if you like." As the resort's receptionist,

Sally handled a large bulk of the payments and invoicing, while Daniella looked after the purchasing of supplies and day to day running of the resort, so it made sense that Sally would be able to find what Daniella wanted quickly.

Daniella stared at Sally for a long second, before letting out a tired sigh. "Yes, please, that'd be helpful."

Dale suddenly felt a stab of compassion for his mother. She had a strong work ethic, and she worked exceptionally hard to keep this place running, and most of the time he took what she did for granted. It wasn't often she let her fatigue show, so she must be really under the pump to agree to let Sally help her.

Steve cleared his throat and Dale looked at all the people gathered in the kitchen. It was unusual to get all the Stormcloud staff together at one time. But as Dale counted, he realized there was one person missing.

"I'm worried about Karri," Steve said, without preamble. "She was supposed to be helping me stable the horses and secure the equipment in case of flooding, but no one has seen her since lunchtime. I've checked with everyone on the station."

There was a brief silence as everyone digested Steve's news.

"She's probably gone back to Koongarra," Daniella said dismissively. "You know what she's like, always flitting off to visit some relative or other." His mother's eyebrows drew together, her gaze flicking toward the door, as if she were more interested in getting back to the guests.

"Not without letting someone know," Steve argued. "And not in this weather; the road is practically impassable."

Dale tended to agree with him. Karri could be a little… flighty at times. Unreliable was too strong a word. She was a good worker, and had a special way with the horses and the cattle, a kind of empathy with them.

"No one is answering at the community on Koongarra. And I've tried to raise Bryan, but I've had no luck so far," Steve continued. "He might be out moving cattle, so I'll keep trying." Steve paused, almost as if holding his breath. He continued in a rush, "If we haven't heard from her by the morning, I'm calling in the police."

That had Daniella's attention. "What? Really? You'd call Robinson?" His mum almost rolled her eyes at Steve but stopped herself just in time. It wouldn't do to look insensitive. Dale knew Karri wasn't on the best of terms with his mother. Karri was one of their indigenous employees, part of the Kuku Group Initiative to get more indigenous people into employment, of which Stormcloud Station was a part. At first, Daniella had been all for the program and had welcomed Karri with open arms. But her enthusiasm had soured for some reason; Dale wasn't sure why. He guessed that she and Karri had a run in about something, but he was yet to discover what.

"Yes. Karri's ute is still in the parking lot. And one of the ATVs is gone." Steve concentrated on Daniella and for the first time that night, Dale saw his mum focus her full attention on her partner. Her frown turned from impatience to worry as she finally understood the seriousness of what he was saying.

Dale tried not to judge his mother. She was a bloody hard worker, had poured her heart and soul into this resort. As had Steve. But Daniella almost seemed to get consumed by the whole thing sometimes, assuming that her partner and her family would always be there to back her up. She could be a tad flippant with them, especially when they had a full house, and her mind was on other things. Dale thought Steve was a very patient man, overlooking the way she often under-appreciated all that he did for her and for the station. He guessed it happened in lots of marriages, taking the other partner for granted over the years. He hoped that'd never happen to him.

"I heard she was seeing some bloke over at Koongarra," Alek said into the sudden silence.

Steve spun around to face the Polish man. "Are you sure? Who told you that?"

"I heard the same thing," Wazza said from beneath lowered eyebrows. "I wouldn't be surprised if that's where she is. Holed up with her lover, waiting for the rain to ease." Wazza spoke carelessly enough, but Dale wondered why he had such a tight grip on his Akubra, now scrunched in one hand. Wazza and Karri worked closely together a lot of the time.

"Hmm." Steve didn't sound convinced. "I guess so. It seems odd that she said nothing when I asked her to come and give me a hand earlier."

Dale studied both Alek and Wazza furtively. While Wazza and Karri had a friendly relationship, he'd also noticed Alek glancing in Karri's direction more than once. The Polish man's one fault was his conceitedness; he thought he was God's gift to women. Dale wouldn't put it past him to have tried it on with Karri. Could either of them be trying to divert attention away from the truth by saying she was sleeping with someone at Koongarra? And instead, Karri was actually carrying on an affair with one of them?

"She came in here and begged an early lunch from me," Skylar said. "It seemed to me that she wanted to get back to work fast, because she wolfed down the sandwich I gave her. But she never mentioned where she was off to." Skylar's head was tilted at an angle, concern written on her face.

"And I haven't seen her since this morning, when we moved the cattle," Wazza said, his voice also gruff with concern. "Did you say one of the ATVs is gone?" He raised his head and stared directly at Steve, who nodded in agreement. "Could she have taken that and gone cross-country to get to Koongarra?"

Before Steve could answer, Daniella cut in, "It's not as if she hasn't done this before." His mother's tone was almost accusatory. She was correct, Karri had taken off back to Koongarra twice before without telling anyone, but that'd been early in her employment and she'd admitted she was feeling homesick and was having a hard time adjusting to the work. It hadn't happened recently, not in the past six months, at least. But this almost sounded like Daniella was accusing Karri of something? But what? Sleeping around?

"I really don't want to involve the police unless it's absolutely necessary," Daniella added. "I don't want to upset the guests in—"

"Yeah, yeah, I know," Steve exclaimed. "Don't upset the guests, because, God forbid, we get a bad review." His eyes flashed angrily, and Dale thought it might be the first time he'd seen Steve get mad at his mother in public. As if seeming to regret his words as soon as they were out of his mouth, Steve threw his head backward and gave a long sigh. "Sorry," he apologized, then he stalked out the door, heading toward the family suites.

Daniella headed out the opposite door, flicking an apologetic look toward Dale and Skylar as she went. Wazza followed on her heels, his flirty, joking mood from earlier nowhere in evidence now. Alek took off after Daniella and Wazza with a start, as if only just realizing the discussion had come to an abrupt end. Bindi and Skylar went back to their scrubbing, but after a muttered conversation with Skylar, Sally took off her apron and headed out the rear door. Daisy hadn't said a word, merely watched everything unfold around her with a bright, unreadable gaze.

"Do you want to grab a drink? Or would you rather head to bed?" he asked.

"Sleep isn't really on my agenda right now." She cocked her head to the side and considered him for a second. "I'd love a drink. What did you have in mind?"

His mind raced with ideas. If they went to the staff quarters, they were more than likely to run into Wazza or Sally. They couldn't go to the family living area, as Steve would be sulking around in there. And he wasn't going to the main lodge, where they'd almost certainly get dragged into some horrible type of parlor game with the guests.

"Come with me." He beckoned with a crook of his little finger. He led her down the hallway as if they were going to the main lodge, but right before they stepped into the large dining living area, he motioned for her to stay where she was. Ducking around the corner—he hoped Daniella was too preoccupied with speaking with the guests to notice him—he nipped in behind the large bar running the length of the room. He grabbed the nearest bottle of red wine on the shelves below the bar, nabbed two glasses and was back in the hallway in less than ten seconds.

"Where are we going," Daisy asked, as he strode ahead of her.

"To the laundry," he said a little sheepishly.

"The laundry?" Her tone was incredulous.

"I know. But you wait, you'll understand in a second." It might sound utterly ridiculous to hide out in the laundry, but there were many advantages to that utility room. It was a small outbuilding, connected by a covered walkway. It kept them out of the rain and the best thing was, no one would go out to the laundry at this time of night, so it'd be completely private.

Dale led them out a side door and into the dark shadows beneath the walkway. He shoved the door open with his hip, flipped a switch that turned on a set of recessed lighting, and went straight to the rear of the room, past two enormous, industrial washing machines and an equally large dryer, to where a set of shelves filled the length of the back wall. A few wicker laundry baskets were stacked together in the corner and he pulled two out and turned them upside down.

"Your throne, my queen." He parodied a low, sweeping bow and was rewarded by a throaty giggle from Daisy.

She sat down gingerly on the basket, and took the glass he handed her, watching him open the wine and then fill her glass nearly to the brim. He did the same with his and took a seat next to her, clinking his glass against hers. He liked the way she stretched out her long, brown legs in front of her and balanced her glass on her knee.

"It's not that bad in here," she admitted.

"I know. You probably think I'm odd, but it's one of the few places I can get any true privacy this close to the lodge." Of course, he had other favorite spots he liked to go when he needed to think, or to get some much-needed space. But all his outdoor hideaways would be useless after all this rain.

Daisy considered him, her long hair falling across her shoulder. "Not really." She didn't elaborate any further, but he got the impression she might also know a little about needing to get away from people now and then. "Well, that was an interesting discussion," she said quietly. "Is that your normal family get-together?"

"No, not at all." Dale gave a grunt of exasperation. "And I have to apologize. If I'd known what Steve was going to say, I wouldn't have invited you to join us."

"Not at all. It was really quite interesting, and a good distraction. Took my mind off wondering when I'll get back to my place." She flicked her hair away in an unconscious gesture and took a gulp of wine. "So, what are your thoughts on this missing girl?"

Damn, why hadn't he seen that coming? Should he tell her the truth? About his mother and Karri?

CHAPTER SIX

Daisy cast her fishing lure into the billabong in one long, even stroke. She was getting the hang of this. Now all she needed was for one of those big, beautiful, silver fishes to take a little nibble, and…

"Caught anything yet?" Dale called to her, dimples flashing from beneath the brim of his hat.

"No," she said, trying to hide her sulky pout. Four of the other five guests had all caught at least one barramundi so far. Why was she so bad at this fishing thing?

Early this morning, Dale had asked if she wanted to join their group, to try a spot of fishing at the other end of the billabong. The guests were supposed to go on a tour of the old gold mine over at the base of the escarpment, and then on a horse ride in the afternoon, but both activities had been cancelled. As Daisy looked around, she could see why. Any dips or depressions were engulfed in water. It was like they were surrounded by small, shallow lakes. So Alek had come up with an alternative.

At first, she'd refused Dale's offer, asking if someone could take her home, instead. It'd taken him a lot of careful explanation and then some hard truths when she still failed to understand that she would not be returning to Koongarra today. The creek would be impassable. It was frustrating and aggravating and she'd had to stop herself stamping her foot like a toddler throwing a tantrum. Worry for River had eaten away at her all night, and she'd tossed and turned, unable to sleep. She had the spare part for his motorcycle still sitting in the rear seat of her car, so he was effectively stranded until she got home. What would he be doing all alone at the outstation?

If he was actually alone. There was also a nagging doubt at the back of her mind that River might be seeing a girl from the community. He'd kept it a secret, heading off on his motorcycle a couple of times a week and not returning for hours, only giving her vague explanations as to where he'd been. She'd warned him repeatedly that he was taking a risk by constantly visiting the Kuku community. But she couldn't really blame him, they were living such an isolated life. The community itself didn't have a lot to do with the outside world, living as much as possible off the land. The elders ran a dry camp, and they didn't tolerate any trouble. River told her that only a few months ago, two young members had been expelled for beating up a third guy. The elders had also promised to protect her and River's identities as a favor to her mother. It was still a risk, though, to be seen in the community regularly. Daisy knew trust was a slippery commodity, often hard won, but then easily lost.

As Dale had stood waiting for her answer, in a moment of madness, she considered setting off on her own, perhaps borrowing one of those ATVs and making her way across country. To check that her baby brother really was safe. But in the end, she knew Dale was right, and she'd have to control that impatient streak of hers and try to keep the worry to a minimum. She also didn't want to ruin the fragile trust that was growing between her and Dale.

So, after a rather large breakfast—the food here was

amazing, pancakes with native lillypillys instead of blueberries, waffles with wild bush honey, free-range scrambled eggs from their own chicken coop, and piles of small beef chipolatas that Daniella proudly proclaimed were made from station-bred cattle—Daisy had followed the group of half-a-dozen guests trailing behind Dale to get outfitted with a fishing rod and waders.

And now, even though she hadn't had one damn nibble from those pesky fish, Daisy found herself enjoying the peace and quiet of standing next to a billabong, surrounded by lush, green growth, listening to the frogs sing their morning melodies and the cicadas buzzing in the trees.

Dale had loaned her one of his old Akubra's to keep the sun off her face, and she tipped it backward to stare at the blue above. Who would've thought that after such a wild, wet, and windy day yesterday, that the sun would shine down like there'd been no storm at all? Clear skies as far as the eye could see. Daisy was learning that was the top end for you.

Dale had showed her how to wind in the lure as it sat suspended just below the surface. He also said she'd know if she had a fish on the line, because when they struck, they pulled like a steam train. Winding her lure up, she moved a few yards farther away and cast her line out again to a slightly different spot. She'd listened as Dale told her and the other guests that most of the barramundi in the billabong were stocked by them. But after a big rain and flooding like they'd just had, wild fish often found their way into the waterways, which helped to keep the breeding stock strong. He hinted that he'd seen a few fish over three feet long, which had the man with the double chin and another corporate-type man—Daisy thought of him as the Silver Fox of the troupe— impatient to get fishing. Men and their egos. Daisy gave a quiet huff of aggravation.

She heard the swish of grass right before Dale appeared at her shoulder. "Would you like a few more tips on how to cast the lure correctly?" He gave her a wicked grin as he fixed her with his intense gaze.

"No, thank you. I'm getting the hang of it just fine." She pulled her line in and recast to prove her point.

He moved in a little closer so he could talk quietly in her ear. "I had a good time last night, thank you."

"No, thank you for sharing your hideout with me." She stared up into his eyes for a second. Surprisingly, she'd enjoyed her time sitting in the laundry with him. Who would've thought a laundry could be such a place for escape? She'd finally relaxed for the first time that day—perhaps the wine had something to do with it—and the little room had felt intimate and welcoming.

It'd been nice getting to know Dale, too. He was lovely. Way too lovely for her, but she allowed herself that small indulgence and enjoyed their time together.

"I really liked our…enlightening conversation." She said no more, merely raised her eyebrows. He understood by her facial expression alone what she was hinting at. Dale had opened her eyes to some of the goings on at Stormcloud Station. He'd told her things that perhaps he shouldn't have. But they'd clearly been eating away at him for a while, and it seemed he had no one else to talk to. He was worried about Karri. Had told Daisy that all was not well between his mother and the young woman. That he'd overheard Daniella talking about firing her to Steve one night. Something had happened between the two women that Dale couldn't put a finger on. He was worried that perhaps her mother had said something to Karri to drive her away.

"So, you think your mother might be the cause of her disappearing like that?" Daisy had asked him, mind-boggling at the idea of the poor, young Karri being harangued by the indomitable woman and feeling so overwhelmed that she fled to Koongarra, even in the middle of a huge storm.

"I don't know. I hope not."

"Surely, your mum would've said something when Steve mentioned he was going to call the police?"

"Again, I really hope so. If not in front of all of us, then at least she might've told Steve in private." Dale's face had pulled back into a grimace of unease, and she felt sorry for him. Wondering at the same time how it would feel to not trust your own mother one-hundred percent. It was perhaps an indicator of how Daniella operated. It seemed running the resort came before anything else in her life. Including her family. Daisy's heart went out to Dale as she began to have an insight into his life, and the fact that it might not have been all sunshine and roses, as she imagined. Neither had hers, but for different reasons. At least she had an affectionate family environment. And she knew her mother loved her unconditionally. It was a bit of a cliché, but Dale fit the bill of the poor little rich kid more, now that she was getting to know him.

They'd talked some more, and she'd tried to steer the topic away from herself as often as possible. The fewer lies she told, the better. Dale mentioned Steve was sort of a stepfather to him, although he and his mum were never married; they'd lived together for over seventeen years. Steve had a daughter of his own from a previous marriage, Julie, but she was six or seven years older than Dale, and they hardly saw her out here on the station, as she had a career and a life in Brisbane. She'd also been intrigued to find out that Dale's biological father owned a large cattle station up in the north of Western Australia, but his mum had left him when Dale was only two. So, cattle ranching was in his blood. And he had two younger half-brothers who lived with his biological father, who he hardly ever saw, either.

They stood in silence, both contemplating the billabong. She was about to ask him if Steve had indeed called the police this morning when a voice split the air. "Hey, Dale," the Silver Fox called out. "Joanna's got her line snagged."

Daisy looked over to where the older couple were wrestling with a fishing rod. The Silver Fox's wife was dressed in such a low-cut top her breasts were on the verge of popping out, and Daisy couldn't help but stare at the tight jeans and brand new, shiny boots the woman was wearing.

To go fishing.

It took all types, Daisy reminded herself as she looked down at her more sensible waders. They'd all been offered a pair, as Dale warned them the area would be waterlogged and boggy after the rain. Joanna had turned her nose up at them.

Dale gave a quiet sigh. "No rest for the wicked," he said, and reeled his line in.

"Be right there, Jack." His voice was bright and unconcerned. No one would know he wasn't fully invested in every one of his guests' entertainment.

Damn that Joanna, Daisy had been enjoying their conversation. Probably enjoying it too much, if the truth be told. She watched Dale's retreating backside as he high stepped over the tall grass along the edge of the billabong. He wore the same uniform as yesterday, jeans and a button-up shirt—except the shirt was a light blue today, instead of dark blue—and he'd swapped his cowboy boots for waders like hers. His shirt sleeves were rolled up to the elbow, exposing tanned arms and a hint of a nicely bulging bicep. He was taller than her, but not by much, and she guessed he was probably a smidge over six foot. It was the way he walked, stalking along with the grace of a hunting cat. Each movement economical and neat, as if everything he did was intentional and well-thought-out. He also had a way of giving her his entire focus, zeroing in on her with his intense, brown eyes. It should've been unnerving, but Daisy merely found herself wanting to drown in those luscious, deep pools.

He was an enticing package.

Although, it was a package she *should* be ignoring. She was in no position to even look at a man sideways. Technically, she was on the run from the law, consorting with a wanted man. She was supposed to be keeping a low profile. Which she would still be doing, if she'd just listened to the damn weather report instead of heading into town to do River's bidding.

And there was Troy to consider. Although, these two months apart from him had cemented in her mind that she was happier without him. Even when she eventually went back to Perth, there would be no future with Troy. He was too lost in his own world of self-entitlement. They were on separate paths. She didn't love Troy anymore, and if she was truthful, she hadn't loved him for a while now.

A part of her wished she'd never run into Dale Williams last night. It'd be so much easier if she were safely back at the outstation with River, never having met him. Because this could get complicated, if she let it. She saw the way Dale looked at her. Saw how he'd pulled away suddenly last night when their fingers touched as she handed him his phone.

She turned around so she could no longer see Dale, who was now helping Joanna, by gently taking her rod so he could untangle the line. So she could no longer see those long, tanned fingers as they deftly unwound the line. And no longer see his muscular forearms flex as he drew the rod backward and forward through the air. Strong forearms, that could easily wrap around her waist, pull her up into that hardened chest so she could reach his lips and…

Sheesh. She needed to get her hormones under control. *Think about something else, Daisy.* She needed to stop that hot, raw feeling rising through her belly as she watched Joanna touch Dale deliberately, flirtatiously on the arm. She was *not* jealous.

River. Their trouble with the law. Their strife with The Black Kings. They were more than enough to keep her occupied. Her mother had no further news to give her last night when she'd called. She'd kept the call short and to the point. Told Evana that she and River were safe and asked if there'd been any further inquiries from the cops. Had there been any more media coverage, or more questions? Daisy breathed a sigh of relief when Evana told her that things seemed to have died down over the past month. There'd been no more mention of anything on the news about the dead man. Which didn't mean the cops weren't still working on the case behind the scenes, but at least people's attention had been diverted. She didn't mention anything about her current predicament; that would merely send her mother into a spiral of panic. Nor did she mention Steve might've recognized her. It could well have been a case of mistaken identity.

There was a sharp tug on the fishing line. Daisy snapped her attention back to the present.

A fish. There was a fish on her line. It tugged again, harder, almost pulling the rod out of her hands. She gave a little squeal of delight as she leaned backward against the weight of the fish. She knew nothing about barramundi, but this felt like a big one.

Taking a step backward, Daisy braced her legs and planted the butt of the rod into her hip to give her better purchase.

"Have you got one?" Dale called, lifting his head from where he was tying on a new lure to Joanna's line.

"Yes," she squeaked. She dared not look away from the commotion in the billabong, and the large, thrashing fish leaping out of the water, churning it up in a frantic bid for freedom.

Dale was almost at her side when the line went slack, the tumult in the water stopping suddenly. Daisy stared at the now calm billabong. The fish was gone.

"Oh, no!" Her loud exclamation was full of disappointment. "Did I do something wrong?"

"It happens," he replied with a shrug. "They're a canny fish. They don't want to be caught."

"Damn," she muttered. She'd been so sure she was taking fresh barramundi home to the lodge for Skylar to cook for dinner. Skylar said she had the perfect recipe for it. Daisy had had a quick chat with Skylar in the kitchen this morning, after she offered to help with the cleaning up. She was really impressed at the way Skylar was so determined to use native bush foods in her all her cooking. But Skylar had bemoaned the fact it was often hard to source some of the less familiar ones. She'd been researching how to grow some of the local native shrubs, like the ones that produced the wattleseeds, and even the ones from farther afield, in her own special garden. But her time was so limited, Skylar had eventually given up on the idea. It made Daisy wonder, and she decided she might do her own research on the topic, if she ever got back to her own computer.

Dale's two-way radio crackled to life. He carried it in a holster strapped around his back and over his shoulder. He'd told her it was common for station hands to wear them like this out on a muster, and it was also a requirement that they took one whenever they were out with the guests.

"Mamma Bear to Yogi, are you there?" Daisy could hear Daniella's crackly voice over the radio.

He leaned his mouth toward the radio and pushed the button. "Yogi here, what's up?"

"Get all the guests up to the lodge. Pronto."

"Ah…okay, we'll just—"

"No. Get back here now, Dale. This is an emergency."

Dale's lips thinned. "On our way, Mamma Bear."

"That doesn't sound good," Daisy commented, winding her line in furiously.

"No, it doesn't," was all Dale said in reply. Then he painted on a bright smile for the other guests. "Sorry, folks, something has come up and we need to go up to the lodge."

There were cries of "no" and "I haven't caught one yet" but Dale cheerfully ignored them, chivvying everyone good naturedly to get moving. "We can return this afternoon," he promised. "The fish won't go anywhere."

Daisy wondered quietly to herself what could have upset Daniella so considerably. The woman sounded clearly rattled on the radio, not that Dale had admitted it.

It took them five minutes to get the rods reeled in and then they followed Dale, single file, around the edge of the billabong. Daisy was glad for her waders, as they passed through a few big puddles and the rest of the ground was filled with sticky, red mud. Daisy cast a sideways glance at Joanna's once-pristine boots and gave a little smirk when she saw they were looking a lot worse for wear. Joanna and another woman—Daisy thought her name was Patricia, she was here with her daughter—asked endless questions as to what was going on. Why did they have to return so suddenly? Dale merely shook his head and said he was as in the dark as they all were. It was a somber party that finally dumped their waders in a pile by the front door and paraded into the main living area, where Daniella and Steve were waiting for them.

"Take a seat everyone." Daniella waved everyone toward the tables, including Dale when he tried to approach the bar where she and Steve were waiting. "The rest of the guests will be here shortly. Then we'll bring you some refreshments." Some of the other guests had opted to stay at the lodge this morning, hanging out by the amazing infinity pool on one of the comfy lounge chairs, or taking an impromptu cooking class with Skylar, who was showing them how to bake her famous pumpkin and wattleseed scones.

Dale pulled out a chair next to hers and sat down slowly, his frown getting deeper by the second. They waited in silence as more guests arrived, filling the seats at the table.

What the hell was going on? Daniella stood, stony-faced and unsmiling near the bar. And Steve looked positively sick, his handsome, tanned face had taken on a green pallor, like he was about to puke his guts up at any moment.

People began to mutter between themselves.

Skylar and Bindi came in carrying covered trays of what Daisy assumed were freshly baked scones from the class this morning and placed them on the bar. A coffee urn and kettle were already set up, along with cups stacked up neatly. Sally followed behind, carrying two jugs of milk, which she set down next to the urn. They looked as confused as everyone.

Wazza arrived through a side door, but stayed in the background, leaning against the far end of the bar. He hadn't bothered to remove his hat, but Daniella didn't even seem to notice. Daisy tried to get a good look at Wazza's face, to see if he knew something the rest of them didn't, but it was hidden in the shadow cast by the brim of his hat.

"Right, I think everyone is here, now," Daniella said a little too forcibly.

There was a pause, and Daniella looked to Steve. He stared back at her, standing so still as if he were paralyzed, the silence stretching on between them.

Daniella closed her eyes for a second, then took a deep breath. "I'm not really sure how to say this, so I'm just going to come out with it."

Everyone sat forward in their chairs.

"A body was found in the creek this morning. Down by the

old mine site. We think…actually we know… It's Karri. She's dead." Daniella's last words were said on a sob and she covered her mouth with her hand.

You could've heard a pin drop; the silence was so complete.

Then there was a collective intake of breath, and everyone started talking at once.

CHATPER SEVEN

Dale sat motionless in his seat. Completely paralyzed. The words were like rocks being thrown at his head, but he couldn't move to dodge them. No. It couldn't be true. This was some sick hoax. He wanted to stand up and shout, to refute the words; tell his mother to take them back. To make it not so.

Daisy turned toward him, her eyes huge, seeming to swallow her entire face.

"No," he whispered. "That can't be true." Her hand landed on his arm, as if to steady him, and that's when he noticed his own hands were shaking. Oh, Jesus. Poor Karri. She couldn't be dead. Could she? He put his head in his hands, no longer able to look at Daisy. What did this mean for him? For the resort. For his mum and Steve?

People were firing questions at Daniella and Steve, talking over the top of each other.

"How?"

"When did this happen?"

"Are you sure she's dead?"

"Who found her?"

They were all valid questions, and Dale raised his head slowly. The rest of the Stormcloud team seemed as shell-shocked as he was. Wazza hung his head, hiding his face behind his hat, both hands clenched into fists at his sides. Skylar and Bindi clung to each other, tears quickly replacing astonishment on their faces. Sally stood a little apart from the other two women, washing her hands together in agitation. He should go to his sister and comfort her. He caught her eye, and she shook her head in disbelief and then glanced over toward Daniella. He should also go to his mother, offer her his support. But his legs seemed to be made of lead. He couldn't make them obey him.

While Dale struggled to stand, Steve seemed to regain some of the implacable stoicism he was famous for, and took two steps toward Daniella, slipping a hand around her waist, offering her his moral and physical comfort. Daisy's hand landed on his arm, and he covered it with his own. The human connection was good, a beacon of light in a suddenly pitch-black room. It kept him grounded to this moment, otherwise he felt as if his brain might implode.

"We'll try to answer all your questions," Steve said, his voice echoing through the rafters. "This is a tremendous shock to us all. If you'll all please sit down, we'll tell you what we know so far."

Most of the people who were standing sat down slowly, their faces white and pinched.

But IT Man and his wife remained on their feet. The man's face was going an interesting shade of purple. "I don't want to sit down. I want to go home. This is atrocious. I need to get my wife out of here. We are not staying one second longer."

"You need to sit down, sir." Steve let go of Daniella and strode toward the tables. "No one is going anywhere. At least, not for a while."

The man looked like he was about to argue, pointing his finger at Steve's chest.

Daniella spoke above the growing murmurs. "Senior

Sergeant Robinson will be here soon, and he wants to talk to all of us. He's flying in by helicopter, while his senior constable will be arriving soon afterwards by car. We need everyone to stay where you are until he gets here."

"Why does the senior sergeant want to talk to us all?" Patricia asked from the rear of the room. "You're making this sound as if we're all suspects or something. I agree with Thomas, here." She pointed toward IT Man. "I want to go home as soon as possible."

"I'm really sorry, but you can't leave yet." Steve stood a little taller, projecting his voice to the back of the room, so there would be no confusion as to what he was saying. Dale was impressed at Steve's steadfastness, because he knew he was too shocked to move, let alone try and calm their equally shocked guests. Steve probably had more time to process this news, he and Daniella had obviously known for a while. "The police have been very blunt about what they require from us. They have a protocol they need to follow. We have no choice in the matter."

"Thomas, sit down." IT Man's wife tugged on his sleeve. "Like Steve said, they have little choice." Thomas sat ungraciously, shaking his head and muttering loudly, something about *what kind of shithole resort do they think they're running here?*

"Jesus Christ, listen to all these people. A woman is dead, and all they're worried about is themselves. All they need to do is answer a few questions, then they can get back to their selfish, little insulated lives," Dale whispered.

When Daisy didn't answer, he glanced over at her, noting she hadn't moved beside him since Daniella had declared the police were on their way. His hand still covered hers, the connection warm and real.

Daisy didn't seem to hear him. Her eyes flickered around the room, as if looking for an escape. "No! I can't," she whispered back. She got to her feet and took a step toward the door. Everyone turned to look, and she seemed to realize people were staring at her. Dale grabbed her hand and tugged, gently coaxing her to return to her seat.

"Sorry, you can't what?" he asked gently, keeping hold of her hand.

"I can't talk to the police." Her green eyes, which were large to begin with, seemed to take up her whole face. She chewed frantically at her bottom lip and he could see her jaw muscles working as she ground her teeth. What was wrong with her? Was she another one of these selfish people who cared more about their own lives than that of a dead girl?

"Why not?"

"Oh, God." Her wandering gaze finally found his, and he saw naked fear swimming in their depths. What was going on? Was she afraid of the police? There was only one reason Dale could think of for someone to not want to talk to the cops. But Daisy wasn't in trouble with the law. Was she? So what could her problem be? He was at a loss for how to help her.

Unless…

No, that was plain stupid. Daisy had nothing to do with Karri's death. That was an absurd idea. As far as he knew, she'd never even met the dead woman. It was uncharitable of him to be thinking such things, just because she was an outsider. A newcomer to the area. It was mere coincidence Daisy had appeared on the scene the day Karri went missing. He pushed all those thoughts away.

"What do you mean? What's wrong?"

She continued to stare at him mutely, enormous eyes like green pools, reminding him of the billabong on a calm day. Her whole body was radiating tension, like she was a caged animal about to turn violent. Her eyes glazed over, and he guessed there was some sort of internal battle going on in her head. His unease morphed into growing alarm. Why wouldn't she answer him? No normal person was this afraid to talk to the police.

"I… I can't tell you," she replied, so quietly he almost didn't hear her. Then, as if a sudden thought hit her, her blank gaze cleared, and she sat up straighter. "I mean…it's nothing. Don't worry, there's nothing wrong."

"Dale, can you come and help us serve the refreshments, please?" His mother's voice rang out, breaking the tension between him and Daisy. She snatched her hand away from his. Dale didn't want to leave her, he needed her to tell him what was going on. Something wasn't right, and it was important he find out what.

But Daniella called out again, more impatiently this time.

"Go on," Daisy urged. "Your mum needs you."

He stood up slowly.

"I was just being silly, don't worry." But that fake smile she pasted on her face didn't fool him for a second. Something was terribly wrong, but if she wouldn't confide in him, then he had no idea how to help her. And he had no way of stopping those insidious voices warning him to be careful of her.

By the time he reached the bar, Skylar, and Bindi had uncovered the trays of scones. He gave Skylar a quick hug. They might not always see eye to eye, but they'd invariably been close. He knew she would be taking this as hard as he was.

"How about some of those answers you promised us?" a man's voice rang out from the front table. It was the guy who'd come barramundi fishing with them, Jack, and his wife Joanna. Dale didn't disagree. He had millions of those exact questions, all clamoring for answers.

"Sure." Steve ran a hand through his hair and glanced at Daniella. And then, surprisingly, at Wazza. "If you'll stay seated, we'll serve you at the tables, and I'll fill you in."

Dale doubted many people would want the refreshments, but he guessed it was his mother's way of maintaining a version of normality. And it probably helped the two women keep calm, having something to do.

"I'm not sure how many of you know, but Karri went missing yesterday around lunchtime. We were worried about her, but this…wasn't an uncommon occurrence for her." Steve didn't elaborate, the guests didn't need to know details about Karri's past actions. "Anyway, when I still had no word from her or her family this morning, I called the local police station and lodged a missing person report with them. Senior Constable King said it was too soon to do anything, but noted it down, and told me to get back to him if she still hadn't turned up by this evening."

Dale nodded, along with a few other guests; those who'd been here for a few days had probably met Karri out on one of the guided horseback rides.

"Warwick…" Steve turned and tilted his chin at Wazza, "Went to continue work on a fence that he'd started repairing yesterday afternoon."

Wazza lifted his gaze to look at Steve, the anguish clear on his face now. Then it hit Dale. Oh, Jesus, Wazza had been the one who found her. The man looked positively sick. What a horrible thing to have been confronted with.

"Wazza…sorry, Warwick found Karri floating in the flooded creek, near to where he'd been fixing the fence. He pulled her out and commenced CPR."

Dale could imagine Wazza frantically trying to breathe life back into Karri's inert body. They'd all been drilled in their first aid skills; his mother had demanded it. The policy was to do CPR first, ask questions later, because you never knew, miracles could happen.

"But she'd been in the creek for too long, and he was

unable to resuscitate her," Steve continued in a monotone voice.

Wazza hung his head again, and Dale thought he heard the big man utter a soft groan of despair.

"How the hell did she get into the creek?" Thomas asked belligerently.

Steve ignored the other man's tone. "We don't really know. After Wazza called me on the two-way, we found an ATV submerged in the middle of the creek. We don't want to speculate, but she could have perhaps been trying to cross the creek and got washed off her bike by a surge."

The sound of a helicopter broke the midday air above the lodge. Senior Sergeant Robinson had arrived. The station had a helicopter landing pad out behind the stables. Stormcloud used a local helicopter company to ferry guests in from Cairns, as well as to help with the cattle mustering. The landing pad was a three-minute dash on foot, or a thirty-second drive if you took one of the vehicles.

Steve turned toward Dale. "Come with me, please." It wasn't really a request, and Dale knew it. Dale scrutinized Steve's back as he turned toward the rear door. Why had Steve chosen him in particular? Dale couldn't very well say no. He cast one more look at Daisy, who sat alone at the end of the table, staring out the window and chewing her lip. She looked about ready to bolt at any second and Dale had taken two steps toward her, when Steve's voice commanded him. "Now, Dale. I need you with me."

Dale hoped fervently that Daisy stayed put as he followed Steve through the doorway.

Steve jumped into his Land Cruiser, started the engine, and the vehicle was already moving before Dale was fully in the passenger seat. He pulled the door shut as the vehicle picked up speed. Steve was clearly rattled. He was a stickler for safety. He'd never normally even start a car unless everyone had their seatbelts on first.

Without preamble, Steve said, "I wanted you to know, before the senior sergeant questions people. Karri had a large wound on her head." Steve wouldn't look at him, kept his eyes fixed on the muddy track leading them around the back of the hanger.

Dale took a few seconds to digest Steve's words. "What do you mean? Did she hit her head on a rock when she was washed downstream?"

"Possibly."

What was Steve not saying? "How else would she have gotten a head wound?" It suddenly occurred to Dale what Steve was hinting at. "Oh, fuck. Do you mean someone could have hit Karri over the head? Do you think she was... murdered?"

"I'm not speculating anything," Steve replied, his voice expressionless. "That's the senior sergeant's job." Steve's hands gripped the steering wheel so tight, the knuckles were bulging through the skin. "And I don't want you passing this on, especially not to the guests. I just wanted you to know, that's all. So you're not taken completely by surprise when the police ask you what you know."

"Oh, God." Dale closed his eyes. This couldn't be happening. "Who would want to hurt Karri?"

"Like I said, I'm not going to speculate—"

Dale interrupted him as his mind flew to the obvious scenario. "But if that's true, does that mean...?" Dale could hardly believe he was about to say this. "Does that mean we have a murderer here? On the station?"

Steve finally looked at Dale. His lips were drawn together in a rictus and his eyes were dark and haunted. That look told Dale everything the other man was afraid to say.

CHAPTER EIGHT

Senior Sergeant Robinson walked into the room and it was all Daisy could do not to throw herself under the table and hide. The highly recognizable blue shirt and dark-blue dress pants with all the insignias had her heart was running around in her chest like a frightened jackrabbit. She hunched her shoulders and pulled her hair across her face, keeping one eye on the cop marching up to Daniella.

That'd been over half an hour ago, but the cop had stayed by the bar, talking earnestly to Daniella and Steve. Almost as if he were waiting for something; almost as if he were keeping an eye on them. Daisy had sweated profusely as she watched the police officer from a distance. When were they going to start this questioning? She needed to get it over and done with, before she lost her nerve.

Oh, fuck, there was another one. She had to grab the seat with both hands to physically stop herself from standing up and sprinting across the room and out the door.

A soft groan left her lips as she watched the second cop go over and greet Daniella, offering her his hand. Two cops were worse than one. They were twice as likely to recognize her. This one was younger, probably the constable Steve had mentioned earlier. The head-honcho's sidekick.

How the hell could she have gotten herself into this situation? This was the worst kind of bad luck imaginable. The police were the absolute last people she wanted to talk to. Her mind raced, looking for a way out of her predicament. But her brain was screaming at her to get up and run, which was no help. Because if she ran now, it'd be like she was pointing a blinding spotlight at herself.

She needed to calm down. If she stuck to her cover story, then maybe, just maybe, she might get out of this unrecognized. She ran over the details of her fake ID in her head one more time.

Dale had been hovering behind his stepfather since the first cop arrived. Now, he was leaning in and talking to his sister. He still looked pale and shocked. It was a terrible thing to happen to this poor family. If she wasn't so caught up in her own problems, she'd feel sorry for him. And she should feel sorry for the poor girl who was dead. Unfortunately, all she could feel right now was fear and frustration at her predicament.

Dale's gaze landed on her and he said something to his sister, laying his hand on her shoulder briefly, before turning and walking toward her.

"Senior Sergeant Robinson wants to go out and look at the scene; at the body. But he's going to leave Senior Constable King here, to take statements from everyone," Steve announced to the gathered group as Dale sat heavily beside her. There were grumbles of dissent from around the room. They weren't happy at having been made to wait so long already. "So, because this will take a while, Robinson has agreed to let all the guests return to their rooms, rather than keeping everyone cooped up here all afternoon. We'll come and get you when you're needed."

There were sighs of relief from some guests. Daisy mentally gathered herself together, it was no use showing

Dale how mixed up she was feeling. She glanced up at Robinson for a second. He wore a sober frown, and she wondered if he ever looked anything but grave. He must be in his fifties, with pale-blue eyes, and a large dent in his chin, made more obvious by his clean-shaven appearance. Tall and imposing, Senior Sergeant Robinson clearly took his job seriously. At least the younger one, King, let loose a smile now and then.

Daisy put on a brave face before shifting her gaze to Dale. "That might make some people a little happier, letting them back to their rooms. But not everyone," she whispered cynically, tilting her chin toward IT Man and his wife. As she pushed away her own fears and her mind cleared, something began to nag at Daisy. "Why are they questioning everyone? Isn't this a simple accident?"

Dale suddenly wouldn't look her in the eye. Was there something else going on here? She knew little about police procedure—and maybe the Queensland cops operated completely differently to the West Australian ones—but surely, they didn't round up everyone in the vicinity and take statements for a tragic accident. Unless it wasn't an accident. There was something hinky happening here, she could feel it in her bones. At least she could honestly say she'd never met the girl before. Hopefully, the cops wouldn't even look at her twice once they knew she'd never set foot on the station before last night. That single thought helped to calm her racing pulse a little more. Yes, if she could convince the police she was an innocent bystander, that her presence here was mere coincidence and she'd been caught up in something she had nothing to do with, they'd let her return to Koongarra and be none-the-wiser as to who she really was.

"Is there any chance of me getting home this afternoon?" She knew it was a long shot; that she was making a severe imposition on Dale for asking, but she needed to get out of here. Even as she spoke, she thought about other ways to get home to her brother. Would someone from the community be able to come and collect her? But how would she get hold of them? "Could someone else take me, if you can't?" she asked.

Dale's next comment put paid to any idea of getting out of here. "Sorry, Steve drove down to Corella Creek this morning, he was hoping to get across so he could check those cattle I moved yesterday. He says it's still too high; too dangerous to cross."

She was stuck here for at least another night.

Sheesh. It was going to be a long afternoon. She stared out the window at the billabong, wishing she could be there, fishing, with not a care in the world.

Sally made her way over to their table. "The cop asked me to hand these out," she said, placing a photocopied page with an image on it on the table in front of them. "It's a picture of Karri," she said by way of explanation. "The cops want to make sure everyone knows who she is…was."

"Thanks, but I already know what Karri looks like," Dale said, woodenly.

"Yes, but she doesn't." Sally waved a finger in the air in front of Daisy's face. Daisy finally looked down at the paper in front of her.

Oh. Shit.

She managed to stifle her gasp of surprise and cover it with a cough.

She knew that girl. The face staring back at her from the page was familiar. Daisy had seen her at the community a few times, but had never caught her name. But more than that, she was the one who'd shown them to the outstation on the day they'd first arrived. Said she was heading back to work, and it was on her way, and so they followed her trail of dust over the bumpy, dirt roads as she led the way in her beat-up Holden Ute. The girl hadn't even stopped to see if they got into the place okay, had merely waved through the window and driven off. Daisy had never twigged that the girl meant she worked at Stormcloud Station. River had noticed her, too. She'd caught his gaze following her around the community, before she even offered to show them the way. Then he'd watched the trail of dust long after her ute had disappeared.

It was one more lie she was going to have to tell the police.

* * *

Daisy pushed the food around on her plate. Her appetite had deserted her, and she watched Dale do the same thing. She glanced up at the rest of the station staff sitting at the table. Most of them seemed to pick at their meals, as well. Skylar had been too upset to come up with one of her gourmet meals tonight. It was steak and chips and salad for everyone.

All the guests were eating in their huts tonight, leaving the dining area free for the staff to sit and chat. To mull over the day and finally talk together as a group without being interrupted. And mourn for their dead colleague. Wazza seemed particularly upset. He sat without speaking, staring out the large windows into the dark.

IT Man and his wife were flying out first thing tomorrow morning. Daisy had overheard him saying he couldn't wait to get as far away from this cursed place as possible. The sooner the better. Which was a shame for Stormcloud Station. This whole death was going to affect them. Affect their reputation, perhaps for a long time to come.

"Why did Senior Constable King ask all those odd questions?" Daisy's head jerked up as Sally Tsun broke the silence that'd settled over the group, speaking from her seat next to Skylar.

"What do you mean by odd?" Dale queried.

"I don't know. Things like, did I know if Karri had any enemies. Anyone who might hold a grudge against her. I thought this was an accident. I thought she got washed off her ATV." Sally's dark eyes were troubled. The petite woman had stopped making any pretense at eating and pushed her plate away. Her glossy, black hair was still up in its neat bun, as always, but there were deep worry lines etched around her eyes.

"They asked me the same thing?" Daisy said. But it'd taken her a while to process the question because she'd been so freaked out that the cop would recognize her. At first her answers had all been robotic and strictly calculated. She was also busy pretending she'd never met the girl before. Her rote reply was that she'd only been on the station less than a day, and she'd never met the dead woman before. She forced herself to look the senior constable in the eye as she said this. And it'd worked. Well, at least she thought it had.

But as she went over the interview in her head afterwards, his probing questions had become surprising, as well as unsettling.

She was now fairly confident that the senior constable hadn't recognized her. Because surely, if she was showing up as a wanted person on their system, he would've arrested her? Right? She'd gone over and over his reaction to her during the interview. He'd remained calm, brisk—but not uncaring—and recorded all her answers on a pad of notepaper. Not a flicker of awareness that she was anyone else than who she said she was passed over his face. Not an ounce of suspicion. So, he was either superb at hiding his reactions, or he genuinely didn't know who she was.

Both she and River had altered their appearances as much as they were able. He'd dyed his normally blonde hair, jet black. Which'd been a shock to Daisy the first time he came out of the bathroom with his new look. People commented that River's looks were an unusual combination for an indigenous person, his light-colored eyes, blonde hair and dark brown skin. But it wasn't as uncommon as people thought. Because their culture had interbred since the days of the convicts, there were often throwbacks, a mixture of DNA. There was no way to change River's eye color, but he'd taken to wearing sunglasses wherever he went as well as toning down his normal attire of gangster-rap baggy pants slung low around his hips, oversize hoodies and lots of bling around his neck. Even his best mates would hardly recognize him now, in his conservative attire of jeans and button up shirts, which went along with his new consultant persona.

She'd gone almost the complete opposite to River. Dyed her normally dark auburn hair a honey blonde, always keeping it tied up in a ponytail or braid, instead of left loose to flow over her shoulders. River told her she should cut it off, but try as she might, she couldn't force herself to shear off her long locks. And she'd toned down her clothing, going for shorts and casual tops, instead of the elegant dresses and corporate suits she often wore to impress at the legal firm where she was interning. Her face was also devoid of any makeup now. Half of her missed the theatrics of applying makeup; the way it made her look. But the other half didn't miss it all, especially not in this tropical heat and humidity.

But a good cop should be able to recognize her facial features, nonetheless. Shouldn't they? So, she was fairly optimistic she'd gotten away with it.

Her fears hadn't been completely laid to rest, but at least they'd subsided to a low rumble in the base of her gut, instead of a wild animal trying to claw its way out of her throat. The most likely scenario was that the West Australian cops hadn't alerted the Queensland cops, because they had no reason to suspect that River had fled to the other side of the country. Or perhaps, even if they had listed River on the Queensland wanted lists, these ones up in the top end didn't have the time to study their lists carefully, never dreaming anyone would hide up here in the middle of absolutely nowhere.

Besides, she was hoping the cops never even found out that River was here. She'd failed to mention her work colleague, Ryan, and King had failed to ask her if there was anyone else staying with her at the outstation. Daisy knew she was skating on thin ice, and might get herself into hot water if—when—the police found out about him. But she hadn't lied to King; not really. It was a lie of omission. The cops might eventually find out about River, but maybe by then, they might be long gone. She'd been tempted to ask Dale not to mention her colleague to the senior constable, but knew that would raise far too many suspicions if she did. All she could do was hope that no one else thought to mention him in their interviews. She'd soon know if they had, because King would surely question her again if he found out she'd been withholding information.

After King had finished questioning her, he led her back into the main dining area, beckoning Bindi over to take her statement next. As Daisy had watched him follow the other woman back into the room they were using for interviews, she noticed Skylar track his movements from across the large space. While Skylar's face remained pale and drawn, her eyes told a different story. She watched King like a hawk, and Daisy caught the flash of longing in her stare. That'd been interesting.

Once she thought about it, Senior Constable King was very good-looking. She hadn't taken much notice during the interview, but now she could look at him without that fear of discovery, she could understand Skylar's attraction. He had the most amazing blue eyes she thought she'd ever seen on a man. So bright blue they rivaled the skies above Stormcloud on a clear day. Short curls of straw-blonde hair covered his head. But even with his serious police face on, she could feel her fingers itching to touch those blonde locks, to see if they were real. If she didn't know better, she would've thought he belonged on a white sandy beach somewhere, a surfer God brought to life right here in the Stormcloud dining room.

"They asked me that, as well," Skylar added, pulling Daisy out of her musings. Skylar fixed her gaze on her mother. "So, come on, spill it. There's something else going on here that you're not telling us."

Daniella looked at Steve before she answered. It was only after he nodded his agreement that she laid her knife and fork aside and carefully wiped her mouth.

Daniella was an attractive lady—Daisy didn't want to add the qualifier *for her age*, because that would be stereotyping the woman, and Daisy hated stereotypes—always dressed neatly in jeans and a long-sleeved, checkered shirt, with her bobbed, brown hair tucked neatly behind her ears to keep it out of the way. Daniella had a way of looking at you, with dark blue eyes, that seemed to evaluate everything in a single sweep of her gaze. She was obviously highly organized, clear-headed, strong, and determined. Driven might be one word that summed her up nicely. Daisy definitely wouldn't want to get on the wrong side of Dale's mother. But she almost seemed at a loss for words tonight. Which Daisy figured might not happen very often.

"If I tell you, this doesn't get repeated. Not to anyone. Not to the guests and not to the neighbors. And especially not to anyone over at Koongarra." Daniella speared Daisy with her sharp gaze at her last words.

Daisy nodded her promise. She wasn't likely to tell anyone, because this story was getting more and more complicated every day. So much so, it was hard for Daisy to keep it all straight in her head. What she was and wasn't supposed to tell people. She was completely onboard with Daniella's wish that the fewer people who knew about the details, the better.

Everyone had stopped pretending to eat and were all watching Daniella with mixed versions of interest.

"Karri had a large wound on her head—what did King call it? A contusion?" She looked to Steve for confirmation. "When Wazza first pulled her out of the water, he thought she must've hit her head on a rock, or a large, submerged log. But Steve wasn't so sure. He thought it could've been from something smaller, like the end of a metal pole, or a hammer."

Sally Tsun gasped and covered her mouth. Skylar and Bindi followed suit.

"And after the senior sergeant examined her, he confirmed it looked more like Karri had been struck with some kind of object or weapon."

Which meant only one thing. Karri had possibly been murdered. This brought on a whole other level of complication, especially to Daisy's life. The last thing she needed was to be involved in another murder investigation. Daisy held in a moan of distress. This was terrible in so many ways.

She slid a sideways glance at Dale. He didn't look surprised by the revelation. So that was why Dale had been avoiding her questions earlier. He must've already have known about the blow to the girl's head.

"Can they really tell the difference?" Sally asked, but her voice was barely above a whisper, so that Daisy had to lean across the table to hear.

Daniella inclined her head. "King said they'd know more after an autopsy."

"They're going to autopsy her?" It was Bindi's turn to sound horrified. "Her family won't allow that."

Bindi's outburst surprised Daisy, but she was correct. Traditional Aboriginal laws didn't allow for autopsies. Some Indigenous people believed that if a body was interfered with, then the spirit would be prevented from moving forward. Although, that rarely stopped the police procedure, if they thought it was warranted. A lump formed in Daisy's throat as she thought about this young woman's family. The Kuku community would already be involved in the Sorry Business, traditional ceremonies and practices conducted to mourn the passing of a loved one. This news would rip them apart and cause even more heartbreak.

"Hang on," Wazza's voice rang out around the table. "I want to get this clear in my head. Are we saying that Karri was killed? By someone on this station? Why would anyone do that? No one here is a murderer." He stood up, pursing his lips in confusion. The hat that was never far from his side was swept onto the floor, unnoticed, as he spread his hands on the table and leaned forward. "You can't seriously be telling me that there's a murderer running loose on the station, somewhere." Wazza grunted, like the notion was completely preposterous.

No one answered, and he sat down heavily, retrieving his hat from the floor.

Daisy felt sorry for the guy. He didn't want to believe it was true. But Daisy knew it could very well be. She'd seen it happen. Had witnessed it first-hand helping her brother. People weren't always what they seemed. One of these people sitting around this table right now could be hiding a deep, dark secret. Hell, she was probably the worst offender at keeping secrets. If anyone found out about her duplicity, she had no doubt they'd see her in a completely different light.

"That's an utterly ridiculous notion," Daniella said, primly taking up her knife and fork once more. "I trust everyone on our staff one-hundred percent." Daniella cast her cool gaze around the table. "But you can see why I don't want the guests hearing this information. It'll panic them even more.

They're already distraught enough about a death on the station. If this gets out…" Daniella didn't need to finish her sentence, Daisy knew enough to realize they'd start leaving in droves. And not come back. The luxury resort's reputation would be tarnished.

Death was one thing.

Murder was a whole other ball game.

CHAPTER NINE

Dale clinked his glass against the rim of Daisy's, but it wasn't so much of a celebration as an acknowledgment of their predicament. They were back in the relative seclusion of their laundry hideout. Daisy had already gulped down half of her glass of red wine by the time he'd taken one sip.

"I needed that," she said, smacking her lips. A drop of ruby liquid trembled at the corner of her mouth. He watched it, fascinated. Her mouth was like a pale, pink bow, lips plump and soft, turned up at the corners. A sensual mouth, full of dark promises. Then her tongue came out and licked away the droplet.

She turned dark eyes toward him, and he almost choked on his wine, glancing down at the floor, instead.

Quick, he needed a safe topic of conversation to refocus his thoughts. "I reckon the creek will be low enough tomorrow morning to attempt to cross it." He blurted out the first thing that came to mind. Damn, why had he said that? Dale didn't want Daisy to go home. Even with everything that was happening on the station, he enjoyed having her around; enjoyed her company. He'd had fun with her barramundi fishing this morning. Loved their comfortable banter. She was easy to talk to. When she let those walls of hers down, that was.

"Am I actually allowed to go home?" Daisy eyed him over the rim of her glass. "The way the cops were talking this afternoon…?"

"Yes, yes, you are." He hurried to allay her fears. "The senior sergeant said everyone was free to leave." Robinson had confirmed with Daniella late that afternoon, after he'd finished interviewing everyone. He made sure they had listed everyone's contact details, so they could get more information at a later date, if need be. Robinson also said he'd be heading over to Koongarra tomorrow to talk to Karri's family. Dale assumed the senior sergeant would include Daisy's work colleague in his investigations, even though the man had been nowhere near Stormcloud, he supposed the police would look at everyone in the area if they suspected a murder had taken place.

Thinking of Ryan reminded Dale about Daisy's response today, where she'd freaked out at the thought of talking to the police. But sitting here in the laundry right now, she appeared completely normal. Back to the bold, undaunted woman he was coming to know. Whatever fears had been bothering her earlier seemed to have evaporated. He decided not to confront her about her earlier display. Why break the sanguine mood?

"That'd be great, thank you." Daisy sighed and leaned backward against the wall, closing her eyes. "You don't know how worried I've been. How worried poor Ryan must be about me."

"Hm," he replied absently. His mind was preoccupied with the idea of Daisy being terribly worried about Ryan. Of Daisy and Ryan…together. The thought had struck him earlier, and it'd returned, niggling like a barking dog in the recesses of his mind. If he wanted to put those doubts to rest, then he really needed to ask. It was now or never. "So, you and this Ryan guy…" he hesitated, twirling the stem of the glass between his thumb and forefinger.

Daisy's eyes opened, and she regarded him with an inscrutable stare, then took a careful sip from her glass.

But he'd started, and he really needed to know. "Are you… ah…you know, together?"

She choked on her wine, spluttering as she leaned forward. "Oh, God, no!" Her response was so spontaneous, he knew she was speaking the truth. "He's my…" She stopped and seemed to gather herself. "He's *like* my brother. I would never…we would never—" She was still sputtering, and he patted her on the back. But in his mind he was doing a small victory dance, because the way she'd been talking about her colleague, he'd almost been sure there was something going on between them. Now he knew there wasn't, he felt lighter.

"Sorry," he apologized. "I just thought…"

"Well, you can stop thinking it," she said, trying to laugh through her coughing fit. "We're purely platonic. But that doesn't mean I don't worry about him." She rubbed a hand around the rear of her neck, tipping her head from side to side as if trying to work out the knots. "I'm a ball of nervous tension." She chuckled, but he could hear the genuine strain behind her words.

"Hm, maybe you should get a better form of communication sorted out, so this kind of thing doesn't happen again." It seemed a little odd to him that the university hadn't sent them out with a sat phone. Weren't universities supposed to be flush with money and sticklers for protocol? Maybe his version of those academic institutions was all wrong.

"Yeah, maybe." Her reply was drowned by another long gulp from her glass. Her fingers kept working at her neck. He knew exactly how she felt. His own shoulders were as rigid as a board. There wasn't a lot he could do about his tight muscles. But perhaps he could help Daisy lower her stress levels.

"Sit down here." He pointed at the floor in front of him.

"Pardon me?" She gave him the side eye, glass stalled halfway to her lips.

"I'll give you a shoulder massage. I've been told I'm good at it." He winked at her, then immediately regretted it. He could never really carry off the cocky, self-assured flirt, not like Wazza, anyway. She was going to refuse, and he'd look like a stupid asshole.

He took a big gulp of his wine and was about to tell her not to worry, when she said, "Oh…all right. That'd be nice." She placed her wine on the floor and settled cross-legged on the cement, beneath his make-shift basket chair. Daisy had her hair up in a long ponytail, and he wished she'd left it loose, like last night. She was wearing the same pair of borrowed denim shorts she'd had on last night, but today, she'd paired them with a dark-blue tank top—another one of Paula's shirts that she'd left behind—to go fishing for barramundi this morning. The tank top left her shoulders bare, and at first, he was careful to keep away from all that alluring, brown skin, concentrating on keeping his fingers on the fabric only. He dug his thumbs into the soft tissue between both scapulas and her spine, and she dropped her head forward and moaned.

"Oh, yeah, that's the spot. How did you know?"

"That's where all my knotted muscles bunch up, too. I'm not doing it too hard, am I?"

"Nope," she mumbled, her chin on her chest. "You're doing it just right."

He tried to ignore that innuendo and let his fingertips explore the contours of her back further. She was slim, he could feel every bone and rib below her skin; feel the bump of each ridge of her backbone. He liked the sense of her body beneath his hands. Yielding, yet solid at the same time.

His fingers walked up to the muscles that ran along between the base of her neck and her shoulders and began to knead them, and she moaned again, the sound vaguely erotic. A flicker of heat flashed through his veins. The crotch of his jeans got a little too tight, and he shifted to ease his growing erection.

He needed a distraction from how good her body felt beneath his hands. And a distraction from reality. He didn't want to talk about everything that'd happened today. It was too raw, too painful.

"Tell me something interesting about you."

She stiffened slightly beneath his hands. "Like what?"

"Like, are you a dog or a cat person? I can tell a lot about a person depending on their favorite animal."

She gave a quiet laugh, and her shoulders loosened again. "I'm a cat person. But not in that creepy, old cat lady kind of way." He could feel the rumble of her laughter through his hands. "We're not allowed one where I live at the moment, but I want to get one when I move out. My family still has a cat, a brown Burmese we inherited from the previous owners. She's old now, but still so beautiful and graceful. I love how independent cats are. But Burmese cats love to be around people, too. Coco used to sleep in my bed with me, her head up on my pillow and the rest of her body tucked under the covers next to me. It was so cute."

Dale listened to the sound of her voice. Listened to the nostalgia in her words. The slightly raspy depths of her tone. Listening to her speak of her early life, imagining her tucked up in bed with her cat, eased some of his own tension.

She still had her head tipped forward, her hair falling to either side and exposing her long, slender neck. Almost against his will, he stroked a finger downward, following the curve over her shoulder. She made an appreciative sound, like she was enjoying his touch. Her skin looked soft and inviting. He found himself leaning over, inhaling the aroma of her hair. It reminded him of the billabong, fresh, with a hint of the crushed grass they'd been standing in as they fished. She had an earthiness about her; there was no artifice. She wore no fake perfume to confuse him. It was merely her.

His lips landed lightly on the back of her neck, trailing kisses along the bumps of her spine. She stilled beneath him, as if she'd stopped breathing. But she didn't tell him to stop, or shake him off. Should he take that as permission to keep going?

His mouth worked down the side of her neck and over to the mound of bare skin at the top of her shoulder. Her skin was warm and welcoming. He trailed his fingers down her arm to her elbow, letting his lips follow. Her skin was faintly salty, but he liked the taste. Slowly, Daisy lifted her head and turned her face toward him. Stopping his lazy exploration of her arm with his lips, he looked up to meet her gaze. Large eyes regarded him as she twisted farther around to stare at him directly.

Would she stop this? Tell him he was dreaming and to get away from her?

Her tongue came out to moisten her lips as she stared at him. Then her mouth collided with his as her hand came around his neck to tug him in. Scooting off his basket, he got down on his knees on the floor, pulling her up to meet him. They were both kneeling on the cement, their bodies hard up against each other as they kissed. She was hot, opening her mouth to his, and his cock bulged against the zip of his jeans uncomfortably. She ran her hands up beneath his shirt, digging her nails into the soft skin of his lower back, making him shiver with desire. She wasn't holding back; she was making it abundantly clear that she wanted this as much as he did; wanted him as much as he wanted her.

He broke their kiss, staring down at her for a second, panting like he'd just sprinted a hundred meters. Green eyes so dark, they were almost black, regarded him in return. She was breathing nearly as heavily as he was. What was happening here? It felt like he was losing all his self-restraint. As if another version of himself was in the driver's seat tonight. An audacious, rebellious version who didn't care about the consequences of what he was doing. A version being driven by a passion so strong it practically obliterated his logical mind. This woman had taken control of his senses. And he liked it.

They came together at the same time, lips clashing. He fumbled under the hem of her tank top, running his fingers up the contours of her stomach to cup one breast through her bra in his palm. She gasped as he squeezed gently, and he loved the feel of the soft, rounded plumpness. His cock went so hard, he thought it might bust loose from his jeans. He pressed his erection into the curve of her hips.

He turned, then slowly lowered himself to the floor, bringing Daisy with him, not letting go of her lips for even a second. Daisy followed him down, using his body to cushion herself as she half-fell on top of him.

The sound of shattering glass cut the air. Daisy raised her head and swore softly.

She must've knocked over her glass of wine with her foot, and it'd splintered into tiny pieces on the cement.

The moment was broken into as many tiny pieces as the glass lying at their feet. Her eyes lost their soft fervor, the look replaced by the sudden realization of their reality. They were lying on the hard floor of the laundry building. About to do something they probably shouldn't.

Slowly, Daisy levered herself off Dale and stood, offering him her hand to help him up, a regretful smile playing over her lips.

Damn, he probably shouldn't have let this get so far. Dale made a silent vow. If he ever made love to Daisy, it wouldn't be like this. It would be somewhere worthy of making love to her. Because she was a special woman.

"Sorry about the glass," she said.

He waved away her apology, looking down at the broken glass and wine all over the floor. "Not a problem." He hesitated. "Look, I'm sorry. I shouldn't have started that. We were both upset by what's happening and this probably wasn't the right place or the right time, or…" He trailed off, suddenly afraid to look at her.

"Don't apologize for kissing me," she retorted. His head snapped up, and he stared at her. "I would've stopped it if I wanted to. That was one of the hottest kisses I've ever had, and I'm not afraid to own it." She stared at him, as if daring to disagree.

A slow smile formed on his lips. "I'm glad about that. And I'll own the fact that I was enjoying myself way more than perhaps I should've been."

"Good."

"Good." At least they agreed on one thing.

"Let me clean this up. Do you have a dustpan and broom?"

Dale opened a tall cupboard and fished out the dustpan and a mop. "If you sweep up the glass, I'll mop up the wine." He hoped the red wine wouldn't leave a stain and give away their late-night exploits.

"I should get to bed," Daisy said, as she tipped the shards into a nearby trash can.

"Sure, I'll walk you over." Dale rinsed out the mop and returned it to the cupboard, hiding his faint disappointment behind a smile. He shouldn't be disappointed that Daisy wanted to go to bed. And that she didn't want to stay here with him. Perhaps do some more kissing. Because he hadn't been mistaken when he said that it was the wrong time and wrong place for them. Even though Daisy had admitted the kiss had been hot as hell, it didn't mean they should necessarily repeat it. Dale had too many other things going on right now. And she was merely concerned about getting back to her work and her colleague, probably hoping to leave all this madness behind.

They emerged into the dark night, and he was immediately hit with the heavy, humid air. The rain might've washed the place clean, tamped down all the dust and given the station a new, green tinge, but it also ramped up the sultry, sticky atmosphere.

Daisy followed him across the rear grassed area toward the staff quarters, her footfalls silent behind him. He wished he knew what she was thinking. Stopping at the main door, he held it open for her. The others must already be in their rooms, asleep, as no light came from under any of the doors. He checked his watch; it was later than he expected. Dale didn't blame them, it'd been a long, terrible day.

"Goodnight," he whispered as she took the small step up to the door.

"Goodnight." Surprising him, she leaned in and kissed him lightly on the lips. "Sleep tight," she murmured, then she was gone.

He held the door open until she got to her room and flicked on her light, then he gently closed it and stomped off toward the side entrance to the family wing. Somehow, he doubted he would *sleep tight* tonight. How anyone could sleep after what they'd been through today was beyond him. But there was one tiny silver lining. He could distract himself from thoughts of murder and deceit by dreaming of Daisy's lips instead. He smiled as the moonlight beamed down upon him.

CHAPTER TEN

Daisy stared out the windshield at Corella Creek. It didn't look much different to two days ago, when she'd been crazy enough to try to cross it in her little Corolla. She'd been lucky Dale had come along when he had, otherwise… It didn't bear thinking about. Recalling her car, she swiveled her head to look for it.

"Where's my car?" Surely, they'd left it up on the little rise beside the road on the left. But it wasn't there. Had someone stolen it?

"Lefty already came and towed it away. I rang him yesterday. Sorry, I forgot to tell you."

She stiffened in her seat.

"He's good, he's repaired quite a few water-damaged vehicles in his time. If he can't fix it, no one can," Dale prattled on from the driver's seat, seemingly unaware of her sudden discomfort.

How could he have done that without asking her?

"As long as he doesn't discover any major damage, it should only take a day or two." He glanced over at her expectantly, and she had to quickly rearrange her face into a smile.

"Oh… Thank you." She bit her lip to keep the rest of her

words in. Damn, how was she going to afford that? She had barely enough money to keep them fed, let alone pay for towing and repairs. She was a poor uni student, who could scarcely make ends meet. And she'd used most of her meager savings on this escape trip to Queensland. Her mother had given her some money to help, but not nearly enough to pay for repairs to a car.

For some stupid reason, Daisy had been hoping against hope that she might hop in her car and drive on home. And all that stuff Dale had said about car engines not doing well after being dunked in a muddy creek was all a lie.

But it'd been a false hope, and she was faced with the reality of no car and no way out of here. At least, not in the near future.

Dale had been so good to her already, rescuing her out of a flooded creek, letting her stay at the resort, organizing for her car to be fixed, driving her home. He'd even handed her a satellite phone as they hopped in his car this morning, saying it was a spare one that she could have on loan until she sorted out proper communication. It was lying in her lap, glaring at her. She couldn't very well say anything now.

The car would have to stay at the repairers until she could come up with the money. She'd have to take a chance and contact her mother again, perhaps she'd loan them some more. Because she needed that car back as soon as possible.

Daisy was determined to get herself and River out of here. They couldn't stay in the area, not knowing she was on the police's radar. Not now the cops would be swarming all over, looking for a potential murderer. They needed to leave today. Tomorrow at the latest.

It was lucky she'd grabbed the motorcycle part for River, otherwise it might be on its way to town inside her Corolla. He'd still be able to repair the motorcycle. Maybe if it came to it, they could both hop on the motorcycle and flee that way.

Dale had been peering out of the windshield for the past few moments, studying the rushing water in front of the truck's bumper. "Hold on tight, I'm going through," he blurted.

Was it really safe? Obviously, he thought so. Daisy grabbed the bar above her head and braced her feet hard against the floor of the cab. The vehicle surged forward; the water rising quickly up the doors until it formed a bow wave in the front, so they resembled a boat more than a land-bound vehicle. She held her breath. Water trickled in through the door sill.

Then they were through the creek, driving up the other side, tiny waterfalls cascading from the undercarriage.

"Easy," Dale said, but Daisy caught the sigh of relief he tried to hide. He'd been worried about it, as well.

They drove in silence for a few miles, Daisy taking in the scenery, and at the same time screwing up her courage for what was to come. Dale was about to find out she hadn't told him the whole truth about more than a few things. She'd been tossing up getting him to take her up to the community and then seeing if she could get a lift to the outstation from someone there. But that could potentially take hours or even days, and she wanted to check on River as soon as possible. She regretted not telling Dale where she lived, she'd come to feel she could trust him, especially after that hot kiss last night. But there was no turning back time, she'd have to live with her choices.

Dale had his window down, leaning his elbow on the sill and driving with one hand. His hat was tipped backward on his head; it suited him, made him look like a cowboy straight out of a western movie. A bit dark and mysterious. He looked happy and relaxed, much as he had yesterday morning when they were fishing, before they got the terrible news about Karri. He flashed her a smile that lit up his dimples for a second, and her heart did a double take. Sheesh, he was good-looking.

Daisy knew a moment of regret. What might've happened between her and Dale if circumstances had been different? She was desperately attracted to him. Even just sitting in the same truck cab as him had all her senses tingling. She wanted to reach out and lay her hand provocatively on his muscular thigh, the one she could see bulging nicely beneath his jeans. Run her fingers up to the waistband, lift his shirt and find the naked skin so she could dig her fingernails in again, like she had last night. Watch him react the same way.

He was attracted to her, too. There was no doubt about that.

Could they have made something work? If things had been different?

"The turnoff is coming up soon," Daisy said quietly.

"What?" Dale slowed the truck. "I thought you said you were staying up with Bryan?"

She'd never told him that, but she had let him make the assumption, and she suddenly felt guilty. But when it came to protecting River—and herself—she couldn't allow remorse to make her weak. So instead of apologizing, she said, "No, we're actually staying at the old outstation. Do you know it? It was the temporary residence in the back paddock, for the manager while they built the current homestead."

"Yeah, I know of it. Haven't been up there in years, though. If I remember rightly, the place is pretty run-down."

He'd hit the nail on the head. The place had been allowed to fall into disrepair, but that was fine by her. She and River just needed a place to shelter and hide out for a while. It didn't have to be a five-star hotel, as long as it was safe.

She gave a nonchalant shrug. "It's does us fine. It was only meant to be temporary accommodation. We've nearly finished our work here, anyway."

He gave her an unreadable glance before turning onto the

side road leading to the back paddock. The turn off to the Koongarra main residence was a few miles farther along the main road. That interior road went much deeper into the station, while their old outstation was in the middle of the property, leaving a good twenty miles between them and Bryan's place. The community was situated farther north again, and could be accessed from either Commonage Road, that ran along the top boundary of the Koongarra station, between the small townships of Nychum and Mareeba, or via the same road that led to Bryan's residence, taking a left-hand fork about halfway to the main homestead. River had found a much more direct route to the community, by taking a disused trail that'd been cut through the woodland savannah, which joined up with the main interior road right before it forked. Which meant that Bryan never had to know when River visited the community.

But it wasn't Bryan that was worrying her. It was River. Specifically, how he was going to react to seeing her and Dale arrive. She had no way of knowing how he'd coped over the past two days without her; worrying if she was all right. He'd probably be upset, and rightly so. She crossed her fingers and hoped he remembered to stick to their story.

This road was already in bad repair, but after the heavy rain, large potholes had opened up, and some of the road edges had washed away. It'd be tricky getting her Corolla down here now.

"Wow, you need to get Bryan onto grading this road for you." Dale's hands were tightly clamped around the steering wheel as he negotiated their bumpy path toward the outstation. Daisy rolled her eyes. Bryan certainly wouldn't see this as any sort of priority.

She stared through the sparse scrubland which opened up as they came over a small rise. Tall, spindly eucalyptus trees were scattered randomly across an open Savanah of brown tussock grassland, with a rotund bottle tree breaking the monotony here and there. River's mate from the community, Yindari, had told them that this was called the back paddock, and when the station was running fully stocked, there'd be cattle running in the area. But it was being spelled at the moment. And it seemed to be thriving, especially after the rain. The brown grasses were showing tinges of green, and the trees seemed to stand straighter, reaching upward toward the sun. Puddles of standing water left over from the storm glinted like scattered sequins in between the trees.

Squinting, she thought she could make out a flash of dull red through the trees. Yes, there it was, the faded, red metal side of one of the shipping containers. They were nearly there. She grasped her hands tighter together in her lap.

"Over there," she tipped her chin toward the buildings.

"I see it." Dale followed the road through a thick copse of trees, and then they emerged into the cleared area around the buildings. Dale pulled up in the middle of the gravel clearing. Daisy tried to take everything in in one glance, checking for damage. A large puddle of muddy water stood at one end of the clearing, where the ground was slightly lower. The shade cloth that'd been strung between two of the containers now flapped feebly in the breeze, hanging by one corner. But everything else seemed to have withstood the storm. There were no trees down nearby, just a few small branches and lots of leaf debris scattered around; the slight elevation of the containers seemed to have saved them from any flooding damage.

The door to the main building burst open and River leaped down the two small steps toward the truck.

"Dinnarri, where you bin? I was worried out of my mind, man."

Dale flashed her a bemused look, his hand resting on the door handle. Shit, River had used her proper name. Daisy plastered a smile on her face and hopped lightly down from the truck.

"Ryan, I'm so glad to see you." Her use of his cover name and the professional tone in her voice stopped him in his tracks. Which was good, because she knew he'd been about to scoop her up in an enormous bear hug; one thing she loved about River was the way he had no problem showing emotion. "Have I got a story to tell you," she continued, hastening to her brother, who was clearly trying to calculate what was going on by the shocked frown on his face. She pulled him into a quick embrace, that she hoped looked more like two work colleagues who'd been worried about each other than a sister who was terribly glad to see her bother in one piece. But she needed to make sure for herself that River was alive and well. To feel his solid body beside her. He was wearing shorts and a T-shirt, not the professional clothing that was supposed to support his new persona, but Daisy couldn't really blame him; he wouldn't have been expecting company.

"I'm glad to see you, too, Daisy," River replied, finally comprehending that he needed to carry on the charade.

"This is Dale," Daisy said, gesturing toward him as he alighted from the driver's side. "He rescued me from the creek when my car got stuck in the flood."

River narrowed his eyes at her. "You tried to cross the flooded creek?"

She ignored the censure in his gaze, and said, "And then he let me stay at Stormcloud Station to wait out the storm." His eyebrows flew up to meet his hairline at this statement.

"Stormcloud Station, huh?" River pursed his lips, and she wanted to roll her eyes at him. Why couldn't he just stay cool about the whole thing? She'd explain it all to him later. "Nice to meet you." He extended his hand and stepped toward Dale. "And thanks for saving my…colleague. She can be so reckless sometimes."

Daisy nearly snorted in scorn. She was hardly the reckless one of the two.

"Hm, yes, I guess she was being a little reckless that day. But I think she was mainly worried about getting home to you," Dale replied, flashing his dimples. His gaze raked over her and Daisy felt abruptly hot. Was he flirting with her? "So, I'm not sure I'd class her as reckless. More like someone who was doing what needed to be done." Dale realigned his broad shoulders and took a small step closer to River. What the hell was he doing? Was he protecting her honor or something? That was the last thing she needed, Dale and her brother squaring off against each other.

"The food and the spare part are in the back of Dale's truck," Daisy squeaked. "Do you want to give me a hand to bring them inside?" she prompted, when River stood staring between her and Dale, lips pursed in consideration, a dark edge appearing in his gaze. "Dale was kind enough to let me store the food in their cool room, so it should all still be good to eat." The quicker they got rid of Dale, the better. She didn't want either of the men doing anything stupid. And she didn't need anyone protecting her honor, either.

"Sure thing," River said belatedly, the scowl not leaving his face. He pulled a box out of the rear seat of the truck as Dale held the door open, but continued to glance backward as he ferried it into the building.

Daisy went to grab the second box, but Dale beat her to it. "I've got it."

She let him do his chivalrous thing with a quiet sigh, snagging her backpack and the bag with the spare part from the front seat and following him across the bare ground. All she really wanted was for him to leave, but it looked as if he was coming inside, whether she liked it or not.

It took her eyes a few seconds to adjust to the dim light

inside, after the bright morning sunlight. River was already storing the fresh food in the small refrigerator. It was slightly cooler inside, but not by a lot. River had already turned on the two fans standing in opposite corners, but all they were really doing was moving the tepid air around.

This temporary homestead consisted of two shipping containers, adjoined end-to-end to make one long, thin room, and a third at right angles, forming a wing that jutted out behind the main room, which had been divided into two small bedrooms. A kitchenette took up most of the far wall directly ahead as you stepped inside, with a small round table and four chairs to sit and eat. Farther down the long room was a musty old couch, two winged chairs that'd definitely seen better days, a television that was straight out of the seventies mounted on the wall, and a stereo set that might have come from the same era as the TV. Scuffed linoleum lined the metal floor; Daisy had tried scrubbing it with soap and water when they first arrived, but no amount of washing was going to get rid of the holes and burn marks.

All their electricity came from a bunch of solar panels on the roof, which stored the power in a small cluster of batteries. If they ever needed to supplement the power, they could fire up a generator, but it was loud and smelled of diesel fumes, and they hardly ever used it.

For a fleeting second, Daisy felt a spike of shame. This place certainly came nowhere near the majestic Stormcloud lodge. What would Dale think of her living in this hovel? Then she remembered it didn't matter what he thought. She tilted her chin up and pretended to ignore him as he did a slow perusal of the place.

"I would've thought the university might've found you some nicer accommodation," Dale quipped.

But she wasn't taking the bait. "Thank you for your help," she said in clipped tones, hoping he'd get the message he was no longer needed.

"Sure, no probs."

But she could see the questions hovering on his lips. "Will you be all right here, especially after all that's happened—"

"And thanks for organizing my car to be towed," she broke in. He'd been about to ask if she was okay here, in this shabby place. It was sweet that he was worried about her. But she needed him gone. And she didn't need him blurting out the details of the murder to River. She'd fill him in with her own version once Dale was gone. River turned around from where he was placing packets of pasta in a cupboard and opened his mouth to say something.

She almost pushed Dale out the door and down the steps before either of them could say any more.

She closed the truck door as he settled himself behind the wheel. He stared at her out the open window, tipping his hat a little farther back on his head, so he could look her directly in the eye. "I'll call you on the sat phone when your car is ready."

"Thank you, that'd be good." She had no idea what she was going to say when he called her. Or even how she was going to arrange to pick up the car, assuming she found the money to pay for it. He needed to know none of that, however.

She waited for him to start the truck and was about to take a step backward so he could drive off, when he said, "I don't like you out here. So isolated. With no form of transport. It doesn't feel right." He lowered his brows, those warm dimples nowhere to be seen.

"I'm fine. We're fine." Daisy smiled at him brightly. "Ryan will have the motorcycle fixed by this afternoon, so it's not as if we're completely stuck. We can always ask someone at the community to come and drive us around if need be," she added. Even though she knew this to be a stretching of the truth. The community would be completely consumed by their Sorry Business, getting ready for Karri's funeral. She and River would be the least of their concerns.

"Hm." His grunt didn't sound totally convinced. But thankfully he finally put the vehicle in gear and drove the truck in a slow circle, so he was facing back down the road.

"Bye." She waved vigorously. *Please, just go.* She needed him to take his compassionate gaze that was turning her insides to mush far away, so she didn't have to think about him.

He waved a hand out the window and moved off down the road. Daisy let out a sigh, her shoulders dropping in relief. He was gone.

She was grateful Dale hadn't mentioned River's lapse when they first arrived and ask why he'd called her Dinnarri and not Daisy. She had a flippant answer ready, something like Dinnarri was her professional name, but she never used it, only her mother called her that. But it was a problem. Because now he knew her real name. Hopefully, he kept it to himself and never mentioned it to anyone else. Especially not the cops.

"Who was that guy? And why was he looking at you like that?" River pounced on her as soon as she came through the door.

"That's not important," Daisy said a tad huffily. She was already over the worry for her baby brother that'd eaten her up inside while she'd been confined at Stormcloud. And she was at the stage of letting her sisterly annoyance show. "I need to tell you what's happened over at Stormcloud. Because it could affect us. We might need to get out of here, like today." She took a seat on the battered couch and River followed her lead, slowly lowering himself into a wing chair, as he seemed to catch the gravity of the situation.

There was no point in sugar-coating it. "A girl died

yesterday at the station. One of the station hands found her in the creek. But there's a question whether her death was accidental, or not."

River's dark eyes widened with shock. "That's terrible."

"Yes, it was. But the most terrible part about it, at least where we're concerned, is that the police are involved. I had to give a statement."

"Oh, shit."

"Exactly." River finally seemed to grasp how bad this was.

"I didn't mention anything about you to the cops," she said. "But it's probably only a matter of time before they find out you're here and want to interview you." She could hardly believe how many lies she was telling to protect River. It was eating her up inside. Up until now, although she knew what she was doing was wrong, she hadn't had to lie to a police officer. Now, it felt a little like she crossed some invisible line. She was in this too deep to get out unscathed anymore.

"Do you know who this girl was? Did she work at the station?" River asked, leaning in closer.

"Yeah, well, it gets worse. When they showed me a picture of her, I recognized her. She's from Koongarra, we've seen her around a few times."

"What's her name?" River had gone extremely still, fixing her with a stare that frightened her.

"Karri something or other. Why?"

"No, it can't be." River's wail of anguish shocked her.

He jumped to his feet. "You're wrong. You're telling me a lie. Karri can't be dead."

What the hell was going on? How did River know this Karri girl?

Oh, shit. It finally dawned on her. Was this the girl she suspected he'd been having an affair with?

And if it was, could the police somehow link him to this murder?

CHAPTER ELEVEN

"Your car is fixed. You're lucky there wasn't too much damage. Lefty said we got it out of the water in time." Dale smiled to himself as he imagined Daisy's excitement at the news on the other end of the phone. It'd been two days since he dropped her back at the outstation. She'd be desperate to get her car back. And he was desperate for her to have it back. It was dangerous to live in such isolated country with no means of reliable transport. Even if she had her workmate to look after her, things could still go wrong quickly out here. She didn't seem to understand that. But then again, why would she? A city girl, with no experience living on the land, she'd have no idea how rapidly things could go bad.

"Oh…ah, thank you. That's great." Was it his imagination, or did Daisy not sound as enthusiastic as she should? "I'll have to arrange to get into town somehow and pick it up. Thank you so much for all your help."

What? It sounded like she was blowing him off. About to thank him and hang up.

"No, no, you don't understand. Your car is already at Stormcloud. I drove into town with Steve yesterday. Lefty said it was ready, so I drove it home again. It was too late to call by the time we got back last night." He hoped he'd done the right thing. But the silence on the other end of the phone was making him doubt himself.

"Oh, sheesh…um, you didn't have to do that." She fell silent.

Why was she acting so cagey? And a tad ungrateful, if he wasn't mistaken.

He heard her take a deep breath. "What I mean is, thank you. I'll get Ryan to drive us over on the motorcycle and we can pick it up. But, Dale…" He wondered what was behind her hesitation. "I'm not sure I can pay you back for the repairs just yet."

Was that all that was concerning her? She didn't have the money. "Don't worry, your insurance should cover the cost. I can wait until they pay you out, that's not a problem."

He heard her hesitation again, and it suddenly became blindingly clear to him. Waiting for the money wasn't the problem. The car wasn't insured. What kind of person would drive an uninsured car into the isolated north Queensland countryside?

He jumped in before she even had time to answer. "But even if you aren't insured, aren't you doing a consultancy for the uni? Surely, they'll help you pay for it?" He'd been wondering why she wasn't driving a university vehicle. Didn't they have a fleet of cars? Or at the very least, they could've hired her a proper vehicle.

"This is, ah… a private consultancy. We're doing it off the books."

Of course they were. Things were just not adding up with Daisy. But he couldn't very well call her out on a few vague suspicions. It was time to end this line of conversation. He had a more pressing reason to contact her. "I'm sure we can sort something out, don't worry about it. There's another reason I'm calling. Steve and I went into town at the senior sergeant's request yesterday. It seems the autopsy has turned up some interesting findings, and he wants to come out and talk to all the staff involved again." Dale assumed that the police would also contact the guests who'd been on the station at the time, all of whom had left by now.

There was silence as Daisy digested this additional information.

"He and the senior constable are coming out to Stormcloud tomorrow," Dale continued. "I wanted to warn you, they'll be coming your way at some stage. They said they'll be re-interviewing everyone over at Koongarra, as well. I was going to lead them out to your place, in case they got lost." That was a bit of a lie. He didn't need to show them the way, he could just give directions, Senior Sergeant Robinson was an old hand at negotiating this country, and they didn't need his help. But Dale wanted to see Daisy again. Needed to see her. This was the best excuse he could come up with. Her coworker hadn't seemed that keen on Dale, and he got the feeling that Ryan wouldn't take kindly to him turning up unannounced. There'd been an aura of animosity coming off the guy, and Dale wasn't sure why. Was Ryan perhaps keen on Daisy? She'd assured Dale there was nothing going on between them. But maybe Ryan wanted more than Daisy did. The other guy was good-looking, with the same dark skin as Daisy. Dale wasn't sure why that confused him as much as it did. There was no earthly reason why two indigenous people wouldn't do a consultancy together. But his gut told him there was something a little off, even though he couldn't pinpoint what it was.

"No." Her exclamation was so loud he had to move the phone away from his ear. "No, don't bring them here. They don't..." She seemed to be searching for an excuse, which was odd. "I'd rather talk to them at Stormcloud, if that's okay. I'd feel more at ease there. They can interview me at the same time as everyone else."

It was an odd request, but then if he wanted to see her, it was even better if she came to him. Especially if Ryan wasn't around to interfere. Maybe Robinson would interview Ryan later, with the rest of the indigenous community. The senior sergeant was more concerned with the statements from the people who'd actually been on the station at the time of the death. Dale also found it a little odd that she hadn't asked about the new findings from the autopsy and what they meant. She seemed more worried about the police coming to the outstation than she was about a murdered girl. Again, Dale felt the stirrings of unease deep in his gut. The other day, when he'd dropped Daisy off at the outstation, something had felt…off. He couldn't put a finger on what it was exactly, but a niggling voice had asked him why a university would put up two of its staff in practically derelict accommodation. On the drive home, he couldn't help wondering if perhaps he should've checked the outbuildings for Stormcloud's stolen ATV. But that would be ridiculous, because he trusted Daisy. Even though he'd only known her for a few days, he was convinced she was no thief. That Ryan bloke, on the other hand…Dale wasn't so sure about him. He rammed the disloyal feelings down into a box and closed the lid. Of course, neither of them had stolen the ATV, or taken the missing meat, or any other such nonsense.

"Sure, I can arrange that. I'll pick you up after lunch tomorrow. How does that sound?"

"That works," she agreed. "I can collect my car from you afterwards."

"Yep, kill two birds with one stone." Belatedly, he decided he probably shouldn't have used the word kill, and he grimaced.

* * *

Dale let out a long, slow breath. That'd been intense. He was completely wrung out. Senior Sergeant Robinson hadn't pulled any punches today in the interview. He searched the living area for a sign of Daisy, hoping like hell she hadn't left yet. He'd made her promise to wait until he was free, but with Daisy you just never knew. He was the last to be interviewed today. She'd been on the list right before him, her expression tense and closed off as he'd watched King lead her into the interview.

There she was, huddled in the corner of the living room, staring out the large windows toward the billabong. Daisy turned green eyes toward him. They were full of misery and a hint of confusion. It seemed the Sarge had been rough on her as well. She looked small and forlorn, dwarfed by the huge windows. Wearing a simple white T-shirt and khaki shorts, with her hair pulled back into a loose braid, the afternoon light on her face made her look younger somehow; more vulnerable.

She had looked pale and drawn even when he picked her up today. That vibrant personality and seductive smile not evident. He put it down to stress about the upcoming interview. But deep down, he could feel something about her had changed. She was withdrawn and would hardly meet his eye, only answering in monosyllables when he asked a question.

He wondered what'd been said during the interview. The police had commandeered the small meeting-room-slash-business suite; a room designed for businessmen who just couldn't leave their work behind. It had a table large enough to seat eight people with a desk in the corner set up with a printer, fax, Wi-Fi modem and computer, and anything else someone might need to stay in touch with the corporate world. Robinson had placed himself at one end of the table, indicating Dale take the seat across from him, and King had leaned against the far wall, watching the proceedings but not participating. It all felt a little different to the first time they'd interviewed him; more intimidating. King, who was normally a friendly and open guy, had a blank look on his face that was unreadable. His blonde, curly hair slicked down flat against his skull today, probably in an attempt to tame his surfer hair.

Had Robinson told her the same things as himself? And if he had, what must she be thinking? Was she looking at everyone with a hint of suspicion? Would she look at him with suspicion? His tongue probed the inside of his cheek where senior constable King had taken the cheek swab. It wasn't painful, merely uncomfortable. Dale had been surprised when Robinson requested a DNA swab, but he'd been quick to agree. After all, he had nothing to hide. Robinson said it was protocol, and Dale, never having been involved in a murder investigation before, believed him. King had performed the procedure efficiently and quickly, placing the sample in a plastic Ziplock bag on the desk. Dale noticed other bags with samples inside already lined up, but then Robinson asked another question and diverted his attention before he could study them carefully.

Dale crossed the room toward Daisy, weaving his way between the tables and chairs. No one else was around, everyone must have returned to their duties after they'd been interviewed. He lay a gentle hand on her shoulder, a form of commiseration. At the first touch of her skin, his mind was bombarded with images of them kissing in the laundry. It was as if that kiss had been a thousand years ago, so much had happened in the past few days. He could still feel her nails digging into his back, her mouth hot and demanding on his. He wanted to reclaim that feeling of passion, of being completely and utterly alive. It was the only good thing to come out of these few days of madness, and he wanted to keep hold of it. Wanted to do it again.

"You okay?"

She merely nodded.

The interview had been tough, because the Sarge had declared that Karri's death was no longer considered accidental. This was officially a murder investigation, and they were all considered persons of interest, at least until they could narrow it down to one suspect. The Sarge wouldn't reveal how he knew these things, but Dale guessed it had something to do with the wound on her head. It was one thing to speculate that Karri might've been murdered. But it was a whole other thing to have that suspicion confirmed.

Dale wasn't sure which hurt more. The fact that anyone could be callous enough—sick enough—to murder an innocent, young girl, or that the police thought anyone on the station was capable of such a thing. He considered Karri a good friend. As did everyone else who worked and lived here. It wasn't right. The Sarge must have it wrong. Karri must have been killed by a stranger. But as the Sarge had so succinctly put it, no one else could've got in or out over those two days. The place was completely shut off because of the floods.

Daisy must be feeling a lot like he was. Scared and confused. Not able to understand how she'd become a person of interest in a murder. Not for one second, did he think Daisy was the killer. First of all, she'd been with him all that afternoon. And secondly, he knew deep down inside she was incapable of such a crime. In a strange twist of fate, they'd become each other's alibis.

Did she feel the same way about him? Did she feel unequivocally that he would never harm another human? He searched her eyes, looking for any form of doubt buried in them; hoping to find trust and not censure. He needed someone to talk to about everything. And over those past few nights in the laundry, he'd felt a deep connection with Daisy. Felt like he could talk to her, when no one else around him would. His mother was going about her day as if this was some kind of minor inconvenience. Perhaps hoping if she ignored it hard enough, it'd all be over soon, and she could go back to running the resort exactly the way she wanted. Steve was also burying himself in work. Steve had never been a talkative one in the first place, one of those strong silent types, who did the work and never complained. Skylar was usually occupied in the kitchen. He'd managed to get her to put down the knives for five minutes yesterday when he checked in on her mental well-being. Apart from being shocked, she also seemed to be in a place of denial, much like their mother. It was like this terrible catastrophe was driving his family further apart; not bringing them closer, as it should.

He'd asked her if anymore food had gone missing, but she waved away his question, saying there were much more important things to think about than a few mislaid steaks. Alek, Bindi, Sally, and even Wazza, had become a tight group since Karri turned up in the creek, almost as if they were sticking together. Dale always had a great relationship with the staff, treated them like an extension of his family. But he could feel a slight disconnect between them, a coolness had developed. Perhaps it was his imagination. But perhaps they feared the family might try to point the finger at one of them and were closing ranks to protect themselves.

Driving over this afternoon to pick up Daisy, he'd devised a plan to get her alone. But now, he was unsure. He almost didn't ask. But maybe it was something they both needed; a way to get their minds off the terrible happenings for an hour or so. Skylar had made him a special picnic to take. All he had to do was get her to say yes.

"Daisy."

"Hm?" She tore her gaze away from the window to look at him.

"I'd like to show you something. Will you come with me?"

"I'm not sure. What is it? I should probably just get back to Ryan."

His stomach dropped. She was going to say no. "I'd like to take you to the top of the escarpment. You get an amazing view of the country below. We can watch the sunset from there, it should be a good one tonight."

"Really?" That seemed to spark her interest.

"Yeah. We can eat dinner up there. Skylar made us something special." Drat, perhaps he shouldn't have said that. Now she'd know he'd been planning it all along.

"Hmm." She gave him the side-eye as she pretended to consider it, while staring out the window. A tiny smile played over her lips, and he knew she was teasing him.

"I really shouldn't. But I've wanted to get up on the escarpment from the first day I arrived. And how can I resist such a gallant invitation?"

"Is that a yes?"

"I guess that's a yes." This time, a genuine smile lit her face, the first he'd seen since he picked her up today. That smile made him feel lighter, took away a small fraction of the heavy cloud hanging over his head.

"Cool." He couldn't keep the wide smile off his face, either. "Come through the kitchen and I'll grab our picnic."

Skylar was in the kitchen, of course. Even though they'd had some cancellations—people who decided that a resort currently under the cloud of a murder investigation wasn't the place they wanted to come—they were still over half full. His sister stopped what she was doing and looked up from her chopping board. A pile of finely sliced, homegrown radishes sat neatly on the board. She must be going to cook her famous char-grilled lamb chops with radish ratatouille and mint and feta tonight. At least Skylar had her cooking to keep her occupied. It kept her completely focussed for hours on end, which helped to hold the horror of what'd happened to Karri at bay.

"Hi, Daisy. Good to see you again," Skylar said, genuine pleasure in her tone. Then she frowned when she suddenly realized why Daisy was here. "Have you been interviewed yet?"

Daisy merely nodded.

"What a fucked-up situation, hey?" Trust Skylar not to hold back on her feelings. "I can't fucking believe they think any of us had anything to do with it." She slammed the knife down onto the chopping board, splitting a bright-red radish clean in half.

"Yeah, I hope they figure it all out soon, so they leave us alone."

"Amen to that, sister." Skylar flicked her blonde ponytail over her shoulder and went back to her chopping board. "Your picnic is in the cool room," she added, raising an amused eyebrow in Dale's direction. He studiously ignored his sister as he opened the door and found the wicker basket neatly tied up with a red ribbon on a shelf at the back.

"Thank you." He gave Skylar a quick hug on his way through the kitchen. "Is there—"

"Yes, I packed everything you asked for, you big loon." Skylar punched him in the shoulder as he let her go.

"Are you coming?" he asked, as he noticed Daisy still standing on the other side of the large kitchen island, staring at the two of them, an undecipherable look on her face. Almost as if she were enjoying their sibling banter. As if she wanted to join in. Did she have any brothers and sisters? And what about her mother and father, the rest of her family? He hardly knew anything about her. Perhaps he could remedy that tonight.

"Yep," she said, refocusing on him.

He grabbed his hat from the rack near the door, and a spare one for Daisy, and led the way outside, the basket swinging from one hand. But instead of heading toward his truck, he took the dirt path up to the machinery shed at the top of the rise.

"Are we walking?" Daisy asked, surprised.

"No. We're taking an ATV," he replied, placing the hat gently on her head. It was now late afternoon, but the sun still had some sting, and the brim would help to keep the setting sun out of her eyes.

"Really? I've never been in one before."

He hesitated for a fraction of a second. She sounded completely sincere, and he hated himself for doubting her for even one second. Why had he ever thought her capable of coming onto their property and stealing one of their vehicles? It was a preposterous idea. He couldn't completely dismiss the possibility of Ryan doing something dodgy like that, however. There was something about that guy that rubbed him up the wrong way. But Ryan was with Daisy, and because of that fact alone, Dale decided he had to believe in him.

"You'll love it." He assured her. Their fleet of all-terrain vehicles consisted of quad bikes, with four wheels and a roll bar chassis. They used them a lot on the station to ferry guests around to the different sites and activities. They were so easy to drive, even the guests could have a go. They were a great way to see the country—open to the sky and the elements, and slower than his truck—they gave the passengers time to take it all in. Twenty ATVs stood in a line right inside the big, open door to the machinery shed. Actually, it was only nineteen now, he reminded himself. This was where they kept all the farm machinery, as well as the many tools, rolls of wire, feeders, drums of gasoline, oil, and all sorts of odds and ends needed to keep a station of this size running smoothly.

"Jump in." He indicated the passenger seat of the first ATV, and he watched as she grabbed the roll bar and swung effortlessly in. He enjoyed watching her move, she had an easy, long-limbed way about her that seemed to pull his eye toward her, no matter where she was.

The path up to the top of the escarpment had been made especially for them to use. Steve had done most of the work himself on their big tractor, using a grading attachment. It wound around the base of the large monolith for a mile or two until it ascended through a low saddle that took them up along a ridge, and eventually led them onto the escarpment.

He watched Daisy out of the corner of his eye as he drove. Wisps of her honey-blonde hair escaped from under the hat and blew around her face as her green eyes sparkled. As they climbed higher, the land slowly opened up below them. He never tired of this view.

"This country truly is amazing. I can see why you love living here." Daisy broke the comfortable silence that'd settled over them.

"Yes, it is, isn't it? You know, I never used to appreciate it this much. I was always itching to leave. Get out there and see what the rest of the world had to offer. Then my mother sent me to Montana. My uncle owns a ranch over there, and I spent nearly two years with him. It wasn't until just recently, after I got back, that I began to see what we have here is really special."

"Sounds like your mother knew what she was doing."

Huh? Dale had never considered that angle before. He'd always assumed Daniella sent him to Stargazer to learn different techniques, so he could bring back any worthwhile practices and implement them here. He'd never thought that perhaps it was Daniella's way of giving him his freedom. Allowing him to stretch his wings. In her own way, perhaps Daniella had tried to give him that gift, and he was suddenly grateful to her.

They passed between two large ironbark trees, and the country opened up in front of them. Daisy gasped. "Oh, wow."

Most people had a similar reaction. The view from up here was spectacular. You could see for many miles in every direction; it was the highest point in the area. Steve reckoned you could even see all the way to the coast on a good day. Dale smiled to himself. That might be a bit of an exaggeration.

He stopped the ATV beneath the shade of a large stringybark. Shutting off the engine, he let Daisy take in the vista. The escarpment dropped away beneath them in a cliff face, a drop of around four hundred yards or more to the valley floor. Undulating floodplains spread out below for as far as the eye could see, broken on the horizon by lots of smaller, razor sharp escarpments that sliced into the blue sky like knives. The red ochre of the earth contrasted with the bright green of the grass, and the more muted olive green of the eucalyptus trees. Sizable areas still contained standing water, which formed small inland lakes in the low-lying areas, left over from the floods, and it shimmered and sparkled, reflecting the growing colors of the sunset.

"This is so much better than I expected," Daisy sighed.

After taking a moment to appreciate the view, Dale left Daisy sitting in the ATV and busied himself, setting up two folding chairs and a small folding table close to the edge, beneath the spreading branches of a eucalyptus. The table was a must out here, otherwise the creepy crawlies—ants, spiders, and scorpions, just to name a few—would descend on the food. He also spread out a large picnic blanket in front of the table, so they could lie back and watch the stars later, if they wanted. He unpacked Skylar's basket, placing two wineglasses, and the special bottle of red wine he asked her to include, on the table. The food was simple, but delicious.

Small, homemade quiches, using some of their very own maple-cured bacon and caramelized onions, also grown in their veggie garden. A freshly made basil-and-pine nut dip, big hunks of sourdough with lots of butter, a plate of locally made vintage cheese and slices of pear, with two individual salted caramel-and-chocolate ganache tarts to finish. Skylar had made these for the guests' desert tonight, but he'd managed to wheedle a couple out of her.

"Wow, this looks like a meal fit for a king and queen." Daisy had sidled up next to him, without him realizing. "You certainly eat well with Skylar around, don't you?"

"Yes, she's definitely one of the draw-cards of the resort. People come just to taste her gourmet food," Dale admitted. "Take a seat. The show is about to begin." He removed the cork from the bottle of wine—it was that old that it still had a cork, one of the large selections his mother had collected over the years. She'd probably kill him if she knew he was drinking it tonight, but he mentally shrugged and poured them both a glass. "Here's to getting out of our own heads for an hour or two."

They clinked glasses, and he watched as she drew in the aroma of the wonderful, old Merlot from the Barossa Valley. It was his favorite. There were only a few bottles left. But he couldn't think of anyone else he would rather share it with. She closed her eyes and took a sip.

"This is amazing." She opened her eyes and gave him an appraising glance. "You sure know how to pick an excellent wine."

It was so nice to have someone else who appreciated his passion for red wine. His mother had got him into appreciating the stuff, and Steve would often share a bottle with them. They didn't drink much red wine in Montana, and he had to settle for beer most of the time. It was good to be back and have access to the family cellar once more. That was one more thing he needed to find out about Daisy. How had she come to esteem red wine? It was unusual to find anyone who enjoyed it like he did, let alone someone his age. He had so many questions for her? Where was he supposed to start? Later. He'd interrogate her later. Now was the time to take pleasure in the landscape before them. It was the whole reason he'd brought her up here.

"I thought it was appropriate. A deep, bold red, to match the sunset." And he wasn't wrong. The sky was morphing from orange to red, then an intense purple, right before their eyes as the sun sank below the horizon. They ate and watched the delight of the setting sun, Daisy sometimes making an appreciative noise when she tasted something new.

As soon as the sun dropped below the edge of the world, darkness encroached like a stealthy hunter, stealing the light quickly, until it was hard to see his hand in front of his face. He dug in the basket and found the small electric lantern they always kept for night-time picnics. Standing up, he hung it on the low branch a little away from them, and it spread a soft, warm glow around them. Just enough light to see what they were eating. And so they didn't stumble around in the dark and fall over the edge. It would also attract the insects, which was why he hung it away from them.

"Sheesh, I'm glad I don't eat here every day. I'd be as large as a house if I had unfettered access to Skylar's cooking."

"I doubt that," he scoffed. "You look pretty damn good to me." Oops, he hadn't meant to say that out loud. But now he had, he may as well own it. "I mean, you're a beautiful woman, Daisy." He put his half-eaten bread back on the plate, and turned to catch her gaze. How would she react now he'd put it out there? She must get compliments like this all the time. Would she shut him down? Or would she kiss him like she had the other night?

CHAPTER TWELVE

Daisy stared at Dale for an endless moment. The air was alive with the nighttime sounds of insects buzzing. She could hear frogs croaking somewhere in the distance. And a flock of tiny finches flew past on their way to roost for the night. Daisy knew the stars were coming out one by one above them, the night sky descending like a soft blanket over the scarp.

But all she could see was Dale's face. His brown eyes piercing through to her soul. He wanted her. He liked her. Over the past month, she'd felt so lost and alone. No one truly understood, and no one knew how hard this had been on her. She was the strong one. Always had been. She supported River because she was the oldest. But he didn't understand that she needed support as well. A bit of compassion wouldn't have gone astray. She craved some human touch; human connection.

And that was what Dale was offering. All she had to do was grasp it with both hands. Not question his reasons and not question the repercussions until afterwards.

Getting to her feet, she came around the table and took Dale's hand, drawing him out of his chair. There was a question in the twist of his lips. Her answer was to stand on tiptoe and take his mouth in hers and kiss him, hard. She knocked his hat off, so she could run her fingers through his short curls, and it lay in the dust, forgotten.

She couldn't seem to get close enough. Her left leg twined around behind his knee and she lifted her hips so she could grind against his. Both her arms wrapped around his neck as she reached up and tilted her head so she could get the exact right angle to gain the best access to his hot mouth.

His big hands trapped her buttocks, pulling her in so tight against him she could feel every rippling muscle of his chest. And his erection. There was no way she could miss that, straining to escape from his jeans. Dale's mouth left hers and he trailed kisses down the side of her neck, and she was sure he left scorch marks wherever his lips touched. She leaned her head backward, giving him better access to the sensitive spot at the base of her throat. A groan escaped her lips as his tongue lapped over her collarbone and into the hollow beneath.

He was setting her on fire. If she hadn't had her leg wrapped around him, she might very well melt into a puddle on the dust. The sensations running through her body were both familiar, but also new. She'd encountered lust before, but this was on another level. This was like a chemical explosion going off in her brain, in her body.

Her fingers found the top button of his shirt. Skin. She needed to feel skin. But the button wouldn't come loose, and in a fit of frustration, she pulled with all her might, ripping the shirt from his body.

He gasped and lifted his head. His dark eyes fixed on hers, pupils dilated. Daisy didn't have time to wonder at her brazenness. Her mouth found one hardened nipple, and she sucked it, letting her tongue roll around the edges.

"Oh, God, Daisy," he croaked, the sound of his voice sending shivers right through her core. Then he picked her up in his muscular arms and it was her turn to gasp in surprise. Before she knew it, he'd let her down gently on the picnic rug, covering her body with his own. The stars twinkled above, so bright they hardly needed the small lantern.

She was desperate to get his shirt off. To get him naked. She'd never been this desperate before in her life. Not even with Troy. Something in Dale called to something deep within Daisy.

The buttons on his jeans popped open as her shaking fingers pried them undone. The belt buckle was a little harder to manage, but she soon had that unfastened, as well. She pushed on the waistband, taking the pants down over his hips, and he helped her by obligingly shimmying them further down past his ankles. She took the opportunity to remove her shorts and pull her T-shirt over her head, leaving her wearing only panties and a bra. Dale had on his ripped shirt, but Daisy found that no hindrance. In fact, it was kinda sexy.

Hot skin connected with hers as Dale lay down on top of her again, his mouth colliding with hers. A sudden shiver of tension ran through his body and he broke the kiss, staring down at her. His lips never moved, but his eyes asked the question, nonetheless. *Are you okay with this?* They seemed to say, *Are we going too fast?*

Maybe they were. But nothing had felt this right, ever.

She nodded, her fingers digging into the small of his back, urging his mouth onto to hers. It was all the permission he needed. He lowered his head, his delicious tongue working down her chest, over the top of the lacy fabric of her bra. The heat of him sent tiny electric impulses straight to her belly. And then lower. Between her legs, which was sizzling with anticipation.

"I hope you have a condom, because I'm not sure I could stop, even if you don't," she whispered in his ear. Her voice sounded harsh in the soft night air. She didn't want to speak, all she wanted was to feel, to be.

He said nothing. Perhaps he couldn't even talk. But the crinkle of a foil packet as he reached over toward his jeans told her as much as his words could've.

She'd never made love outside before. Preferring the comfort and order of a roof over her head and the predictability of soft furnishings below. This was new to her. Something she could hold close to her heart, treasure for the rest of her life.

Dale rolled away for a second to sheath himself, and then he was back.

She used those seconds to remove her own panties and bra, and then pushed him down and slid on top. It was her turn to take charge. She wanted to watch his face. Without waiting, she straddled him, lowering herself down over his cock.

He made a guttural sound in the depths of his throat, animalistic and primal. They moved together, his gaze on her face, his hands on her hips, urging her on.

Slowing the pace, she took control of the rhythm. He was close, she could tell. So was she. They'd been heading towards this ultimate, inevitable ending for a few days now, and neither of them needed long to reach the peak tonight. Once more she rose up and then sank down onto him, slowly but surely. Dale threw his head back, the ecstasy overtaking him. She arched her spine, rising and falling with his rhythm. And she felt it, too. Her own orgasm rising to crescendo. It hit her like a wave, bowling her over, and she closed her eyes and dug her nails into Dale's chest, holding onto him like he was her lifeboat.

Collapsing onto his chest, she lay there contentedly for many unheeded moments. Until at last, she found the strength to roll onto the picnic rug beside him.

She hadn't noticed before, but sweat covered her body. A slight balmy breeze tickled her naked breasts, cooling her. Still panting from exertion, she turned to look at Dale.

That had been intense. Almost like she was drowning, and Dale was the only one who could save her.

They lay entwined in each other's arms, looking at the stars through the leaves of the stringybark. For the first time, Daisy wondered if they were safe from prying eyes. But she decided Dale wouldn't bring her here if they weren't. Maybe a possum, or perhaps an owl flying overhead might've seen them, but otherwise they were completely alone.

"I've never done it outside before," she finally said.

"How was the experience?" he asked in mock seriousness.

"I can definitely recommend it. Perhaps I should put it in a review for the resort. One more thing the guests have to try before they leave."

He gave a soft laugh. "Not sure my mum would agree with that one."

"No, probably not." She snuggled beneath his arm, laying her head on his shoulder. "But truly, that was… as amazing as it was unexpected."

"I know," he agreed.

They lay in silence again.

But it wasn't long before Dale broke their peaceful bubble. "This whole…police investigation is tripping me out a little. I can't decide what to make of it all. It's like I've suddenly been thrown into a rushing whirlpool, and I can't figure out which way is up, and which way is down." His fingers traced gentle circles on the naked skin of her shoulders. His tone was light, but she could feel how desperate he was to talk about it. To make sense of what was happening at his family home.

She wished she could have a frank conversation with him.

She wanted so much to confide in him. To pour out her whole sordid tale. She couldn't do that, however. She couldn't put River's life at risk. Even though she felt like she could trust Dale, it wasn't only her tale to tell.

While Karri's death had definitely been playing on her mind over the past few days, she wasn't as desperate to figure out who the killer was. Not like Dale. Her motivation was driven by how deep the police investigation would go, and how she could remain as far off the radar as possible. How River could remain off the police radar. And by doing so, they'd also hopefully remain off The Black Kings radar.

Daisy was still coming to terms with River's revelation the other morning, that he'd known Karri. And not merely as an acquaintance, either. No. River and Karri had been sleeping together. Carrying on an affair right beneath her nose. All those times he said he was riding his motorcycle over to the community, he'd actually been meeting up with Karri. Or, on the few occasions where she'd left him alone at the outstation, she'd come out to visit him. When Daisy asked how he'd contacted her, he sheepishly showed her a small cell phone, and admitted that he'd bought it right before they left Perth. He knew he wasn't supposed to have one, which was why he hadn't told Daisy about it.

River said he was in love with Karri.

River also swore black-and-blue that he had nothing to do with her ending up in the creek. And she believed him.

Daisy had burst into tears when he said this. Because River had kept all this from her. Had lied to her. Lied about the phone. Lied about why he was going to the community. All lies of omission, but still lies, nonetheless. She'd cried because she wondered how much deeper into the shit they could actually get. And because River was crying, as well. He was heartbroken at Karri's death. But after a while that sorrow turned to anger, and he began ranting that he was going to find out who did this to her and exact his revenge. Which scared her more than anything else.

Her brother's revelation made her all the more desperate to get away from here. But when she'd suggested they take what they could fit on the motorcycle and flee, he'd flatly refused. Said it was too dangerous, and they should at least wait until the Corolla returned, before they made any decisions to leave. But Daisy knew that part of River's reluctance was because he was distraught over Karri's death and wanted to find out more about her killer. Perhaps a part of him wasn't ready to move away from this place where he'd supposedly fallen in love with her. Worry had nearly driven Daisy insane over the previous few days. Every nerve in her body was crying out for her to leave, to find somewhere safer. But River wouldn't budge, and part of her knew the motorcycle wasn't an ideal getaway vehicle, either.

While none of this was an excuse for Daisy's actions tonight with Dale, perhaps it was an insight into the reason she'd allowed this lapse of judgement. Had allowed herself this small luxury. To make love with Dale for this one time only. She would never see him again after tomorrow. Now they had the car back, she would not let River talk her out of leaving. Even if she had to hog-tie him, she was getting him in that car and driving away.

Daisy could reveal none of this to Dale, however. One thing she could say was that she knew without a doubt he wasn't the killer. Apart from that, she couldn't help him figure out who it was. She hardly knew these people, had no idea of their true personalities or motivations. He'd be able to answer that question better than her.

"Have you ever had a cheek swab done before? It was kind of an odd feeling, wasn't it?" he asked.

"No, I haven't," she replied a little dreamily. She was enjoying the feeling of his fingers on her skin, so it took her a few seconds to realize what he said. "Wait. They took a sample of your DNA? Why did they do that?"

Dale's fingers stopped their leisurely exploration. "I don't know. I assumed they were taking everyone's DNA." He shrugged a shoulder lightly underneath her ear.

"Well, they didn't take mine." She sat up, suddenly feeling cold. Why would they take his DNA and not hers? There was only one explanation that made any sense. "Were they only taking DNA swabs from the men?" she asked.

Dale sat up next to her. "Why would you say that?" Confusion hovered behind his eyes.

"Did you ask anyone else if they had a sample taken?" She reached for her bra and top, lying in a crumpled mess on the corner of the blanket.

"No, I didn't," he said a little defensively. "Why would I…?" his words trailed off, and the confusion cleared from his face. "There were four sample bags, including mine, on the table. I saw them after King did my swab." He also reached for his clothes, but he stopped with his jeans halfway up to look at her. "If they'd tested everyone, there should've been nine samples. Which means you're right, they only did the men." Their gazes met, and she stared into his brown eyes.

"So, if they're only testing the males, what are they looking for?" Dale mused. "Do you reckon they're going to test all the male guests who were here at the time, too?"

"I don't know about the guests," she answered. "But I'm wondering if she was raped. Would there be enough evidence left after she spent twenty-four hours in the water to determine that?" Daisy was thinking aloud, trying to gather her thoughts. She used the time she took to pull on her shorts to come up with another option. "Either that, or she was pregnant."

Neither of those scenarios was good for River. He'd told her the last time he'd seen Karri was two days before she drowned. Could DNA evidence last that long? Could it withstand being submerged in filthy water for that long? She was no forensic expert, but she hoped not. But if Karri had been pregnant…That was a whole different ball game. At least the cops didn't have River's DNA in their system. She needed to get him away from here before the cops found out about him, and pulled him in for questioning, too.

"Shit, I never even…Oh God, do you really think that could be true?" Dale was staring at her, dumbfounded.

"What else could it be?" She wanted to be wrong, but gut instinct told her she was right.

She needed to get home. Needed to talk to River. Her shirt had got stuck halfway on, she'd put her arm through the wrong hole, and she almost ripped it in her haste as she pulled it off. Making a loud noise of frustration, she twisted the top around in her hands until she found the right opening and slipped it on. Then she packed up the food into the basket.

Dale hadn't seemed to pick up on her distress, however. He was still putting on his shirt, head tilted up to study the stars as he considered their conversation. "The Sarge said he was going over to the community tomorrow morning, as part of the investigation. I wonder if he's going to test all the men over there as well?"

Shit, that was all she needed. Someone in the community was sure to mention that she and River were on the property. Then the cat would be out of the bag. Her movements became jerky and uncontrolled, and she rammed items willy-nilly into the basket.

"Can you please take me back to the lodge? I should be going."

"What?" Dale returned his gaze from the stars and seemed to realize for the first time that she was in a desperate hurry to leave. "Oh, sure. I'll just put the chairs in the ATV."

She already had the basket packed and was standing waiting for him. He glanced at her once as he folded the chairs. There were questions in his glance, but he was too much of a gentleman to ask them. He was probably wondering if she regretted their steamy interlude. What a shame it had to end this way. It would've been nice just to snuggle on the blanket with him forever.

She looked away. Let him think what he would; she could never tell him the truth, so none of it really mattered.

Once they were in the ATV and on their way back down the escarpment, with the powerful spotlights on the front lighting their way, Dale filled the silence with more of his musing. "Perhaps it's a jealous lover thing. Maybe they'll discover it was someone over at the community, all along."

"Maybe," she said noncommittally. "But isn't there the whole problem of how they got on and off the property without being seen in the middle of the flood?"

"True," he agreed.

The rest of the trip was spent in relative silence, each lost in their own thoughts.

She wanted to lean over and touch him. Tell him he was amazing. That their time together had been amazing. And she was going to miss him terribly when she left.

When he pulled the ATV into the machinery shed, she was of half a mind to kiss him goodbye, feel his lips one more time and brand them into hers forever. But she remained sitting straight up and staring forward, feeling like the churning emotions inside her chest were going to implode.

"Thanks for a wonderful night," she said, trying to inject warmth into her voice. "Thanks for showing me that view, I'll treasure it always."

"No probs." He was avoiding her gaze, damnit. He'd caught onto her aloofness. But it was for the best. "I'll show you to your car," he added woodenly.

Dragging her feet through the gravel, she followed him down the path from the shed toward the back of the lodge.

All the lights were blazing, which meant everyone was still awake. Probably finding it hard to sleep, and she didn't blame them. She should go in and say her farewells, but she couldn't face any of them. Instead, she followed Dale around to the guest parking lot, which was lit by many small solar lights.

There was her car, all white and shiny. Lefty must have washed it and cleaned out the interior for her.

"I'll follow you home," he said.

"What? Why? There's no need for—"

"I'm going to make sure you get home safely, whether you like it or not." His voice had such a hard edge, she was sure he hated her. The last thing she wanted was for him to do another kind thing for her. It'd break her heart, because the only course of action was to push him away now.

"Fine," she sighed. "Do whatever you want." As long as he didn't demand to come in and make sure everything was all right. She had no idea how River would react to seeing Dale again. Now that Karri was dead, everyone was a suspect in River's eyes. Even though she'd assured him there was no way Dale could have murdered Karri because she and Dale had been together all that afternoon.

A small part of her was thankful for the presence of Dale's big truck behind her as she negotiated the road between the lodge and her home. She'd never admit it, but her near-failed attempt across the creek when it was flooded had freaked her out. Corella Creek was practically back to normal, with a small flow of water coming across the concrete causeway. She was glad for the truck's bright lights, which illuminated the whole creek bed. She'd also never crossed the creek in the dark before, and it would've been scary if she had to do it on her own.

She let out a sigh of relief when they finally pulled into the clearing next to the outstation. But that sigh of relief quickly turned to worry when she noticed none of the lights were on in the shipping containers. Surely, River would still be up, it wasn't that late. And he'd want to speak to her, to find out what the police had asked her this time.

River had set up a security light that came on whenever someone approached the homestead, but everything else was dark.

Stepping out of her car, she glanced over at the small lean-to River had built to cover his motorcycle.

The motorcycle was missing.

CHAPTER THIRTEEN

Dale turned his truck around. He'd done his duty and made sure Daisy got home in one piece. A security light had flashed on when they first arrived, but the rest of the place was in darkness. Ryan must be asleep already. Which was odd, because it wasn't that late. Then he saw the worried frown on Daisy's face. She stepped out of her little Corolla and rushed across to yank open the door to the sea container, not even bothering to close her car door behind her. Lights flickered on inside. What was going on? He stepped on the brake and rolled his eyes to the ceiling with a sigh. *Keep driving. This is none of your business.*

She'd made it abundantly clear that she regretted what they'd just done together. Her sudden rush to get dressed and head home after they made love. And the ride down from the escarpment had been a chilly affair. She could hardly look him in the eye after they alighted from the ATV. Her reaction had hurt. More so than he'd like to admit. On the drive over to the outstation, he kept telling himself what they'd done had merely been sex. A onetime affair, and he shouldn't let himself get so wrapped up in her.

Daisy reappeared at the door, a look of terror on her face, a piece of paper flapping in her hand. "River," she screamed.

"Where are you?" She took off into the dark at a sprint toward the large metal shed meant to house the farm machinery, an amorphous shape in the night.

Who was River? Did she mean Ryan? Was her colleague missing? And why was she acting so wild?

Dale turned his vehicle off and leapt out, jogging after her, not confident enough of the unknown terrain to move at the same speed as Daisy. He was only halfway to the shed when she reappeared, her white T-shirt glowing in the light of the stars. "He's gone," she cried. Then she did something totally unexpected. She sank to her knees and put her head in her hands.

He also sank to his knees amongst the leaves and sticks and put his arms around her. She was sobbing uncontrollably. "Who's gone? Do you mean Ryan? I'm sure he hasn't gone too far. I'll help you find him." He stroked the top of her head as if she was a distraught kitten, hoping to soothe away her sobs. It shocked him to see her like this. This was all a little surreal, both of them kneeling on the ground in the dark. How could a workmate cause her such distress? He hated to see her in such pain. When he found this bastard, he was going to have a stern word for doing this to Daisy.

"No, we won't find him. He's gone." She shoved the scrunched-up piece of paper at him and continued to cry.

Dale did his best to smooth out the paper with one hand, while he kept his other firmly around her shoulders. He lay the sheet on the ground and pulled out his phone, turning on the flashlight app. It was a handwritten note.

Dear Dinnarri,

I know how much trouble I've put you in. I'm sorry I dragged you all the way over to the other side of the country. I'm leaving, going somewhere you'll never find me.

I'm going to find this bastard who killed Karri, and I'm going to give him a taste of his own medicine.

You're free now. You can go home. I'll be okay on my own. Don't try to find me.

Love you. River.

None of it made much sense. Apart from the fact her colleague seemed to want to mete out his own form of vigilante-style justice. He could join the queue; Dale felt the same way, and he assumed Steve, and probably Wazza, all wanted a piece of the guy, if they ever found him.

What kind of trouble had he put Daisy in? And what did he mean about dragging her across the country? There was also the use of that name, Dinnarri, again.

Daisy was still crying, but her sniffling had become less noisy, and she lifted her head from his shoulder. Wiping the back of her hand across her eyes, she sat on her heels, breaking their contact.

"I need to look for him." She began to get to her feet, still wiping away tears.

"I'll help you," he said, also standing and dusting off his pants. He had no idea where to look. All he knew was he couldn't let Daisy go out alone. Not in the state she was in. She needed a friend by her side. "But all of this makes little sense. You have to tell me what's going on. Then I can help you."

She stared up at him, those big, green eyes red from crying, her face blotched with tears. She shook her head. "I can't tell you." Her voice was small and forlorn, more like a small child than a grown woman. What was so terrible that she couldn't confide in him? There was obviously a secret eating her up inside. He'd felt that she was holding something back from the first day he'd met her. That he wasn't seeing the true Daisy. And this was the reason. It had something to do with this Ryan, or River, or whatever his name was.

"Yes, you can. You can't go out looking for him on your own. You need help."

"No, I don't." She dropped her head and wouldn't look at him.

He took Daisy by the shoulders, tilting her head up with a finger under her chin, until she finally met his eyes.

"I want to help, Daisy. Let me help."

"I…" Daisy bit her lip in consternation. His eyes were drawn magnetically to her mouth. The same mouth he'd been kissing less than an hour ago.

He felt it the second she gave in. Her shoulders dropped, and she blew out a long breath. "Yes. Okay. I need to tell someone. Come inside. It's a long story."

Daisy scuffed her sneaker-clad feet through the leaves and debris. The standing puddle of water had disappeared from the end of the gravel clearing, the dry earth quickly soaking up what was left of the water. Red mud was reverting to dry, choking dust. It was almost as if the flood had never happened. She stomped up the stairs and led him into the building.

"I'm going to make a cuppa. Do you want one?" she asked, filling a battered, steel kettle and placing it on the gas stovetop. With a practiced flick of her wrist, she struck a match and lit the blue flame.

"I'll have a strong coffee, please. Black." Dale pulled out a chair at the round table, sitting down and leaning backward so he could watch her move around in the small kitchenette. She took a tissue from a box on top of the refrigerator and blew her nose, then straightened her hair, which'd come loose in her mad dash to the shed.

He watched and waited. It was hot in here. The place must've been shut up all day, and it was stuffy. Sweat was already beading on his brow. As if reading his mind, Daisy turned on the two fans standing in each corner and then opened all the windows. They brought almost immediate relief, as the hot air was pushed outside.

The kettle whistled, and she took it off the stove and filled two mugs. Then she turned slowly to stare at him.

Breaking the silence, she said, "That man you thought was my colleague is actually my brother, River."

Dale pursed his lips. He hadn't been expecting that.

"Okay," he drawled, trying to figure out where this was all going. That might account for why she was so upset. She was clearly close to her brother. But why all the subterfuge? He said nothing more, giving her space to explain in her own time.

Daisy poured milk into her tea and stirred it slowly. The look on her face told him she might well be searching for the courage to tell him the rest. She drew in a deep breath. "We're not doing environmental consultation, and we have no connection to the university in Melbourne, either."

"Okaaaaay." This time he drew the word out a little. It seemed as if almost everything Daisy had told him was a lie. But why? And why was it such an elaborate lie? "Let me guess. You weren't born in Darwin, either." He tried, but failed, to keep the sarcasm out of his voice.

She brought his mug of coffee and her cup of tea over to the table, setting his down in front of him.

"No, I wasn't." She looked directly at him. "We're both from Perth. My whole family is in Perth. I go to uni in Perth."

Some of the brother's cryptic note was making sense. At least now he understood what it meant when River said he'd dragged her all the way across the country. This was about as far away from Perth as you could get.

"So, what are you doing here in the middle of nowhere?"

She hesitated, twirling the cup in her palms. "My brother got involved with the wrong crowd." She sighed and lifted her gaze to the ceiling. "He tries hard to do the right thing, but he always seems to land in trouble."

Uh-oh, this didn't sound good. It sounded like...

"He's wanted by the police in Western Australia. But it's all a big misunderstanding."

Yep, that was exactly what it sounded like. The boy was mixed up in something illegal. And he'd somehow dragged his big sister into it.

"So, I got him out of there as fast as I could. He's innocent. But the cops say he's involved in the crime. An accessory to the fact. But he never hurt that man. He told me he tried to get them to stop."

A sudden worry niggled at the back of Dale's mind. "What kind of crime are we talking about?" he asked warily. It was suddenly very important that she answer this question. This was the crux of the whole matter, and a sudden lead weight settled over him as he waited for her reply.

"It's in connection to murder."

Dale's heart stuttered in his chest. No. This couldn't be. His blood ran cold. Surely, that was too much of a coincidence. The boy was under investigation for a murder in West Australia. And now, he just happened to be here when another murder occurred.

"Holy fuck," he whispered.

"It's not what you think." she hurried to correct him. "He's innocent, I know he is. And I know how bad this all looks. But there's no way he would hurt Karri, either."

Dale wasn't so sure. He had to applaud Daisy's conviction, but she was severely biased. She could be wrong. And if she was wrong… There was no point in arguing with her. He needed time to think over these revelations and come to his own conclusion. The coincidence was remarkable. It all began to make horrible sense to him. Why she'd been so desperate to get across the flooded creek. Why she'd looked so terrified when the police had arrived. Why she hadn't wanted Senior Sergeant Robinson to come to the outstation; because she needed to keep River hidden. And now he knew about their connection, he could see the similarity between them. Even though River had light-brown eyes and dark hair, they had the same, heart-shaped face, the same high cheekbones. But there were so many other things that needed clarification.

"Why did you go on the run if he was innocent? Why didn't you just go to the cops, explain how things went down?" he asked.

She stared at him as if he'd just sprouted horns out of the side of his head.

"You're joking? The cops would've had him locked up quicker than you could blink. They can't see past the color of our skin, most of the time."

He was shocked by her statement.

"Don't give me that look, you know the cops are biased. They stereotype us. Perhaps Robinson and King are exceptions. But come on, can you honestly say that most cops don't take a second look whenever an Aboriginal walks in front of them?"

He stopped to consider her words. "I didn't realize it was that bad," he answered truthfully.

"No, well you wouldn't, would you?" She arched an eyebrow in his direction.

He was about to argue, to deny he was racist. But then he stopped and thought about how he might look through her eyes. How he'd never experienced racism in his life. And how perhaps he was biased by his white privilege. There was a lot to unpack in that one statement, and Dale decided to shelve the argument for another time. There was plenty to think about in what Daisy had just told him, without going down that rabbit hole.

"But there is more to it than just being wanted by the cops," Daisy said quietly into her mug.

There was more? What more trouble could this boy possibly get into?

"It's the reason I agreed to bring him here. His life's in danger." She stopped and lifted her haunted gaze to stare at him. "There's a gang. They think he betrayed them; turned some of their members over to the police. Which he didn't," she added hurriedly. "I couldn't bear the thought of those thugs coming after him. Torturing him. Perhaps even killing him. And my family was in jeopardy while he was in the city. Those thugs don't care who they hurt in the process of exacting revenge."

Dale could hardly believe his ears. He stared at Daisy as if were speaking some kind of foreign language. He thought he'd been getting to know her. But this was like some story he'd read in a sensationalist newspaper. This kind of thing didn't happen to normal people.

Who was this woman sitting in front of him?

Another thought occurred to him. "Is your actual name Daisy?" He remembered the name written on the letter tonight, and the time that he'd returned Daisy after the flood and River had called her something else in his rush to make sure she was okay. For some reason, this was the worst betrayal of all. He didn't even know her real name. If she couldn't even tell him that, how in hell was he to believe anything else they'd shared was true? His heart beat heavy as a drum, a lead weight settling inside his chest. Was there nothing about this woman he could believe in?

"Yes. And no," she replied.

What was that supposed to mean?

"The name my parents gave me, and the name I use, is Dinnarri. But Daisy used to be my nickname. When River was very young, and he couldn't pronounce my name properly, I became Daisy. I haven't used it in nearly fifteen years. I chose it because only my very close family would ever know I used it."

Dale exhaled on a loud breath. It *was* her name. For some

stupid reason, he felt lighter. When he'd whispered her name as they were making love, it'd felt so right. Her name was a part of her, and it spoke to him.

Daisy sat opposite him, passing her mug of tea between her hands. She looked like she had the weight of the world on her shoulders, and he finally had an inkling why. When she looked up, the dark smudges beneath her eyes were more pronounced, her pretty mouth turned down, pain and anguish pulling at the corners. She'd been suffering this whole time, and he never knew. This brother of hers had a lot to answer for.

"Come here." He stretched his hand across the table. After a millisecond of hesitation, she took it and let him draw her up from her chair and lead her into his lap. Draping an arm around his shoulders, she settled into his chest, accepting his proffered comfort. Her tears had dried, but the misery was still simmering near the surface. He could almost feel the pain radiating from her. His body responded immediately to having her close. To how soft and pliant she was in his arms. To the way she needed him. To her sudden vulnerability. He wanted to be the rock she clung to in her stormy ocean.

"I don't know what to do," she mumbled into his neck. "I'm scared River will do something reckless. He's not good on his own. I need to find him. But I don't know where to start looking."

He couldn't believe he was about to say this, but he did, anyway. "Come back to Stormcloud with me." He certainly wasn't leaving her on her own out here. Not with a likely murderer on the loose. And not with her unstable brother gone missing.

His feelings for her were in complete turmoil. He'd been so sure they had a connection as they lay under the stars together tonight. He'd even go so far as to call it the start of something great, as if he might well be teetering on the edge of free-falling into space, where only she'd be able to catch him. Afterwards, she'd turned so cold and aloof, as if it'd all meant nothing. She'd just revealed that everything he thought he knew about her was a lie. That she was on the run from the police. And helping her brother hide from a rabid gang. He had no idea how he was supposed to feel about her now. But his emotions in turmoil aside, all he knew was that he couldn't leave her to suffer alone in isolation. He needed to know she was safe, and the only place he could protect her was at Stormcloud.

"What?" Her head came up suddenly, and she gave him a look that reminded him of a startled fawn. "I can't do that."

"Why not?"

She went to stand up from his lap, but he trapped her with an arm around her waist. This was important. He wouldn't let her fob him off, treat him with disdain as she had earlier.

"I mean it, Daisy. You'll be safer if you come to the station. Your safety is important to me." He drilled his gaze into her as he said these last words, letting her see his sincerity. Letting her see his vulnerability. Letting her see his need to help her.

She stopped struggling, instead, her head tilted to one side as if considering him. If she flatly refused to come, he'd even consider staying here with her. But that was a last option. They needed him back at the station; the work to keep the cattle station up and running didn't stop because there was a murderer on the loose.

"What if River comes looking for me? I have to stay here." She was still arguing, but the heat had gone out of her words.

"We'll leave him a note. Where is the sat phone I gave you? We can leave that with the note, and he can call you if he needs to."

Daisy didn't look convinced. "I don't want to impose on you and your family. Again."

"It's not an imposition, if it's to keep you safe." He could see her wavering. He was getting to her. He knew how stubborn Daisy could be, and so, perhaps somewhere deep down, Daisy was a little glad she had an excuse not to stay here on her own. "Why don't you go and find that sat phone," he said gently.

Finally, she nodded, and he released his grip on her slim hips. She stood up, and he immediately missed the weight of her on his thighs, and the warmth of her arm around his neck.

He tried to gather his thoughts as he watched Daisy do a quick search of the living area. A slight frown settled over her face and she disappeared into first one bedroom and then the other.

"I can't find the sat phone. It's not in the drawer where we usually leave it, and it's not anywhere else in the house," she finally revealed. "Maybe he took it with him."

Of course he did, that selfish prick. He'd taken the phone as insurance and left Daisy with nothing. It was typical of a person who only thought of themselves. And the more Dale learned about this brother of hers, the more he disliked him. Instead, he said, "That's a good thing. He's a smart kid. Now we know he has a means of communicating. If he needs help, he'll use the phone."

"I guess so," she intoned. He could see the confusion tumbling around in her head. But she clearly desperately wanted to believe Dale, that she finally nodded, and said, "I'll pack a bag. Can you wait for me?"

He wanted to say he would wait for her forever, but that was a silly sentiment, and he wasn't even sure where it'd come from. "Of course. Take your time. There's no rush."

Daisy headed into the bedroom and Dale stayed seated, waiting for her.

He needed to decide what to tell his family. He was hoping

to convince her on the drive back to confide in Daniella and Steve, at the very least. He was pretty sure they would keep the secret, if he begged them to. But was it right for him to ask them to do this? To keep such a monumental secret? And if she refused to tell them, it was going to be a heavy burden for him to bear. The implications for him and for the station were mind-boggling. What if River *had* played a part in Karri's death? Daisy seemed to have a blind faith when it came to her brother. But what if she was wrong?

CHAPTER FOURTEEN

Daisy sat on the bed, head in her hands. It was late, past midnight. But there was no way she was going to sleep. Dale had shown her to the same room in the staff quarters as before. He'd hovered protectively in the doorway for a few minutes, until she quietly shooed him away, telling him she would be fine. Her bag sat unpacked at the end of the bed, because she had no strength to put away her clothes in the closet. Because doing so would mean admitting defeat. She'd turned out the bedside lamp, not wanting to disturb anyone else, and was now sitting in the dark.

Should she have revealed her secret to Dale? It'd do no good second-guessing herself now. He knew about her and River, and she had to mitigate the risk; make sure he told no one else. At the last second, she'd withheld the most vital bit of information. She was about to reveal River's link to Karri and tell Dale that River had been sleeping with her, but something had made her keep her mouth shut. Perhaps she could feel Dale's cynicism at her story, and knew if she mentioned Karri's connection to River, then he'd want to believe River was involved in her murder somehow. Which he wasn't, she was absolutely certain about that. At the same time, she needed to come up with some sort of plan for herself. Should she stay in the area, in case River reappeared?

Where had he gone? If only he'd waited to talk to her first. But then, that was River. Always jumping in feet first, and thinking later.

He'd been the same, even when he was little. But their parents always excused his behavior, justifying his pranks as just being a boy, and that was the way boys were supposed to behave. But the behavior continued, even after River was old enough to understand the consequences of his actions.

One time, when Daisy had confronted him, River had flown into a rage. He'd yelled that no matter what he did or how hard he tried, he could never live up to her eminence. She was the favorite child, and he was always overlooked by his parents.

He was only fifteen, and she'd been nineteen, old enough to know better. But the revelation of how he viewed her had cut deep. Because it simply wasn't true. Was it? His words had needled at her psyche, and perhaps she'd come to believe them a little. It was possibly one of the drivers making her want to help her brother now. That guilty stab, every time River ended up in trouble or on the outs with their parents, she subconsciously felt was her fault. She'd begun using his own reasoning to excuse his destructive behavior. It'd been a bone of contention between them ever since. A simmering, unhealed sore, festering away.

Perhaps it was time she did something about it. When she saw River next—if she saw River—she decided she'd have it out with him once and for all. He needed to take responsibility for his own actions.

The sound of a voice outside the window made her lift her head from her hands. Daisy tilted her chin, straining to hear better. It sounded like a woman, the tone low and urgent. Perhaps speaking on a phone, because there was no other answering voice.

Who was out there at this time of night?

And was it really her problem?

The one-sided conversation continued in an indistinct murmur until curiosity got the better of Daisy. She tiptoed to the window. It was already open a crack, and she slid her fingers underneath the frame and lifted it slowly. It slid nearly a foot before the frame caught and made a small grinding noise. Instantly, Daisy stopped, yanking her fingers away. Had whoever out there heard her? Craning her neck to get as close to the opening as possible, she tuned in to the conversation. The person talking hadn't paused in her discussion, and Daisy let out a quiet sigh of relief. They mustn't have heard her stealthy window opening.

It took her a few seconds to figure out the voice was that of Sally Tsun. Even though the petite woman had spent most of her life in Australia, there was still a hint of a Vietnamese accent. Daisy dare not poke her head out the window to confirm her suspicion, however. Sally might see the movement, even in the darkness, and she'd give herself away.

"I can't just up and leave. That's the most stupid suggestion you've made yet," Sally hissed. "Everyone would be immediately suspicious if I did that. We have to have a legitimate reason for me to leave." Sally stopped speaking, and Daisy assumed she was listening to whoever was on the other end of the phone. "I don't care what you think, Johnny. You're the smart one. Come up with something and quick. Maybe my grandmother died, I don't know."

What was all that about? Who was Sally talking to?

Daisy strained to hear more of the conversation, but Sally must've moved towards the back corner of the building, and her voice became indistinct, a low buzz in the night air, and Daisy could make out no more.

That was odd. It sounded like Sally wanted to leave the station. She didn't know the woman very well, but she'd never heard her mention Johnny before. Was he her boyfriend? Daisy didn't blame Sally for wanting to get out. This whole murder situation was freaking everyone out. Dale had mentioned they'd had some cancelled bookings today, with guests deciding they didn't want to holiday at an eco-resort that was under the cloud of a murder investigation. Daisy thought that was fair enough. But she couldn't shake the feeling Sally was up to something. Perhaps she should mention it to Dale in the morning.

She stumbled toward the bed and lay on top of the covers, not even bothering to get undressed. She knew she wouldn't be able to sleep, but fatigue was dragging her muscles down. At least if she lay on the bed, it was a form of rest. She closed her eyes, but that was a mistake, because she was immediately bombarded by images. Not images of River, as she might've suspected, but images of Dale. Hovering over her, the night sky bright with hundreds of stars behind him, his eyes full of dark passion as he lowered his mouth to claim hers.

* * *

Daisy's eyes sprang open. She'd fallen asleep. Although, she didn't know how that'd happened. A pale streak of light peeked in beneath the curtains. It must be early. There was a knock at her door. Was that the sound that'd woken her in the first place?

"Come in," she croaked, rolling over and sitting up. The door cracked open, and Dale put his head in.

"Sorry, I wasn't sure if you'd be awake," he said apologetically.

"I can't believe I actually fell asleep. What time is it?"

"It's only five-thirty. The sun isn't even up yet. But that's good you got some rest."

"Yes." She nodded, dragging a hand through her tangled mat of hair. Sheesh, she must look a mess.

"Steve called an early staff meeting this morning. He wants to address a few of the issues and rumors that've been going around, before the guests get up. You know…about the murder." Dale still hesitated over the word. Even now, none of them truly wanted to admit that one of their own had been murdered. "I thought you might like to come along. Then you can spend the day with me. I'm taking a group of guests over to the old mine site. Skylar will have breakfast ready for us," he added as extra incentive.

"That'd be great," she answered quickly. Any information she could garner at the moment would be helpful. Perhaps Steve might have more information from the police about who the prime suspects were. Plus, the call of Skylar's cooking could not be ignored. "Give me two minutes to get changed."

"Good." He pulled the door shut behind him, and Daisy quickly dug into her bag, grabbing the first clean outfit she could lay her hands on.

Stripping off her clothes, she chucked them in a heap next to the bag. Then, as she reached for a fresh bra and panties, she stopped. It was strangely erotic, her standing naked in the middle of the room, while Dale was right outside, only a flimsy piece of wood between them. A part of her wanted to open the door and invite him in. Wanted to see the flare of hunger in his eyes when he saw her standing there. Exposed and unguarded.

Last night she'd been so sure it was the last time she'd see Dale. And now she'd been given another chance, but wasn't sure what to do with the opportunity. The pull of him was strong. Even through the door she could feel his presence. What was she supposed to do with this gigantic pile of steaming emotions?

Pushing away the confusing residue of lust and attraction from her mind, she fastened her bra, pulled on a clean T-shirt and a pair of denim shorts, then slipped her feet into her sneakers. She opened the door with one hand, while pulling her hair into a ponytail with the other. She probably looked terrible, and needed a shower, but at least she wasn't wearing the clothes she'd slept in.

"Thanks for waiting," she said, following Dale's broad shoulders down the hallway. It was getting lighter outside, the first streaks of pale indigo painting the horizon before the sun rose. She loved this time of morning, when the air was cooler, before the heat of the day descended. Wazza's dark form strode across the area between the staff quarters and the lodge right in front of them. She could tell it was Wazza, because he had his eternal hat on his head. He stopped and held the door open for them, giving Dale a nod of greeting, and shooting her a surprised smile.

"Didn't know you were coming back," he said, bringing up the rear.

"Neither did I," she answered cryptically. There was no time for any more conversation, as they entered the kitchen and found everyone else milling around.

Skylar was bustling around as usual, pulling a tray of bacon out of the oven, and flipping fried eggs out of a skillet and piling them on a large plate. Bindi was buttering a pile of toast, and Sally was setting out plates and cutlery for everyone. Seeing Sally jolted her mind to the overheard conversation tonight. The diminutive woman showed no signs of fatigue from her late-night phone call. Her hair was done neatly in the same bun she always wore, her black skirt and charcoal shirt perfectly ironed. She looked ready to start the day, with no sign that she was planning on leaving.

Steve leaned against the countertop, deep in conversation with Alek, his hands painting a picture of something in the air. Alek glanced her way, a look of confusion flashing across his features before he returned to his intense conversation with Steve. Daisy studied Alek for a second. Dale had mentioned that Alek was a bit of a ladies' man. He'd certainly looked her up and down the first time they'd met, but she'd shut him down with a glare that told him she wasn't in the least interested. Had he ever shown an interest in Karri? She needed to remember to ask Dale later.

Daniella had taken a seat on one of the barstools that lined the rear of the countertop and was rapidly tapping away on her iPad.

Neither Daniella nor Steve looked shocked to see Daisy, so she assumed Dale had already warned them she was back. On the return drive last night, Dale had tried to convince her she should let him tell his mum and Steve the full story regarding River. But she'd balked at the idea. It was bad enough that Dale knew. The idea of anyone else finding out made her feel sick. So, they'd settled on a convoluted version of the truth. They'd tell everyone that River—Ryan—had suddenly been called home by a family emergency. That he could be gone for up to a week, and Dale had suggested she stay at the station, so she didn't have to be all alone. She felt like a bit of a fraud. And she also felt people would think her weak, afraid of staying out in the bush by herself. Dale had brushed those fears aside, telling her few women he knew—especially ones brought up in the city—would ever agree to stay in that rundown outstation in the first place. Let alone stay as a woman on their own.

Everyone was talking quietly between themselves, the buzz of conversation filling the kitchen. Daisy stood and listened, not taking part in any of the discussions. Dale went over to talk to Steve and Alek about where they were going to move the cattle out of the high paddock. Daisy tuned out that exchange.

"I need you to find some more documents for me," Daisy heard Daniella say to Sally over her shoulder.

"What? Why?" Sally's face took on a pinched air of concern.

"I've just had another email from Mr and Mrs Peterson," Daniella said with an impatient wave of her hand. "They're saying we overcharged them for their stay back in October. That's two people now, who say we've got the invoicing wrong. Perhaps we need to take a look at our financial software. Could there be a glitch in it somewhere?"

Sally moved closer to Daniella, so she could peer down at the iPad on the countertop, and Daisy could no longer hear what the two women were saying.

Dale didn't seem to have noticed the tense conversation between his mother and the receptionist, continuing his chat about the right concentration for a salt lick, of all things.

"Don't let the food get cold," Skylar announced.

"I don't need to be told twice," Wazza said with a grin. He snagged a plate and began piling food onto it. Steve and Alek moved toward the middle countertop, jostling Wazza in a friendly bid to be the first to the food. Daniella looked up, but went straight back to tapping away, with Sally looking unsure whether she should grab some food, or continue to hover by her boss's side.

Dale came over and nudged Daisy with his shoulder and indicated with his chin that she go ahead of him. Daisy didn't need to be told twice, either. Her stomach had been grumbling ever since Dale mentioned Skylar cooking breakfast. She piled grilled tomatoes and tiny little sausages with two fried eggs onto her plate. Dale dragged two of the barstools next to the wall near the rear door. She took one, and began shoveling food in, watching Dale as she ate. Watching the way he and Skylar traded insults in an easy banter and the way he leaned in to whisper something in his mother's ear. He cared about these people, and he wasn't afraid to show it. She'd experienced the same thing last night in his arms. The memory caused a sharp pain of longing to shoot through her.

"Right," Steve said through a mouthful of food. "Let's get this meeting started."

Dale took the seat next to her, giving her a quick wink of solidarity. His shoulder touched hers as he raised his fork to his mouth. The top of her arm flooded with warmth.

"I wanted to hold a bit of a debriefing session. I should've done this days ago, and I apologize. But we've been caught up in this whirlwind, and it's put us on edge. From today onwards, I hope we can all be on the same page. We need to be consistent in what we tell the guests. And we need to be telling them the truth, not rumors we've heard from other members out in the community." Steve turned his gaze toward Sally. She met his gaze, head held high, but Daisy could see a slight red tinge climbing her neck. Steve didn't enlighten them any further, but Daisy guessed that perhaps Sally had been talking about Karri's rumored boyfriend over at Koongarra. Daisy stared at the other woman. Sally couldn't possibly know the truth—that River was Karri's secret lover —but the fact the woman was spreading innuendo and half-truths made Daisy decidedly uneasy. What could Sally possibly gain from that kind of gossip?

Steve began to speak again, and Daisy swapped her focus back to him, leaving that unanswered question for later. "The death of a trusted friend and employee is never a good thing. Most of us are feeling grief, a deep sense of loss, as well as terrible confusion."

Steve had hit the nail on the head with his sentiments. But this wasn't what she wanted to know. She needed some cold, hard facts. Did they have any suspects? Were the police widening the search? She knew they'd interviewed some of the Indigenous people over at the community. Karri's family especially. Had they become part of the suspect pool? Or were the cops still focused on people who were at the station at the time of the death?

She jiggled her knee, impatient for him to get on with it.

There was a loud knock at the back door. Steve turned a quizzical gaze towards Daniella, as if to say *who would be knocking at this time of the morning*? For the short time Daisy had spent here, she knew that the guests always came in the front entrance. The rear door was more for staff.

"I'll get it." Dale handed Daisy his plate, and went to open the door. There was a brief exchange and then Senior Sergeant Robinson strode into the room, Senior Constable King hot on his heels. Both of them looked terribly sombre, and Daisy's heart leapt into her mouth at the sight of them.

"Morning, Nate," Daniella said, looking as cool and unruffled as ever at having two severe-looking policemen arrive at her breakfast meeting. "What can we do for you on this fine—"

"We have a warrant for the arrest of Warwick Nobles. We have evidence that points to him as the main suspect in the murder of Karri Grainer." The senior sergeant cut her off gruffly. "Everyone remain where you are, please."

Daniella's hands flew to her mouth.

Daisy did the same to stop her gasp of shock. Her gaze fluttered around the room, landing on the man they'd come to arrest. He was leaning up against the wall while he ate. The look on Wazza's face would've been comical, if the situation wasn't so serious. His mouth was open, a fork full of bacon stalled halfway up from the plate.

Dale took a step forward, and King raised a hand in warning.

Ever so slowly, Wazza placed his plate and cutlery on the countertop next to him.

"What's this all about?" he asked, keeping his face open and friendly.

Robinson approached him, King only a step behind. "Warwick Nobles, you have the right to remain silent. Anything you say could be held against you…" the rest of the senior sergeant's words blurred in Daisy's ears.

What the hell? They were arresting Wazza for murder?

CHAPTER FIFTEEN

Dale watched, unbelieving, as King helped Wazza into the rear seat of the police cruiser and shut the door. Then the senior constable slipped into the passenger seat, keeping his eyes directed straight forward. The rest of the Stormcloud staff stood around the parking lot, all equally in a state of shock. Senior Sergeant Robinson put the vehicle into drive, and it disappeared around the corner of the lodge, kicking up a small trail of dust as it went.

Everyone seemed to be frozen. No one moved or spoke for many seconds after the car disappeared.

Steve was the first to break the spell. "Right, I'll follow them into town and find out what the hell is going on." He jangled a set of keys in his hand as he headed straight toward his Land Cruiser. "Daniella, look up the details of a good lawyer and text them to me. We need to make sure Wazza is looked after," he added.

"What?" Daniella looked like a fish stranded out of water. It took a lot to knock the wind out of her sails, but this arrest had completely confounded her. The iPad dangled, forgotten from her hand.

"Wazza is going to need a lawyer. I want to make sure he has the best. We know he didn't do this, and I'll be dammed if the police are going to pin it on him." Dale had never seen Steve so worked up, furious anger clearly visible, a rage of boiling lava just beneath his skin. Steve jumped into his vehicle and took off, wheels spinning in the dirt, without even waiting for an answer from Daniella.

Daisy stirred beside him. She looked as shocked as the rest of them, and without thinking, he took hold of her hand. The comforting gesture was as much for himself as it was for her. Right at that moment, Skylar, who was on Daisy's other side, glanced down and saw their hands entwined. Her blue eyes came up and met his, a question in their depths. It seemed the cat was out of the bag when it came to him and Daisy. He wasn't bothered about it right now.

In the rear recesses of his brain, Dale understood Daisy might well be cheering on the police, at least silently in her head. This arrest might mean that River was innocent, as he claimed to be. It certainly took the pressure off River. Dale wouldn't be so quick to jump to conclusions, however. The police could have the wrong man. He hoped the police had the wrong man.

"What are we going to do? What shall we tell the guests? How are we going to run this place if we're down two station hands?" Daniella said, her voice rising to a wail.

"Let's go back inside," Dale suggested. "We don't need anyone else hearing this." Reluctantly, Dale released Daisy's hand, taking his mother by the shoulders and steering her through the back door. He pushed her onto one of the barstools and removed the iPad from her hand.

"I can't believe this is happening." Daniella leaned forward, hands on her knees, and began gasping for breath. Oh God, was she hyperventilating? She was a woman who never lost her cool, and seeing her this way made Dale want to lose it, too. She was right; this didn't feel real. But it was. His body went numb, he couldn't think straight, and his arms and legs felt like they were made of lead.

Daisy stepped forward, placing a hand on his mother's hunched shoulders, rubbing small circles and murmuring, "It's okay. You'll be okay. Take some deep breaths, that's right." After a few seconds, Daniella took Daisy's advice, dragging in deep lungfuls of air. "That's good. Now let it out slow and steady. You're doing well," Daisy encouraged. The sight of Daisy helping his mother, while he stood back and watched on as helpless as a fool, finally snapped him out of his funk. Moving to his mother's right-hand side, he put a hand on her shoulder. The contact felt a little odd; he rarely touched his mother; she wasn't the sort for public shows of affection.

"None of us can believe this is happening," he said gently. "But we'll get through it, we always do." He knew his rote response wasn't strictly true, but it was what his mother needed to hear at the moment. Daniella nodded, and kept doing her deep breathing, her eyes fixed on the floor.

"Thanks," he mouthed, leaning forward to catch Daisy's gaze. The corner of her mouth curled up in reply.

Then he glanced up and saw Skylar's worried frown. They both hated to see their mother this way. Skylar said, "I need a strong coffee. Anyone else need one?" There were murmurs of agreement, as people arranged themselves around the centre island in the kitchen.

"Will we, though? Get through this, I mean? What does this mean for Wazza?" Sally blurted. She was tapping her fingers on the bench in an agitated manner, her gaze darting from one person to the next. "What does this mean for all of us? What if we've been living with a killer in our midst all along?" He couldn't blame her for her blunt questions, they were all terribly anxious and worried.

Dale wasn't sure how to reply. Skylar placed a mug of coffee in front of him, and then one in front of Daisy and his mother. It was so like Skylar, keeping everyone fed and watered. That was how she dealt with things, by keeping busy, keeping moving.

Alek had taken a seat at the end of the island, next to Bindi, and he spoke up for the first time since the police had arrived. "Steve seems to believe that Wazza didn't do this. But how can we be so sure? The police must have some sort of damming evidence to arrest him."

Dale glanced at Alek. The man looked positively sick, his pale-blue eyes bloodshot and his long hair greasy, as if he hadn't washed it in days. Why would he be so quick to condemn Wazza? Surely, he knew Wazza wasn't capable of this? Thinking back, Dale remembered Alek had been the first to mention rumors of Karri seeing someone over at Koongarra. How had he known? Did he know more about Karri than he was letting on? It almost seemed as if Alek *wanted* the police to have conclusive evidence. Dale glared at the man.

"Yes, that's right," Sally agreed with Alek. "Maybe this is a good thing. If they have captured the killer, then we can all return to normal, can't we?" Sally's agitated fingers finally stopped their tapping and a small smile appeared on her face. "This is actually good, if the police have their man, they'll stop bothering us." She almost looked pleased with herself, like she was proclaiming their salvation. Why was Sally so quick to agree with Alek? It felt as if both she and Alek were too hasty to betray their good friend and workmate. So far, Bindi had said nothing, merely watching the interchanging with widening eyes.

Before he could voice his doubts, Daisy stood up and glared at Sally. "What about *innocent until proven guilty*? Doesn't Wazza warrant the benefit of the doubt? It sounds like you all have him locked up already."

Sally narrowed her dark eyes at Daisy. "Just who the hell

do you think you are, telling us what to think? You've been here for all of five minutes. I don't—"

Dale jumped in before this erupted into a full-scale argument. "Everyone calm down. We need to wait until Steve reports in. We can't keep jumping to conclusions."

Six pairs of eyes turned toward him, and he could feel the tension in the room ramping up. Daisy was correct, Wazza was innocent until proven guilty.

"I agree with Dale," Daniella said, surprising him. She seemed to have finally recovered her composure. "We should all take this down a notch. Everyone needs to get back to work. The guests will be awake soon. This place isn't going to stop just because one of our station hands has been arrested." Daniella leveled her cool gaze at each of them in turn. His efficient, collected mother was finally back in charge. Dale breathed a silent sigh of relief.

"Steve was going to tell you this morning, before we got rudely interrupted," Daniella continued. "Julie, his daughter, will come out to give us a hand, She's arriving today. She's in between jobs and is willing to help us out. And God knows, we're going to need her more than ever, now that we're two station hands down. Three really, if you count the fact we never replaced Paula. So at least we don't have to worry about our heavy workloads."

That was good news. Dale nodded in approval. Julie was a few years older than him, and while he didn't really know what she did for a job—something to do with marketing—the few times she'd visited Steve at the station, she'd shown she was also good with the horses and had no problem getting her hands dirty.

"Come on everyone, let's get moving. Skylar, have you got breakfast organized?" Daniella snapped. Skylar rolled her eyes, but she motioned to Bindi, who jumped up and they began pulling breakfast supplies out of the cool room.

Daniella glared in Alek's direction until he finally got the hint and disappeared through the door to organize the schedule for the day. Sally followed quickly on his heels, probably to go and set the tables for breakfast. Even though they were currently only half full, it still meant they had over twelve guests to look after.

"And you." His mother rounded on him. "What are you supposed to be doing right now?" There was acid in her voice and her eyes flashed, hiding a growing anger. She hated it when things didn't go according to plan. When she wasn't fully in control. No one wanted to get in her way when she was in this sort of mood. This morning would've been her worst nightmare, and now they were all in the firing line for the fallout of her foul mood. Especially because everyone had seen her lose it earlier.

"I'm taking eight of the guests over to the mine site this morning, we might even do some panning for gold. Daisy's coming with me." He kept his voice conversational, winking at Daisy over the top of his mother's head.

"Yes, well, you might need to do a whole lot more than that today, without Steve here. Don't spend too long gallivanting with the guests this morning." Her gaze fell upon Daisy and he got her meaning immediately. She didn't want him wasting precious time with her. She didn't approve of Daisy. Distaste for the woman standing beside him was evident in the slight curl of his mother's lip. "You're supposed to take over the running of this station one day. Maybe it's time you stepped up. Took some responsibility."

Dale leaned backward to get away from the scorn in his mother's tone. He did everything that was asked of him. He was a hard worker. His mother ran everything like clockwork around here. How was he supposed to compete with that? It wasn't that he didn't want to take on more; it was that she wouldn't let him. She was holding on so tight to the reins that no one could tear them out of her hands.

She was hitting below the belt, especially with Daisy, Skylar and Bindi all listening. He swallowed down all the nasty retorts on his tongue. Now wasn't the time to start a family argument. His mother was stressed beyond belief, as were they all. She was taking out her anger on him and saying things she didn't mean. That was all.

"Come on, Daisy, let's get this tour organized." He turned on his booted heel, not waiting to see if she followed him.

He stomped up the pathway to the machinery shed, Daisy trotting at his heels. Sometimes he wondered why he stayed. He didn't need to take the shit from his mother. He'd done everything she asked of him. She was the one who told him to go to Montana, when he'd wanted to travel the world, instead. Not that he was begrudging his time at Stargazer Ranch, he'd enjoyed every second. But that wasn't the point. The point was, his mother controlled his life. And now she seemed to have taken a disliking to Daisy, as well. Well, she would not control his love life, that was for sure. He stomped harder up the path, raising small puffs of dust as he went. Why did he put up with her shit? Perhaps he should just up and leave. He hadn't truly been happy here since he returned from Montana. Maybe he should find a job at another station. Perhaps even work for his biological father at his station in Western Australia. Wouldn't that make his mother blow steam out of her ears? Let Skylar or Julie take on the weight of responsibility for a while.

"Are you okay?" Daisy puffed from beside him, trying to keep up with his long-legged stride. Glancing down at her, some of the heat of his fury dissipated. His mother always knew just how to press his buttons. Today was going to be difficult enough without his mother in his head. He wasn't going to let her get to him. Not today. Not while he had Daisy by his side. Even though his life was going to shit, and even though Daisy's life wasn't going as planned, either, it was good to have her here with him. She was sweet and compassionate. Worried about him. Hell, she'd even helped his mother when she'd panicked. And then her mother had repaid her with barely disguised scorn. Daisy was a good person, even if she'd told him all those lies. She'd done it to protect her brother. Would Skylar have done the same for him? He hoped so.

For the second time that day, he reached out on impulse and took her hand. "I'm not sure any of us will be truly okay today, but thanks for asking."

She smiled, showing a row of white teeth, and her green eyes sparkled in the early-morning light. A small piece of the leaden weight on his shoulders lifted at the sight.

"That was some heavy stuff," she said. "Sally seems very keen to believe Wazza is guilty."

"Yes, Sally can be a bit judgmental. Things are black or white with her. Alek wasn't very supportive, either," he added.

"Yeah, I guess I don't know either of them very well." She hesitated for a second, and he wondered what else she wanted to say.

"But?" he prompted.

"I'm not sure whether this means anything or not. Sheesh, especially not after they just arrested Wazza. But I overheard Sally on the phone talking to someone called Johnny last night. It sounded as if she was planning on leaving the station. Like soon. Did you know that?"

"Nope." That was an odd revelation. But not completely surprising. Sally wouldn't enjoy being associated with everything that was going on at the station. She was a straight-down-the-line type of person, she wouldn't want her reputation sullied by association with a murder.

"Do you want to learn to drive an ATV?" he asked,

changing the subject. It was all too much for his mind to handle, and he had more pressing matters, at the moment.

"Yes, please," she said, flashing him a smile full of white teeth.

"Let me give you a quick lesson." He led her into the machinery shed. "The keys are over here." He showed her the wooden board at the rear of the shed where the keys were stored. He still hadn't found the time to install that damn lockbox. He really needed to do that sooner rather than later, or he'd have Steve breathing down his neck.

"Each has its own numbered tag," he explained. "Most of our ATVs are dual person. We had them especially built and shipped up from Sydney. But we also have three single-person ones. They're usually used by the staff, if we need to run an errand or round up cattle, something like that." He didn't add that they used to have four single person ATVs, and that one had gone missing recently.

They spent the next ten minutes doing laps around the machinery shed, as Daisy got the hang of driving. The ATVs weren't hard to master, which was why they let the guests drive them. But he enjoyed showing Daisy how to drive, and he drew the lesson out for as long as possible. She almost had him laughing once or twice, until he remembered Wazza was locked up in jail.

Daisy helped him bring out five of the two-seater vehicles and line them up, ready for the guests to arrive. Two guests in each ATV, and one for him and Daisy. Skylar should have a couple of large picnic baskets ready for them to take out for morning tea. But she'd still be swamped with the breakfast rush. He'd leave it for half an hour or so, before they went to collect them. The tour wasn't scheduled to start till nine am.

"We have half an hour to kill, I can take you up and show you the stables. I need to feed the horses, anyway." That was normally Steve's job, but with him occupied in town, Dale didn't have a problem stepping up.

"That'd be nice, thank you. I'd also love to have a shower if I have time before we leave."

"Sure," he agreed. "It'll only take fifteen minutes, then you can head down for a wash, and I'll collect the food."

The stables were a three-minute walk farther up the small rise away from the lodge. They passed beneath the branches of a stand of river gums, their white bark offering a stark contrast to the lush, green grass now sprouting beneath.

If only his stupid imagination didn't keep going off on a tangent, showing him images of himself pulling Daisy into the feed store, where it was dark and warm and private and kissing her until she couldn't breathe.

Daisy broke the silence. "I was wondering. Are the keys to the ATV's always left in plain sight? You don't lock them away at night?"

"No." He gave her a sharp look. Why was she asking that? He hadn't told her about the stolen ATV, so what was she aiming at? "Well, we haven't up until now. I've been meaning to put the keys in a lockbox with a security code. It's on my list of things to do."

"It sounds like a good idea," she agreed. "But right now, anyone on the property could use one anytime they wanted? As long as they knew where the keys were?"

"Yes," he replied slowly, not knowing where she was going with this line of questioning.

"So, you wouldn't necessarily know if someone had used a vehicle? I didn't see a sign-out sheet, or anything."

He stopped walking and turned to face her.

"No, I guess not. But we put a high level of trust in our staff. If anyone needs to use an ATV, they'll tell me or Steve, or even Daniella. It's an unwritten rule, you don't go anywhere on this station, without letting someone know first." Or at least, they'd used to trust their staff implicitly.

Now, he was confused as to who he could rely on.

"Yes, but Karri didn't tell anyone when she borrowed one, did she?"

Whoa, Dale took a step backward, as if she'd slapped him in the face.

"Why would Karri do that?" Daisy continued. "Why would she take an ATV without telling anybody? If she knew the rules, why didn't she tell anyone? Where do you think she was going on that day? Was she going to meet Wazza, but didn't want anyone to know? Maybe the police found some evidence on the ATV. Maybe that's why they were taking DNA."

Was she asking him if he thought Wazza could indeed be guilty?

CHAPTER SIXTEEN

Was Wazza guilty? The debate kept rolling around in Daisy's head. One thing was for sure, Dale hadn't liked it when she made the suggestion. It was good that he was so terribly loyal to his friend. But it wasn't so good if that loyalty blinded him.

The ATV bounced over a large river rock, and Daisy scrambled to grab hold of the leather strap above her head. They were nearly at the old mine site, and she listened as Dale shouted across to another vehicle traveling beside them to keep a lookout for the remains of the wooden mine shaft elevator rising into the sky around the next bend, as it heralded the entrance to the abandoned mining village. Daisy tried to take in the surrounding countryside, but her mind refused to cooperate, it was still dwelling on the events of earlier this morning.

The one good thing about today's arrest was that it took River off the suspect list. She hoped Dale believed her now, that her brother had nothing to do with Karri's death. Daisy had to be careful to keep the relief off her face, as she watched the senior sergeant drive Wazza away. But Dale must've known what was going on in her head, because he shot her a conspiratorial glance when no one else was looking.

The police must have firm evidence to have arrested

Wazza. Some sort of DNA clues to link Wazza to the murder, maybe. But what was it?

She still had a vain hope that River would contact her using the sat phone. She'd tried calling it last night from her cell when they first discovered he was missing, but the sat phone had been turned off. And again, this morning, she'd tried it once more, but with the same result. River might have the phone, but he would not turn it on unless he needed to contact someone.

She stifled a yawn behind her hand. The combination of a late night and an early start, mixed in with the generous dose of stress over River's disappearance and now Wazza's arrest, was getting the better of her.

"I'm feeling the same way," Dale said, flicking her a lopsided smile. It wasn't quite enough to light up his dimples, but the promise was there. She wanted him to smile at her again, the way he had last night. Sheesh, had it really only been last night? So much had happened since then. She hadn't had the chance to process the fact that they'd slept together. That she and Dale had made love under the stars. Maybe it was a good thing. If she couldn't dwell on it, then she wouldn't have time to come up with all the reasons she shouldn't be with him.

"Don't worry, I've got coffee and supplies when we get there." He turned to look at her fully, his brown eyes crinkling at the corners. Oh God, those beautiful, brown eyes, she could melt into them. His fingers rested lightly on the steering wheel, tanned and long. She followed the shape of his wrist up to his powerful forearms, bare where he'd rolled his shirt up to the elbows. She remembered those skilful fingers from last night. How they had played her body, making it sing like a finely tuned instrument.

His Akubra was firmly set on his head, giving him that quintessential Aussie cowboy look. She was wearing his borrowed one again, but knew she didn't look half as sexy in it as he did.

"There it is," Timothy, one of the guests, yelled excitedly. His wife squealed in reply from her seat next to him in the ATV, pointing toward the wooden structure towering high above the trees ahead. They were a young couple on their honeymoon, who'd only arrived yesterday. Timothy had invented some kind of cell phone app and started his own software company that was now worth millions. A wunderkind, by all accounts. The best thing about the couple was they didn't seem to be bothered by the fact that there was an active murder investigation going on at the station. In fact, Timothy thought it was kind of cool. Daisy wasn't sure what to make of his attitude. It was a bit macabre.

The other guests had varying reactions to the news when Daniella filled them in on Wazza's arrest during their morning get together after breakfast. Daniella had wanted to keep everything on the down low. If she had her way, she would've pretended this whole thing was one big mistake. Dale had told Daisy that when Karri's body was first discovered, Steve had talked Daniella into a compromise, and they'd decided that each morning they'd give the guests a brief rundown on what'd happened so far and give them any updates they'd received from police. It was only fair, Daisy thought, that the guests were told the truth. They were giving up their hard-earned money to pay for a stay at a luxury resort, and they deserved to know how that might affect them. Daniella was quick to assure everyone that the luxury resort would go on functioning as normal, and the guests need not worry they'd lose out in any way.

Dale let the young couple lead the way, also waving through two men in their ATV, a father and son duo, letting them go ahead. Two more ATVs were making their way up the side of the riverbed behind them. Dale told the tour group that normally at this stage of the year, there'd only be a muddy trickle in the bottom of the riverbed. But with all the recent rain, it was now nearly full.

"Come on," Dale called. "You're gonna miss out on the chocolate brownies if you don't hurry." The older woman driving the closest vehicle waved to show that she'd heard, but continued picking her way slowly through the boulders, her husband encouraging her from the passenger seat. She wasn't the most confident of drivers, but at least she was giving it a go, Daisy thought. This woman and her husband—Sarah and Michael—had asked a lot more questions about the consequences of Wazza's arrest than the younger couple, but in the end, they too, seemed convinced that everything was under control, and they could continue to enjoy their stay.

Daisy's stomach rumbled at the mention of brownies. She hadn't had a chance to eat much of her breakfast before the police had shown up this morning.

Ten minutes later, all the four-wheel-drive vehicles were parked beneath the shade of an enormous coolabah tree.

"The whole mine site is listed on the Queensland Heritage Register. While it's technically on our property, it's still open and available to the public. This is the old manager's cottage," Dale explained as everyone gathered around him. "You're welcome to take your time and look through it. The local Shire have set it up as a museum, to give you a glimpse of how things might've been back in the twenties and thirties when it was in its heyday. There's also an old cemetery farther up the hill for you to explore. There are still quite a few abandoned miner's cottages scattered around the old township. Please don't go inside any of these, as they're not safe. You can walk around the outside of them, but don't go in." He stopped talking until everyone looked at him. "I mean it, please don't go into any of the other buildings." There were nods of agreement, and Dale continued. "Let's meet at the elevator shaft on the edge of town in, say, forty-five minutes. I'll have morning tea setup for you, and I can show you the old mine shaft, although we can't get down it anymore, it's too dangerous. Then we can go over to the main battery, where they used to crush the quartz stone and process it to remove the gold. Afterwards, we can visit one of the old horizontal shafts. But please don't go near anything that is boarded up or signposted *keep out*. Those signs are there for a reason. To keep you safe."

"Cool, I love all this old historical stuff. Let's go." Timothy took his wife by the hand and they disappeared into the manager's cottage, the father and son duo following close on their heels.

Sarah, the woman driving the ATV, turned to Dale. "Which way to the cemetery? I love looking at old headstones and trying to figure out how those people's lives were affected." Michael rolled his eyes behind her back, but when Dale pointed them in the direction, he dutifully followed his wife. The other couple, two women, Sadie and Peta—who'd proudly proclaimed to everyone who'd listen that they'd been together for over twenty years and had already decided now it was finally legal for them to marry, they were going to come back to Stormcloud to have the ceremony—took off toward the centre of the township. They, too, were holding hands and Daisy had a moment of wistfulness. How would it be when she was that age? Would she be married? Would she still be that much in love? Would it be Dale she was in love with?

What the...? Where had that come from?

"Do you want to give me a hand setting up morning tea?" She almost jumped out of her skin at the sound of his voice, hoping he couldn't see the guilt that must be written all over her face because of her wayward thoughts.

"Only as long as I can have one of those brownies you

mentioned. I'm starving," she said, patting her belly and hamming it up, hoping he didn't notice the flush creeping up her neck. Why ever had she thought that it might be Dale she'd be holding hands with in twenty years?

"It's a deal." Dale retrieved two large wicker baskets from the rear tray of his ATV and handed one to her. Then he dragged out a foldable table, and they walked farther into the abandoned town, following a rocky pathway that wound through the trees. The old gold mine was situated at the base of a small escarpment, a blunt finger of rock, part of the larger range, of which Mount Mulligan escarpment was also a part.

Red rock abounded here. Tufts of dried grass broke through the red gravel wherever she put her feet. It was a sparse country, beautiful, but harsh. Not luxuriant and green, compared to around Stormcloud lodge. Daisy wondered what it might've been like to live here so long ago. It was interesting to get a glimpse back in time, but also a little sad that this place full of such history had been allowed to fall into wrack and ruin. The only sounds were those of birds calling from trees, and the incessant singing of the cicadas. The place felt completely deserted, and she had to force herself to remember there were eight other people in the area. It was a little spooky, and a shiver of fear ran its cold finger down her spine. She didn't know what'd caused such a reaction.

"How many people come out here? Say, on a weekly basis?" Daisy asked, her interest piqued.

Dale shrugged and tilted his head in contemplation. "Our tours probably bring the most consistent numbers. We come out here at least once a week, and usually we have a larger group than this." Dale grimaced at the reminder they were down by half their number of guests. "But this site is deemed one of the local attractions, and so you get other travelers in their four-wheel-drives coming through here. In the high season you could get up to fifty people a week." Dale made it sound like that was an impressive number, and Daisy had to hide a smile. It probably was a good number, considering how isolated they were. But it still wasn't as high as Dale seemed to think it was.

There were an awful lot of places to hide around here. If someone didn't want to be found, they could certainly choose one of the condemned cottages, even though Dale had warned against going inside. Could River have possibly found this place? Could he be hiding out here somewhere? She took another, more careful, look around, studying the rows of collapsing huts. No, she was just being silly. River would be long gone. And he wouldn't have enough supplies to keep him going out here, either. A person would need to be well-prepared if they wanted to stay here for any length of time.

She helped Dale find a flat spot in the shade of the large, wooden structure, away from the covered mine shaft, and helped him unfold the table. The heat was already building, the humidity almost disabling, and she wiped ineffectively at the sweat on her brow. This tropical northern heat took some getting used to.

True to his word, as soon as the table was set up, with a crisp, white tablecloth and empty mugs for the tea and coffee, Dale waved a container of still-warm brownies beneath her nose. "Don't tell anyone I'm giving out favors." He smiled cheekily. If she could've been certain no one was watching, she might even have stood on tiptoe and kissed him, long and hard.

"I won't, I promise." She bit into the brownie and gave a groan of pleasure. "Oh, my, these are to die for. Almost as good as her wattleseed scones."

"I know," he agreed, patting his stomach. "Skylar's food is so good. Like you were saying last night, even though you don't need to watch what you eat, I might have to, or I'll get fat."

"I don't think you have a problem with that," she scoffed, flicking her gaze up his body. Remembering all of that lean muscle from last night.

"You reckon?" he asked, with a cheeky smile. Then he lifted the corner of his shirt to reveal a set of chiseled abs, and her mouth went dry. They were just as good as she remembered, and she suddenly wished they were alone.

"Where are those brownies you promised us?" Timothy called, and Dale quickly lowered his shirt, then turned to face the table. Timothy and his wife were coming up the slight rise from the direction of the cemetery. Daisy shot Dale a look. She was pretty sure the other couple hadn't seen his flirting, but she had to hide a secret smile. Luckily she hadn't given in to her cravings, or they would've definitely been sprung.

Daisy enjoyed the hour and a half, listening to Dale explain how the old gold mine used to work, and then following him a little way into a dark tunnel where he showed the guests how they used to mine with good old-fashioned dynamite, and lots of brute strength. He was an excellent tour guide, imparting enough information to keep her interested, but not bore her to death. He told them that while there was one main shaft going straight down—the one underneath the elevator shaft—a couple of other enterprising geologists had found veins of quartz heading straight into the side of the escarpment, hence there was quite a few smaller shafts leftover from the mining boom. These shafts had been boarded up as the wooden beams supporting the tunnels were collapsing, except for the one he was showing them, which'd been reinforced so tourists could take a peek.

It was much too dark in the tunnel for Daisy's liking, and she was glad when they emerged into the sunshine. Then Dale herded them all toward the ATVs so they could return to the lodge. Skylar would have lunch ready, he told them all.

But Daisy knew Dale was more interested in hearing whether Steve had reported in regarding Wazza's fate yet. It was midday; surely the police would've decided whether to charge Wazza by now?

But Daniella's face told them all they needed to know when they arrived at the lodge. She shook her head at Dale's inquiring look and walked away. Was it a good thing, or not, they hadn't heard from Steve? Daisy couldn't decide. Dale became withdrawn over lunch, which they ate in the kitchen with Skylar and Bindi. Sally was busy with a new couple who'd just arrived, showing them to their accommodation, making sure they were settled in and had everything they needed. Dale hardly said two words to anyone; he seemed to be having an internal debate over something.

Skylar was running one of her cooking lessons for the guests in the afternoon, with Bindi's help, which was good, because it freed Dale to do other things. Given Dale's mood at lunchtime, Daisy was surprised when he asked if she wanted to give him a hand.

"A tree came down in that storm and damaged one of our pumping sheds. We pump water from the billabong to use for the horses and cattle. Steve was gonna fix it this afternoon, but it looks as if I'll be doing it instead," Dale said, as they sat at the kitchen island after finishing their meal. He dragged a hand through his hair, leaving it deliciously rumpled. "I guess I'm gonna be doing a lot more, too, if Wazza..." He didn't finish his sentence; couldn't elaborate all the things it would mean if Wazza didn't come back. They were now effectively down three staff members, with Paula leaving early in the season, Karri dead, and now Wazza in jail.

"I don't mind helping." She had nothing better to do. It was an excuse not to have to make all the decisions she was still yet to find answers for. Such as, should she stay? Or should she head home and leave River to his own devices? "I'm a fast learner, and a bit of dirt never bothered me." Which was true, even though she was born and bred in the city and knew absolutely nothing about living on a farm, she'd never been afraid of hard work. Staying with her cousins and living on country up near Darwin had opened her eyes to lots of things. The harsh reality of eking out a living from the land chief among them.

"Right. Thank you. We might find you that same pair of waders you used the other day when we were fishing. It's going to get pretty mucky."

Dale wasn't wrong. The corrugated iron shed was on the banks of the billabong, which was still gloopy with mud from the floods. The small shed was set up on a block of concrete, which kept it out of reach of even the worst floods. An old tree had toppled during the storm, clipping the corner of the building on its way down. Daisy could see half of its branches were already dead and stunted, Dale told her it was only a matter of time before it came down, and they should've cut it down earlier. It now lay resembling a giant stranded whale, all its limbs shattered, the few remaining reaching for the sky, is if begging for redemption.

"What a shame," Daisy said, eyes glued to the fallen behemoth.

"We'll put it to good use. We'll chainsaw it up and use it for firewood. Nothing goes to waste out here."

Daisy shrugged. That was the circle of life, she supposed.

They spent a hot and sticky afternoon, sweating in the sun, as they pulled down the broken pieces of tin from the roof and one side of the shed, and replaced them with new ones. There wasn't a lot of time for talking, and Daisy found she was all out of words, anyway. It was nice to be using her body, pushing it to its limits, tiring herself out physically, so she didn't have to think about everything that was bothering her.

She wondered about bringing up the subject of Wazza with Dale; it was clearly on his mind. But why rehash all the old information? Until they had something new, there was no point. Daisy knew that Julie, Dale's stepsister, would arrive at the station today, and he hoped she'd help to take up a little of the slack around the station. It was good they had family to call on in a time of crisis.

Finally, they finished the job, and piled all the broken bits of material into the tray bed of Dale's truck. Daisy took the time to survey the surrounding landscape. It was late afternoon, and the cicadas were humming loudly in the trees. The foliage of the understory, as well as the tall, waving fronds of tussock grass, were such a vibrant green. The country was similar in a lot of ways to where she'd stayed in the Northern Territory. The earth was such a deep, ochre red up there. It was red here, too, but more subdued. Distances were vast in Northern Queensland, with large stretches of open woodland as far as the eye could see. If anything, this land was a tad drier, less-lush-rainforest and more grasslands —they called them floodplains. But she could get used to living here. There was a certain peace and tranquility you just didn't get in the city. She could feel the stretch of the earth beneath her feet.

"You appreciate this place, don't you?" Dale's voice broke through her musings. "Have you ever thought about staying?"

"No," she snorted. Then, when she saw his face fall, she amended, "I mean, yes it's beautiful, but no, I'd never stay." What would she do here? Her life was in Perth. She had a degree to finish. Her dream of becoming a leader in environmental law to fulfill.

They drove to the lodge in relative silence, with twilight descending around them. Daisy only had time for a quick wash before dinner. It seemed Steve still hadn't returned from town. She offered to help Bindi and Sally serve the dinner, but Daniella asked her to come and sit at the tables with the rest of the guests.

Dale's stepsister, Julie, had arrived sometime that afternoon, and after Daisy had been introduced, she surreptitiously checked her out as she chatted to Daniella across the table. Julie had short, cropped hair, and projected a very modern and professional look, with a hint of makeup, but not so much that it looked contrived. She had welcoming, brown eyes, and Daisy felt immediately that she'd like this woman. She was also an absolute extrovert and had the table in stitches with some of her anecdotes. Almost the complete opposite of her father. Daisy briefly wondered if she took after her mother.

The meal was delicious, as usual, and it was topped off by an amazing dessert that the guests helped to prepare during their cooking lesson—lychee and wild honey ice cream with white chocolate and grilled mango slices. Daisy sat next to Timothy and his wife and they chatted about what it was like to live in the tropical north. He talked about his grandiose plans to move his entire company up to Cairns, so he could enjoy everything on offer here. His wife rolled her eyes at Daisy behind his back, and she got the idea that while Timothy was a dreamer and a schemer, not many of his plans ever came to fruition. Of course, the topic of the police investigation came up; it was only human nature that people wanted to discuss something as juicy as a possible murder. Their curiosity was piqued. But Daisy tried not to enter into their speculation, noticing Daniella's pained expression. Like it or not, Daniella was going to have to get used to people asking questions. She needed to get over this obsession of keeping it private, the resort's reputation was already taking a beating; it'd do no good if people thought she was purposefully withholding information.

After dinner service was over, and all the guests had retired either to their rooms, or were sitting on the front veranda sipping a nightcap, Daniella gathered all her staff and family together in the kitchen. She shot Daisy a look of displeasure but said nothing as she settled in on a bar stool next to Dale. Julie took a seat next to Skylar; it seemed they got on well together. Bindi, Sally and Alek remained standing, huddled together at the end of the kitchen island.

"I know everyone is wondering about Warwick," Daniella said. "But I'm as much in the dark as—" She stopped speaking when someone opened the back door. They all turned as one to stare as Steve strode in, his face grim. Daniella stood up quickly, watching him like a hawk.

"Julie, great to see you." He swooped in and gave her a quick hug. "Thank you so much for lending a hand." But even Daisy could see that even his pleasure at seeing his daughter couldn't take away the strain on his face.

"I need a drink," Steve said, ignoring Daniella's inquiring look, and heading straight out to the bar. Daisy looked at Dale. Almost as one, everyone in the kitchen followed Steve through to the main lounge. He poured himself a large double whiskey and swallowed it in one gulp, with Daniella looking more and more impatient.

At last, he turned to face everyone. "Wazza has been remanded in custody. They're going to charge him with Karri's murder. They're not allowing him bail, because of the seriousness of the crime."

CHAPTER SEVENTEEN

Dale felt like he'd been punched in the gut. Steve's news had taken them all by surprise. Steve was exhausted. He'd spent the day talking to lawyers, as well as on the phone to Wazza's family. At first, the police hadn't been very forthcoming with any details. But after the lawyer Steve hired—who'd agreed to drive straight to Dimbulah from Cairns, a one-and-a-half-hour trip—presented himself at the police station, they found out more.

The most shocking part of Steve's news was that Karri had been pregnant. Dale could make terrible sense of the reason the police had requested DNA samples from all the men. Worst of all, it turned out that Wazza was the father. Fairly damning evidence. The police were accusing him of murdering Karri because he didn't want her to have the baby, and she refused to abort the child.

Of course, Wazza strenuously denied the charges. Steve said the poor man was a complete mess. By the time the lawyer had arrived, Wazza had already confessed to the senior sergeant he had indeed been sleeping with Karri. But he said their affair ended a month ago, when she started seeing someone else. He never even knew she was pregnant.

Dale couldn't get his head around it. After Steve relayed

the details to them all, he'd told Julie he'd catch up with her in the morning and went straight to bed, saying he'd had a shit of a day, and tomorrow wasn't looking any better. Sally took off in the direction of the staff quarters as soon as Steve disappeared through the door, a frown marring her normally perfect features. Daniella, Skylar, Julie, and Bindi all huddled together, consoling each other and trying to work out how Wazza and Karri had conducted their secret affair. It was wonderful to re-connect with Julie again; he'd forgotten how much fun she could be. She'd buoyed the mood over dinner with her stories and laughter, and even though he hadn't felt like laughing, it was nice to have something else to think about for a while. Skylar looked up from their heated discussion after a few moments, inviting Dale to join them with a quirk of her eyebrow. But Daisy stirred on the stool beside him, and he declined Skylar's offer, saying he'd wanted to make sure Daisy made it safely to her quarters. That statement caused Skylar's other eyebrow to crawl up her forehead, but he ignored it. He led them toward the side entrance out to the staff quarters, but Daisy halted halfway down the hallway. "This is all so fucked up. Don't you think?"

She was staring at him, like she was about to cry. She was right, this was all totally fucked up. He took her in his arms, pulling her close, needing to feel her body warm and alive next to his. It sounded corny and desperate, but he was so grateful that it wasn't him locked up in that cell tonight. One thing Wazza's arrest showed him, was how quickly life could turn on a dime. One minute, you were as free as a bird, the next your life could be turned upside down. He wanted to hold Daisy. Be with her. Feel every minute. She stood on tiptoe and kissed him. For a moment he forgot where he was, and what was going on around them.

"Stay with me tonight," he whispered in her ear. "I need

you. I need to feel your body next to mine." She didn't pull away or shake her head, which he took as a positive sign. Maybe she was feeling the same way. She didn't want to be alone tonight, either. Then she kissed him again, and he had his answer.

Taking her by the hand, they turned and went deeper into the lodge, as he led her toward the family wing. Hopefully, Steve had actually gone to bed, as he'd said. Dale slowed as they approached the door to the family living room. He breathed a sigh of relief when he saw the room was empty, and they tiptoed past. His bedroom was at the far end of the building, while his mother and Steve's room, and Skylar's rooms, were this side of the living room, closest to the lodge, which meant they could talk normally and wouldn't be overheard.

Instead of turning on a light, he drew back the curtains on the large, picture window, revealing a night view of the corner of the billabong with the escarpment rising behind it. The stars were just as bright as they'd been last night, like a painter had scattered glow-in-the-dark paint all over the fabric of the sky.

He swung around, ready to gather Daisy up in his arms, to consume her with his mouth and body. To let himself loose for a few moments from these terrible feelings of guilt and hopelessness.

She backed away. "Actually, I'm not sure, perhaps I should go to my dorm room." Why was she acting so indecisive all of a sudden? After what they'd done last night, he'd seen all she had to offer, and more.

"I'll take you back if you want," he said, approaching her slowly. "But first of all…" He scooped her up and kissed her, letting his lips explore hers. Tamping down on his sudden urge to rip all of her clothes off, he controlled his desire; he didn't want to scare her off. Instead, he let her know by the pressure of his mouth, the way he clung to her, how much he wanted her. After a second's hesitation, she returned his passionate kiss.

Tonight would be different. They could take their time and explore each other's bodies. There was still a burning urgency running through his veins, but this didn't have to be a quick, one-off thing. They had the luxury of a soft bed and all night to spend in it. He was hard already, just thinking about it.

Much like yesterday, Daisy was wearing those tight little shorts that he loved because of the way they showed off her pert bottom to great advantage. When she'd arrived for dinner, however, she'd exchanged her dirty T-shirt for a soft, linen tank top that revealed her bronze shoulders nicely. And she'd changed her sneakers for a pair of tan leather sandals, which she now kicked off, leaving her feet bare.

He tugged on her hair tie, and strands unfurled from the braid, falling down her shoulders. Then he lifted her arms above her head, trapping her wrists together with one of his hands, and sliding the hem of her top up, exposing the taut muscles of her belly. Ever so slowly, he drew the fabric over her arms and then dropped the piece of clothing on the floor at their feet. Releasing her wrists, he dropped to his knees and kissed her belly.

He spent his time exploring the soft skin of her stomach, which twitched and flickered beneath his touch. Ticklish, was she? That was good to know. He undid the top button of her shorts and slowly slid the zipper down, revealing plain, white-cotton underwear. She was a no-frills kind of girl. But he found it sexy as hell. His lips wandered to the waistband of her panties and he kissed his way across the hem. Her hands tangled in his hair and she let out a groan.

These shorts needed to come off, they were hindering his access to the places he wanted to kiss the most. He tugged, and they slipped easily over her hips, pooling in a crumpled heap at her feet. Which left the underwear. Hooking a finger through the waistband, he leisurely drew them down to reveal a perfect triangle of dark hair. Now this was better. Tugging the panties down with both hands, he buried his face in between her thighs.

"Dale," she gasped. But her hands in his hair urged him on, directing his mouth exactly where she wanted it to be. His tongue flicked in and out, tasting her, enjoying the small sounds of pleasure she made as he did so.

"Oh, God," she groaned, and he looked up to see her head thrown backward. He reached one hand up her belly to the dip between her breasts. As if taking his cue, she unhooked her bra, so she was standing naked in front of him. He stopped what he was doing, staring up at her. She was so beautiful in the starlight. Then her hands dragged his head up, and she leaned down to meet his lips.

"Bed. Now," she mumbled into his mouth.

He could do that. In one fluid move, he picked her up in his arms and carried her to his king-size bed, placing her gently down.

"Clothes off," she demanded, holding up a hand as he climbed onto the bed with her. He had no trouble doing what he was told by a woman who knew what she wanted. His boots and socks came off first, flung into the far corner of the room. Then came his shirt. Why were there so many buttons on these things? It seemed to take an eternity to undo them all. But at last, he peeled it off, while Daisy watched him with hungry eyes.

Finally, he dropped his jeans to the floor, only remembering at the last second to retrieve the condom from his pocket and place it on the nightstand. She stared at him; her gaze tracing down his body, from his shoulders all the way to his hips, lingering on his pulsing erection for a few seconds, before continuing all the way down his legs. He liked the way she devoured his body with her eyes.

"You sure are a good-looking cowboy," she said, voice heavy and husky.

"Why thank you, ma'am." He bowed before her, adding a flourish of his wrist. Her laughter died as he crawled onto the bed and covered her mouth with his.

She turned to face him, and they lay side-by-side, staring into each other's eyes. Running a hand up her thigh, he followed the contours of her body. Long-limbed and perfectly proportioned, her darker skin blending in with the night, while his paler skin glowed faintly in the starlight.

He was falling hard for this woman with so many secrets. What was he going to do?

Before he quite knew what was happening, Daisy was on her knees, pushing him down so he was flat against the bed. "My turn," she said. His belly clenched in anticipation.

Using her fingertips, she explored the muscles of his pecs, running a circle around each nipple, and then tracing over each bump of his ribs, until she found his abs. Then she lowered her mouth and followed the same route with her lips, as her hands drifted lower, to find his erection. Stroking it with precise care, she torturously trailed her lips down to meet her hands. Her tongue flicked the tip of his erection and he nearly jumped out of his skin. She was going to drive him crazy. After only a few more moments of her ministrations, he could take no more. He needed to be inside her, or he was going to explode. As if reading his mind, Daisy stopped what she was doing and climbed her way up his body, laying full-length along him so they were connected by skin all the way up.

She'd taken control last night; it was his turn now. He reached for the condom and had it on in a second, rolling her over, using his elbows to hover above her. She arched her body up to meet his, and at the same time dragged his head down so she could latch onto his mouth. He nestled beneath her legs, savoring the anticipation, holding on as long as he could, before he finally plunged inside her.

She let out a sound that was a mixture of pleasure and torment. That sound drove him on. They moved together in harmony for a few strokes. But soon their movements became faster and more urgent, until he was so close to the edge, he knew he was going to lose control.

"Daisy," he cried out, just as he tumbled down the cliff, wave after wave crashing over him. She lifted beneath him, and he knew she was only seconds behind him. Then she threw her head backward into the pillows and let out a series of soft growls, before she went limp beneath him.

He lay on the bed, panting. Wow. So much for taking his time. But Daisy drove him crazy, and they had all night to themselves. They could do this as many times as they wanted.

He turned his head on the pillow to watch Daisy. Her hair was spread out across the bed, eyes closed, still trying to collect herself.

"My mother is going to hate you," Daisy sighed quietly.

"What?" Where had that come from?

"Sorry, I didn't mean to say that out loud." She rolled her head sideways so she could look at him.

"Well, you're going to have to explain it."

"It's complicated. But then, this whole thing…" she waved her arm in the air to encompass them and the bed "…is complicated."

She wasn't wrong about that.

"My mum wants me to marry an indigenous boy. Someone who understands our culture. She has grand plans for me. Wants me to be a beacon for our people, all that kind of shit."

"That sounds like a lot to live up to."

"It is."

"And you're saying that maybe I've put a spanner in her works."

"Seems like you have," she agreed.

He continued to stare at her. What exactly did their conversation mean? Was she saying what he thought she was saying? That she was considering making him a part of her life?

Breaking the growing silence between them, she languidly rolled over and straddled him, saying, "Talking about spanners, how long before your tool is ready for action again?"

"My what?" he sputtered. "My *tool*? Why would you call it that?" He reached for her ticklish spot, and she dissolved into a fit of giggles on his chest. "I'll show you exactly what my *tool* can do," he said, lifting her chin with his thumb and kissing her.

An hour later, Dale lay on the pillow and groaned. Daisy was going to kill him. But it'd be worth it. He closed his eyes and sighed, and Daisy did the same, settling into his shoulder. Suddenly the peaceful air was broken by a loud buzzing noise. What was that sound? Dale opened his eyes. He didn't want anything or anyone interrupting this perfect bubble of happiness surrounding the two of them. But the annoying sound kept going, and he propped himself up on his elbow.

"Oh, shit." Abruptly, Daisy leapt out of bed. "That's my phone." She fumbled in the dark through the pile of clothes that she'd left on the floor.

Daisy was suddenly silhouetted against the starlight from the window as she stood up, phone held to her ear. She was completely naked, and her curves were outlined against the stars. He held his breath. It could only be one person calling Daisy at this time of night.

"Hello? River, is that you?"

He couldn't hear the other person's reply, but Daisy gave a loud exhalation of relief and Dale knew it was her brother.

"Where are you? What—" She cut off her questions and listened intently.

"Yes, I know the place you mean," she replied. Then there was more silence as she listened once more to what River had to say.

What place? Where was River? It was exceedingly frustrating only being able to hear one side of the conversation, and he wished Daisy would put her brother on speaker.

"Yes, I can come now." Daisy glanced in Dale's direction and then quickly ducked her head and turned away. He frowned. If she thought she was going anywhere without him, she'd better think again. "But do you really think this guy is—"

What guy was River talking about? And where did River want Daisy to go? Dale got out of bed and began to quietly get dressed. Not knowing what was going on was driving him mad.

"I don't think that's a good idea. You should wait for me to get there." Daisy raised her voice, obviously upset about whatever River was suggesting. And also, obviously thinking she was going alone. He put a hand on her shoulder, and she flinched, as if only just remembering he was there.

"River, wait… Oh, fuck." She held the phone out and stared at it. "The fucker hung up on me," she said, finally looking at him.

"What's going on?" he asked, keeping his tone as gentle as possible. She was clearly distraught. Shaking off his hand, she began pacing back and forth, offering him glimpses of that luscious backside and slim hips.

She didn't answer, just kept up her pacing, muttering things to herself now and then. He watched until it became too much. Standing directly in her path, he grabbed her by both shoulders. "Daisy, you need to tell me what's going on," he said slowly and succinctly.

"I'm not sure…" She stared up into his face, hesitating.

He knew what she was thinking. "Whatever it is you're planning, I'm not letting you do it alone. Get that through your head, okay?"

She stiffened at his words and glared at him. Trying to stare him down in all her glorious nudity.

He returned her stare, equally determined to win this battle of wills.

Tilting back her head, she blew out a long breath. "Fine. I'm not sure I'd be able to find that gold mine by myself in the dark, anyway."

"River is at the gold mine? Where we were this morning?"

"Yes. He said he saw us. I'm so mad I didn't know he was there."

"You're not telepathic. If he was hiding from us, how the hell were we supposed to know he was there?"

"Yeah, well, that's not the worst bit. River told me there is another man hiding out in one of abandoned shafts. He's been watching him for the past two days. He thinks this man has been living out there. And he might be Karri's killer."

There were so many ideas to unpack from Daisy's statement, Dale didn't know which one to start with. Most importantly, how could there be a man hiding out on their property without them knowing about it? How long had he been there? And how was he possibly connected to Karri?

"River said he was going in for a closer look. We need to get out there and help him. Protect him."

"I'm calling the cops," Dale said, reaching for his phone

"What good will they be?" She stamped her foot in frustration. "They're hours away. I'm going now. Whether you come with me or not."

CHAPTER EIGHTEEN

Dale could call the cops if he wanted to, but Daisy wasn't waiting around for them to show up. River needed her. Besides, River didn't want the cops anywhere near him. If it turned out there was something dodgy going on with this strange man at the gold mine, then she had no problem calling the cops, as long as River had a chance to disappear before they arrived. He was already putting himself in all kinds of danger merely by being on the property. If he was around when the police arrested this guy, he'd end up in jail.

"Well, if you won't let me call the police, then I'm definitely coming with you," Dale growled.

"Fine," she snapped. "Then, let's go."

"As soon as I tell Steve what's happening." Dale was doing up the last button on his shirt.

"No!" she squeaked in alarm. If Dale told Steve, he'd have to reveal River's part in all of this. She was still desperate to save him, if she could. "Please don't," she amended. "What if we leave a note? If we're not home by the time he gets up in a few hours, then it probably means we need help, anyway."

Dale stared at her, his jaw muscles obviously working overtime as he considered her request. "Fine," he snapped, mirroring her earlier tone. "Follow me, and keep it down if you don't want to wake everyone else."

She slipped on her sandals, but Dale kept his boots in his hand as they tiptoed down the hallway and into the living room, where he went over to a desk and pulled out a sheet of paper. He clicked on his phone flashlight app and wrote a hurried note, then left it on the coffee table in full view. Daisy jiggled up and down on her toes, impatiently. But he soon led her to a door she hadn't noticed before leading to outside the building. Without saying a word, he motioned for her to precede him and closed the door without making a sound, then sat down and quickly pulled on his boots.

"It's actually quicker to get to the shed this way," he whispered.

The machinery shed was dark, and she was glad Dale was there, otherwise she might've fumbled around for quite a while before she found the keys.

"We're going to push the ATV down the path for a way," he explained in a hushed whisper. "I don't want the sound of the engine to carry to the lodge. Once we're at the riverbed, we can turn it on."

Daisy nodded, she'd push the ATV all the way to the gold mine, if it meant she could see River.

Pushing the ATV wasn't as hard as Daisy expected, although she stumbled a bit in the darkness. They finally made it to the riverbed, and Dale told her to jump in.

On the ride over, Dale quizzed her about exactly what River had said on the phone and asked which particular abandoned shaft this phantom man was hiding in, so he knew where to aim for; the abandoned township covered a large area, and there were upwards of a half-a-dozen abandoned shafts, all safely boarded up, as far as Dale knew. Daisy didn't appreciate his tone; it was almost as if he didn't quite believe her. But then he hadn't heard the absolute certainty in River's voice. Certainty that this man had something to do with Karri's murder, although what sort of clues he'd found, he hadn't bothered to elaborate over the phone. Dale also hadn't heard the fear in River's voice. It was the fear that was driving Daisy to hurry to her brother. Nothing scared River. He was usually so full of cocky arrogance and bluster, believing he was untouchable. Something about this man was making him afraid.

She really hoped River waited for her to arrive and not do as he'd threatened. He said he was going to move in closer, to see what other evidence he could gather while the guy was sleeping. He also said he had a plan to capture the man. There was only one way in or out of the shaft, so he'd set a trap at the entrance.

Why couldn't Dale drive any faster? She glanced at his profile, seeing the grim line of his mouth and the square set of his jaw. She shouldn't be so uncharitable; he was doing the best he could. He hadn't had to come with her. And he'd had every right to warn Steve and Daniella about what was going on. This involved them, too; it was happening on their property. He was doing all of this for her. To help her.

She wished she hadn't mentioned what her mother would think of him. But it'd slipped out. Because lying there in the afterglow of their amazing sex, she'd been thinking about what her life would be like if Dale were in it. Which was stupid, because no sane person could ever see the two of them together. Even if River wasn't in the equation, and even if she wasn't on the run from the law, her life was in Perth. And his was here in North Queensland, four-thousand kilometers away.

"I'm going to turn the headlights off, so they don't see us coming. It might get bumpy, so hang on. I'm going to stop in the riverbed; we'll have to go the rest of the way on foot."

All good ideas, and she was glad again that Dale was here. She would've been in such a hurry to get to River, she probably would've driven straight into the abandoned township and given herself away. Or at the very least, given River away.

The surrounding bushland was plunged into darkness as Dale turned off the lights. He slowed the ATV to a crawl as his eyes adjusted. It didn't take long for her to make out shapes in the dim light. The tops of the trees were silhouetted against the sky, and large boulders loomed out of the dark. Soon Dale was proceeding with more confidence. He must know this trail like the back of his hand.

An owl hooted directly above them. It was a forlorn sound, and Daisy felt a shiver of premonition run down her backbone.

"We'll leave the vehicle here," Dale whispered a few minutes later. "Grab the flashlight from the glove box," he commanded, and she felt around in the compartment until her fingers closed around the small metal cylinder.

Daisy didn't know how much farther it was to the gold mine, but she hopped out almost before Dale had completely stopped, eager to get there as soon as possible. She stubbed her toe on a river rock and nearly fell.

"Slow down and wait for me," Dale hissed from behind her. "You won't do anyone any good if you fall and break your leg before we get there."

She slowed to let Dale catch up with her, but her feet kept wanting to break into a run. They were so close. She needed to see for herself that River was okay.

"There are also snakes around at night, so be careful where you step."

Snakes. Daisy recoiled into his chest, lifting her feet as if she might magically levitate off the ground. Dale had mentioned they needed to watch out for snakes during the day, but not at night. *Pull yourself together.* She took a deep breath. She was here for River. No stupid snake was going to scare her away.

"And don't forget about the cane toads," Dale added. It was too dark to see, but she was sure that man was smirking at her.

"If it's the shaft I think it is, it's the one farthest away from the town," Dale continued. "It's a good ten-minute walk." Which would make sense. Any tourist poking around was unlikely to go that far out, so it'd be the perfect place to hide. How the hell had River found this guy?

Daisy let Dale take the lead, keeping as close as possible to his heels, not wanting to get lost. What would she have done if she'd come out here on her own? It would've taken her all night to track down River.

For the next ten minutes, all she could hear was the quiet rasping of her breath, and the crunch of their shoes on the ochre gravel. A couple of times they walked straight through a large spiderweb, strung between two trees, and Dale cursed while he wiped away the web. Between the spiders, the snakes and the toads, Daisy was really glad Dale was out the front.

She recognized the bulky shadows of the abandoned cottages as they slid by on the left-hand side. Dale kept them within the cover of the scattered acacia trees, rather than exposing them out in the open. She hadn't seen the large, wooden, mine-shaft elevator in the middle of the township, but that'd be far behind by now, as they continued to skirt the edges of the old village.

They kept going, Dale following a path that led away from the main township, toward the base of the escarpment, running parallel to what would've been the main street when the town had once thrived. It was darker in here as trees crowded in, their branches blocking out the starlight, and the escarpment loomed tall in front of them.

Dale slowed, then stopped in his tracks. He leaned in and

whispered in her ear. "I'm not exactly sure how far down we need to go, distances are hard to gauge in the dark." He raised an arm and pointed down the length of the escarpment. "There are at least three or four abandoned shafts in this direction, but I'm not sure—"

The sound of a gunshot split the air. What the…?

Dale was quicker to react than she was, ducking behind a trunk and dragging her with him.

Daisy covered her mouth with her hands to stop herself from crying out. What was that? Who was shooting? River? Was River involved?

She tried to tear herself out of Dale's arms and run toward the sound, but he held on tight. She was strong. She struggled against him. But he was stronger. She opened her mouth to scream River's name, but a hand clamped over her face before she could utter a sound.

"Calm down," he growled into her ear. "Do you want to get us both shot?" His voice had a hard edge to it she'd never heard before, and it was that hard edge that finally got through her near-hysteria. She relaxed in his arms, letting herself go limp. He was right. If someone was shooting, the last thing they needed was to draw attention to themselves.

But she was desperate to find out what was going on. Dale cautiously released her mouth. They both peered around the edge of the trunk. Lights were flickering in the distance. A flashlight, perhaps. She glanced at Dale and they communicated silently, both agreeing they needed to get closer. Dale took Daisy's hand and forced her behind him as they wended carefully between the trees. She wasn't sure she enjoyed being pushed behind, being told what to do. Dale thought he was protecting her, but she was quite capable of protecting herself. It was her brother in potential trouble out there. She let the feeling drop; it'd do no good to rage against gender bias right now.

As they crept closer, Daisy made out a lone figure pacing to and fro in a small clearing. Closer and closer, and she could see the figure was that of a man, and the cliff face behind him contained a wooden casing, perhaps where the mine shaft was boarded up. Now they could hear him talking, a phone held to his ear. They finally got close enough to see it wasn't River. This man was shorter, stocky, and stalked around with a menacing grace that had Daisy's alarm bells ringing. This man was dangerous; she could feel it. Perhaps River had been right all along.

The man stopped talking, and shoved his phone in his pocket. And then he looked down at something on the ground at his feet. A dark, shapeless lump. The shape moved and groaned.

Oh, God. It couldn't be.

That wasn't River, was it?

She released her grasp on Dale's hand to run toward her brother. But Dale had her around the waist before she'd even gone two steps. She sank down onto the ground, a low sob escaping from deep inside her chest.

Dale cupped her face with his hands and forced her to look at him. *Don't do anything stupid,* his eyes seemed to plead with her. All she could think was that she needed to protect her brother. She'd been doing it all her life. It was ingrained in her psyche, instinctive. He was her flesh and blood, and she would do anything for him. But slowly that all-encompassing dread, that terrible urgency drained from her body, replaced by a hard-edged fear and a cooler head. After a few seconds, she nodded at Dale and he released her.

What were they going to do now? They had to rescue River, there was no doubt about that. But how?

Dale pulled his phone out of his rear pocket and glanced at it. Great idea. She agreed wholeheartedly that it was time to call the cops. Or at least call the lodge and get someone to come and back them up. But then he grimaced and shook his head. He had no signal. Shit. Why hadn't they brought a sat phone? Too late now.

She crawled through the underbrush, snakes and cane toads be damned, needing to get closer, to figure out the lay of the land. Dale was close by, shuffling quietly through the red dirt beside her. Rocks and leaves and sticks dug into her knees. So instead, she used her toes and hands to walk like a monkey across the landscape, making sure she stayed hidden from view by bushes and tall grass. When they were within a hundred yards, she hunkered down behind the wide trunk of a bottle tree, Dale by her shoulder.

Now she could see exactly what was going on. A small, hurricane lamp sat atop a rock near the entrance to an abandoned shaft, casting just enough light to see by. The entrance looked to be completely boarded up. Was this the tunnel River was talking about? River lay on the ground, but he'd stopped moving. He was very still. The other man was pacing around the small clearing, and she could clearly see the gun in his hand.

The man abruptly stopped pacing, and cast a sharp gaze out into the darkness, as if he'd heard something. She held her breath. He continued to stare for many long moments. Then, just as suddenly, he gathered up the lamp and disappeared out of view.

What the...? She frowned at Dale and he shrugged in return, equally puzzled. There had to be some sort of false door, or perhaps the man had disguised the entrance, so that it merely looked boarded-up from a distance.

Everything was plunged into darkness when he took the lamp with him. Daisy couldn't quite believe their luck. The man had gone. And he'd left River lying there. Now was their chance.

"Quick." She motioned with her hand. "Help me get

River."

"Are you completely sure it's your brother?" Dale whispered. She merely nodded. There wasn't a shadow of a doubt in her mind. Even without that owl hooting its premonition, she could feel it in her bones. "But what if that guy comes back?" Dale asked. "Why would he leave River just lying there? Surely, he'll return any second?"

It was true. The man was highly unlikely to leave River lying there. Perhaps he'd ducked inside to get something. Like a shovel to dig a gravesite. The terrible thought spread across her mind like a virus. That was it; she'd do this on her own, if she had to. Drag River across the dusty ground to safety. But it'd be much quicker and easier to move River with Dale's help. She knew she was asking a lot; had already asked a lot from him. But she'd ask again, for her brother's sake. She stared at him, waiting for him to decide.

Dale got to his feet. "Come on. Let's make this quick."

She wanted to hug him, pour out all her gratitude, so he knew how much this meant to her. It wasn't the time, however. Her eyes needed to adjust to the darkness, but she didn't have time, and so stumbled, half-blind in the direction of the clearing. They were making more noise than they should, but that couldn't be helped. She made out the faint outline of the top of the escarpment and they went deeper into the shadows beneath it. Dale was a few feet away; she could hear his footsteps and faintly make out the shape of his head as he stalked through the grass beside her. As they got closer, she slowed, almost feeling her way with her feet, her hands outstretched in front.

She stopped abruptly when she heard a low moan directly in front of her. She'd almost fallen over River because it was too murky to see where she was going.

Dropping to her knees, she felt around until she came in contact with something warm, wet and sticky. It took her a few seconds to realize it was River's blood seeping onto the ground. She recoiled in horror. Steeling herself, she leaned forward again, this time finding River's back, patting her way up his body until she found his head.

She leaned over and whispered, "River, it's me, Daisy." He gave another moan but didn't speak. He was in a bad way. Where had he been shot? In the chest? In the stomach? She couldn't see in the dark.

"Over here," she called quietly to Dale. "I found him. Quick." They needed to get him away.

Dale was beside her. He quickly gathered River beneath the shoulders, and she took up his feet as they lifted him off the ground.

All of a sudden, everything around them was illuminated into stark brightness. Someone had turned a spotlight on them. She made the rookie mistake of turning toward the light and was instantly blinded.

"Don't move, or I'll shoot," a deep voice rang out from behind the spotlight.

Fuck. Dale had been right. It was a trap all along. She'd dragged Dale into terrible danger.

CHAPTER NINETEEN

"Get down on your knees," a voice called from behind the blinding flashlight. It was a man, that was all Dale could tell. His mind was refusing to accept what was happening. That he and Daisy were being held at gunpoint. He scanned the area for a weapon, a means out of the situation.

"Come on, you know I've got a gun, and you've already seen I'm not afraid to use it," the man said, his voice rising to a loud growl. His voice might be loud and menacing, but Dale could hear the panic behind his threats in the high pitch of his tone. This man was as scared as they were. At least, Dale hadn't been silly enough to look directly at the light, but he thought Daisy might have, by the way she was covering her eyes.

"Do it, *now!*" the man screamed.

This time Dale knew he needed to comply. This guy sounded as if he was losing it. He lowered River's shoulders carefully to the ground. Raising his hands slowly in the air, he bent his knees and dropped to the dusty ground. He looked over at Daisy, silently willing her to do the same. They couldn't take any chances. Not until they knew who and what they were dealing with. He let out a gust of relief when Daisy followed suit, admittedly scowling into the spotlight as if she wanted to leap over there and tear out the guy's throat.

The man advanced toward them, keeping the high-powered flashlight trained on their faces. A length of rope landed on the ground near Dale's knees.

"You." The flashlight flickered onto Daisy. "Tie him up."

"What," she answered a weakly, not seeming to understand. "No, I—"

"Do it now, or I'll fucking shoot him in the head."

Daisy jumped and scuttled over on her hands and knees to Dale. Did the guy actually have his gun? It was hard to tell what was going on behind the flashlight. But they'd both seen the weapon in the man's hand earlier, they'd both heard the gunshot and seen the effect on River, so Dale could only assume this man *was* pointing a gun directly at them.

"Turn around," the man ordered. "So I can watch her tie your hands."

Smart guy, Dale thought, as he shuffled around and put his hands behind his back for Daisy. Silently, he willed Daisy not to tie the rope too tight.

And she did a pretty good job, at first, keeping the loops loose enough so that he might work himself free.

"Not good enough," the man snarled. "Do a better job." There was a loud crack and a thud in the dirt nearby, and Dale flinched. Daisy squealed, crashing into his side. The man had fired a warning shot. He meant business. Instinctively, Dale had tried to fling his arms around Daisy—which was hard to do when his wrists were bound behind his back—wanting to protect her. She huddled in tight against him, trembling. She was terrified. Dale hated this guy for what he was doing. For shooting Daisy's brother, and for threatening them. Who was he? What the hell did he want? How could he possibly be related to everything that'd happened on the station recently? At least he'd answered one question—the man was armed and dangerous.

Dale had never been up this close and personal with a proper gun before. One meant for killing people. Of course, the station had a couple of shotguns and a little .22 for getting rid of vermin. He'd certainly never been threatened with a pistol before.

"Do it right," the man grunted, and Daisy slowly peeled herself away from Dale's side. He didn't want to let her go. He wanted to keep her encased within the safety of his body. Forever. A quick glance at her face showed it was streaked with tears, but her mouth was set in a grim line of defiance. She was determined not to let this man beat them. She was terribly attached to her brother, overprotective. But in the short time he'd gotten to know her, he understood Daisy would do just about anything to save River. Including facing up to a stranger with a gun.

Daisy tied the knots as tight as they would go, and Dale didn't blame her.

Then the man ordered her to tie his ankles as well, and so Dale sat and pulled his knees up in front to make it easy for her. All the while, his mind was whirling with strategies and schemes for escape, each one discarded as swiftly as they entered his head. The other guy had a gun, and that gave him the trump card. As Daisy tied his feet, Dale tried to get a look at the man behind the flashlight. He caught glimpses of a full head of dark hair, high cheekbones and eyes so dark they could've been black. He racked his brain to remember if he'd heard the man's voice before, but came up with a blank. There was a slight accent from somewhere in Asia, but Dale couldn't pinpoint exactly where. He was pretty sure he'd never met this guy before.

Once Dale's ankles were secure, the man made Daisy turn around, and he tied her up, as well. Soon, they were sitting side by side in the dirt, bound hand and foot. Taken captive. A groan from off to his left reminded Dale that River was still lying wounded and unconscious on the ground nearby. If they didn't get him help soon, would he die? He couldn't let that happen; it'd destroy Daisy. And if Daisy was destroyed, then part of him would die, as well.

A sound reached his ears, and it took him a second to work out what it was. That was the distinctive burble of an ATV engine. Was it one of theirs? Had Steve woken early and found his note? Perhaps they were saved. But in the same second a wave of relief flooded over him, he remembered there was a gun pointed at them. He had to warn Steve to stay away.

"Watch out," he shouted. "It's a trap."

The man with the gun rounded on him. "Shut the fuck up," he shouted, as the beam from a set of headlights hit them full-on.

Dale flinched and ducked, waiting for the bullet to enter his body. But then the man laughed. "That's funny. Did you think someone was coming to rescue you? Nah, that's not going to happen." The guy twirled the gun in his hand and walked toward the oncoming vehicle. As if he knew exactly who was arriving.

Dale's heart sank. He must have an accomplice. Maybe that's who he was talking to on the phone when they'd first spotted him. It must be a satellite phone, because Dale had already checked his cell and it wasn't getting any signal. That meant this guy was well organized. And well stocked, if he'd been staying out here for weeks, as River suggested.

"You took your time," the man called out.

"I came as quick as I could," a woman answered.

Dale froze. He recognized that voice.

Then the woman strode into the clearing, which was now lit by the headlights from the ATV.

It was Sally Tsun.

What was Sally doing here?

"You need to gag them, Johnny," she said coldly.

Daisy's eyes went as big as saucers, and she glanced at Sally and then at the man she'd called Johnny. Dale's mind raced. Hadn't Daisy mentioned she'd heard Sally on a phone call a few nights ago to a man named Johnny? His stomach roiled, and bile rose up his throat.

Did Sally have something to do with Karri's murder? Was she covering up for this guy?

Dale went to open his mouth to ask Sally all those things and more, when Johnny shoved some kind of rag in his mouth. Dale gagged and nearly choked on the disgusting thing, unable to breathe. Johnny shoved it in harder until it hurt, forcing Dale's head backward and bringing tears to his eyes.

Then he did the same to Daisy.

Sally stood back, arms crossed, watching Johnny. "Tell me what happened," Sally demanded. "How the fuck did you let this get so out of control?"

"Me? Let things get... Don't make me fucking laugh." Johnny went up and took Sally by the throat. "This is all your fault and don't you forget it."

Dale blinked. Whoa, this guy wasn't pulling any punches. He was obviously in control, and he was making sure Sally knew it.

Sally lost some of her arrogance, her mouth pulling up in a grimace as both of her hands wrapped around Johnny's, a pleading look entering her eyes. They stood for many seconds, staring at each other.

"Sure, Johnny, you're right, I stuffed up," Sally finally said, her voice a little strained from his grip on her throat. He let her go. Her body language seemed submissive, but Dale noticed her narrowed eyes, even if Johnny didn't.

There were some odd dynamics going on between these two.

Johnny went over and took a seat on an old, fallen log ten yards away, resting his hands on his knees and blowing out a breath. "Like I said to you on the phone, this idiot showed up in the middle of the night." Johnny waved his gun in River's direction. "I caught him snooping around my stuff. He must've figured out how to get into the shaft."

Sally cautiously approached River. He remained unmoving, and she nudged him with her toe. "Is he dead?"

"Nah, not yet, I don't think." Johnny said it with such pragmatism that Dale got the distinct impression this man wasn't unused to killing.

"Why would he do that? Who the hell is he?" Sally sat down on the opposite end of the log, completely ignoring Dale and Daisy.

She'd do well not to look at him, Dale thought, because he was sure he'd be able to impale her with just his gaze, he was so furious. This woman had worked for the station for over two years. He trusted her. Implicitly. How dare she use that trust against him?

"It wasn't till he mentioned he had a sister named Daisy that I twigged how he was connected."

Daisy's head shot up. She made some grunting noises and struggled to break free of her bonds. Even though it was useless, Dale admired her tenacity. He understood how she felt, because he wanted to go up and punch this man in the face nearly as much as she did.

"He didn't know I had a gun. He tried to pull a knife on me." Johnny gave a theatrical laugh. "Said that he was going to call his sister and this guy," Johnny tipped his chin in Dale's direction, "and they'd come out here and sort me out." Johnny snorted. "That was never going to happen."

"So, you shot him?"

"Yep."

"But he's not dead?"

"Nope."

Sally sighed loudly, but when Johnny gave her a sideways glare, she subsided into silence for a second. "So, what are we going to do with him? And with them?"

Dale stilled. For the first time, Dale felt real fear slither down his spine.

"Well, obviously, we need to get rid of them. And then we need to hightail it out of here. You can't stay at Stormcloud any longer, the gig really is up."

Shit, shit. Did Johnny mean what he said? Or was he just talking tough to scare them? Staring at Johnny, Dale decided he could carry out his threat. He needed to think fast. How was he going to get him and Daisy out of this?

"Do I have time to go and get my stuff? I wish you'd told me that on the phone. I left in such a rush. I don't—"

"No, you don't have time to get your stuff," Johnny yelled, standing up.

"But all my good clothes. And my jewelry," Sally huffed. "Besides, there's paperwork, receipts, and lists of credit card numbers that could incriminate me."

"You should've thought of that before you got me into this mess." Johnny was waving the gun around in the air. Dale was convinced this guy might have a screw loose, the way he was treating the weapon so carelessly. Which made him even more dangerous.

The two were arguing like an old married couple. Dale decided they were in some kind of relationship; boyfriend and girlfriend at the least, perhaps even married.

"The longer you argue with me, the less chance we have to get away. So start fucking thinking. How do we get rid of these two?" Johnny finally said, advancing toward Sally, hand raised as if to take her by the throat again. But she saw him coming and scuttled backward, out of reach.

"Wait." She raised a hand to stop him. "I've got an idea."

"What?" he said, retaking his seat on the log.

"We could drive them up to the lookout in their ATV and run it off the edge. Make it look like an accident."

Dale's blood ran cold. Daisy gave a squeak of alarm and he turned to look at her.

"Ah, I knew there was a reason I loved you." Johnny smiled for the first time that night, and it was a terrible sight to behold. He stood and walked over to where Sally was standing, and grabbing her by the nape of the neck, he pulled her in and kissed her hard on the mouth. Dale averted his gaze.

Even with the man's chilling words reverberating around in his head, Dale knew that was some majorly fucked-up kind of behavior to show your love. But then, these two deserved each other.

"It means one of us will have to walk back and find their ATV first," Sally said when Johnny finally let her up for air. "I drove past it on the way here. They left it in the— Eeeee, I hate those things." Sally jumped sideways, looking down at her feet, where a cane toad squatted, seeming oblivious to her alarm. She swung her leg and aimed a kick at the creature, but at the last second, it hopped into a tussock of grass and she cursed loudly when she missed. Dale felt obtusely happy that her kick had gone wide.

"I'll get it. You stay here with these two, I won't be long."

Sally looked at Dale and Daisy for the first time. "Give me your gun," she said, holding out her hand.

"They're tied up, they're not going anywhere," Johnny said with an exasperated sigh.

"I don't care. I don't trust them." Sally said. "And what about the other one? The brother. Should we tie him up as well?"

"You can, if you want. There's more rope in the shaft." Johnny flicked his wrist in the direction of the boarded-up cave. "I don't reckon he's gonna survive much longer, anyway."

Daisy gave a low moan. Bastard. He wanted to maim that guy so bad.

Surprisingly, Johnny handed over his gun. "Do you remember how to use one of these?" he asked, as he placed it in her palm.

"Of course, I do," she replied huffily.

Johnny merely grunted, then turned and flicked on the flashlight and began walking in the direction of the river and their ATV.

"Right," Sally said with purpose, once Johnny was out of earshot. "I'm going to find some rope, you both stay here." She giggled. Then glanced at them as if unsure, adding, "This gun is loaded and ready to fire." She made a show of raising the weapon and releasing the safety catch, then pointing it first at Dale, then at Daisy. There was a feral glint in her eye. Dale was seeing another side to this woman who'd worked at the station for two years. How had he not seen this streak of crazy before? She'd been good at hiding her true self, that was for sure.

After giving them one more glance, Sally threaded through the clumps of grass toward the entrance to the shaft. Leaning down to grab the small hurricane lamp, she suddenly leaped backward in alarm. "Oh, you little…these fucking things are everywhere." She made a swipe at something with her foot, then gingerly picked up the lamp and sidled around something on the ground, finally disappearing behind the wooden boards. Dale couldn't see, but he imagined it was probably another one of the hated cane toads.

They were alone in the clearing. The bright headlights of the ATV were still shining on them. If they were going to get away, now was their chance. He cast his gaze frantically around the area. What could they use to help them escape?

Daisy made an impatient noise, and he zeroed in on her face. She was making strange grunting sounds and straining against her bonds. These gags made it impossible for them to communicate, which was the whole point. What was she up to?

All of a sudden, one of her hands popped free, then her other appeared, with loops of rope still wrapped around her wrist. She shot him look of triumph, and he knew a second of sheer relief. She was free! Her fingers fumbled with the rope at her ankles, but before she got one knot untied, a flicker of light caught their attention. Shit, Sally was coming back.

Daisy quickly put her hands behind her back, shooting him a wary glance. She'd been so close. But now she had her hands-free, there was still a faint hope that she might escape.

Sally walked over, a length of rope swinging in her left hand, the gun in her other, on open display. She stopped and studied them minutely for a few moments. When she was satisfied that nothing was out of place, she went over to River and rolled him over. River didn't make a sound, which scared Dale. Sally bent down and tied his feet first, making sure she kept them in her line of sight as she did so. Daisy glowered at Sally. He could almost feel hatred coming off her in waves. Sally ignored Daisy's stare, instead, roughly pulling River's arms behind his back, and tying them as well.

Sally stood, staring out into the forest, ignoring them. Which was good. Now was Daisy's chance. If she was going to do anything with her free hands, it had to be now. The sound of an ATV made Dale turn his head. Shit, he'd returned already. Johnny must have run the entire way, he'd made it in a little over five minutes, while the trek had taken him and Daisy closer to ten; admittedly, they'd been sneaking their way through the undergrowth.

Johnny stopped the ATV next to the one Sally had brought. He left the engine running and the lights on.

"Bring the girl over first. I'll tie her in, make sure she's secure," Johnny called to her. What was Daisy going to do? They would figure out her hands were loose. She should've done something to escape already, before Johnny returned. Dale willed her not to try anything. It was too dangerous now.

Sally sauntered over, tucking the gun under her arm as she knelt down, and untied Daisy's feet. Dale was a little shocked at her blasé handling of the weapon. No person with half a brain or half an hour's training would store a loaded gun that way.

Daisy stared at Sally as if she could bore holes through her with just her eyes. Sally didn't react, however. Instead, as she finished untying the last knot and slipping the coils of rope from around Daisy's ankles, she leaned in closer, so her nose was almost touching Daisy's.

"I'm going to enjoy watching you tumble over the cliff," she said, with a smirk.

CHAPTER TWENTY

Daisy's blood thundered around her body. It felt as if she was literally boiling. She'd heard the phrase before, but never dreamed she would be so angry that it'd happen to her. She controlled her body, bending it to her will, so instead of reaching out and clawing this woman's eyes out, she remained still, poised, ready to strike. The slimy animal squirmed in her hand, and she had to tamp down a surge of revulsion. This creature was going to be her salvation, she needed to hang onto it for a few more seconds. The sound of her own heartbeat was unnaturally loud. Could Sally hear it? Would it give her away?

"I killed that little lying, greedy bitch. I'll have no problem dealing with your skinny ass, either," Sally snarled.

Daisy recoiled in horror. What had Sally said? Surely this petite woman with the large smile and pretty, dark eyes hadn't just revealed she was the one who murdered Karri? All this time Daisy had been suspecting Johnny, but it'd been Sally all along. Her mind could hardly comprehend Sally's declaration of guilt. The senior sergeant had been right when he suspected one of their own.

"You're going down. You think you're so special, don't you?" Sally murmured viciously. "Waltzing onto the station like you own the place. Flirting with all the guys, got Dale wrapped around your little finger. You're going to find out exactly how un-special you really are. In fact, yo—"

Sally's tirade was cut off mid-sentence, and she screamed in pain and fear as Daisy lunged at her, shoving the cane toad in her face.

"Argh, get it off me. It's disgusting. Argh, it burns. It's burning my eyes." Sally stumbled up off her knees and backward a few steps.

Daisy had shoved the cane toad directly into Sally's eyes. She'd been counting on the toads' poison stinging like hell—perhaps even blinding her—and it seemed to be doing the job. Daisy knew little about cane toads, but she knew they secreted toxic poison from glands on their shoulders, and she knew Sally absolutely hated the amphibians. Two points in her favor. Daisy frantically wiped her hands on her jeans, hoping to get rid of any poison on her own hands.

"What the fuck is going on?" Johnny called, running toward the clearing.

Daisy was on her feet, ripping the gag out of her mouth. She had to get to Sally, who was still blinded, and wrestle the weapon off her. It was her only chance. But Sally kept stumbling backward, one hand wildly swiping at her eyes, her other hand reaching for the gun tucked under her arm.

Oh, fuck. Daisy dropped to the ground at the same time as the gun went off. Sally was shooting wildly in every direction. One. Two. Three. Four shots. Daisy hadn't counted on her doing that. Oh God, what about Dale? Was he okay? He could be shot.

There was a loud scream, and then a thud as something landed on the ground. Or should she say, someone? She could no longer see Johnny running toward them in the headlights. Where had he gone?

"What have you done?" Johnny screamed. "You've shot

me, you fucking…" His last words ended on a gurgle.

It was as if everything was running in slow motion. Daisy took in Dale as he cowered on the ground, watching the whole scene unfolding with enormous eyes. She could hear Johnny as he thrashed in the long grass right outside the clearing, perhaps struggling to regain his feet. And Sally was staring in confusion, still wiping her eyes, unable to comprehend what she'd just done.

Daisy's job wasn't finished. Sally was still a threat. Daisy was up on her hands and knees, keeping low, crawling across the dusty ground. Too late, Sally saw her coming, and lowered the weapon in her direction, but Daisy took the other woman out at the knees, sending her crashing onto her back, the gun flying through the air and disappearing out of sight beyond the ring of light.

Sally must've been winded, because she lay on the ground gasping like a fish and clutching at her chest.

Daisy pounced, landing with her knees right on the woman's solar plexus, knocking more air out of her lungs. With both hands she pushed Sally's head into the dirt, forcing her face sideways. When Sally reached up to grapple with Daisy's hands, she grabbed the other woman's first two fingers on her right hand and jerked them backward. A scream erupted from Sally, so primal and full of pain that Daisy almost halted. But then she remembered River and Karri. She needed this woman immobilized, so she kept the pressure on, bending her fingers backward until Sally had no choice but to follow the direction Daisy was pulling or risk a broken finger. In one swift move, Daisy forced Sally to roll over onto her stomach as she brought her hand up behind her back, keeping the pressure on.

River had taught her the finger lock move. He said a woman needed to know how to defend herself, and he'd been right. But Sally was strong, stronger than Daisy expected for such a petite woman, and she bucked and kicked out with all her strength. It seemed perhaps Sally was prepared to risk broken fingers to get away from her. Daisy sent the pointy bit of her elbow crashing into the woman's chin, once, twice, three times, stunning her into silence for a few seconds as her eyes rolled back in her head and she stopped struggling.

Those precious few seconds were all Daisy needed. Using the loop of rope still caught around her ankle, she tied Sally's hands behind her back. Then she ran and picked up the other length of rope, which Johnny had used to tie her own hands.

By the time she returned to Sally, the other woman was coming to. Daisy quickly looped the rope around her legs just as they flailed in the air. Sally hissed at her like a venomous snake. Her eyes were red and swollen from the toad's poison, and spittle flew from her mouth as she screamed obscenities at Daisy.

Daisy stood and watched Sally for a few moments, until she was satisfied the other woman wasn't going anywhere in a hurry. Ignoring the curses being flung in her direction, Daisy went over to Dale. She crouched down and removed his gag first and quickly went to work untying his hands. Johnny had stopped thrashing in the grass, and Daisy had no idea whether it was because he was dead, or because he was creeping up on her right this very second.

"Holy fuck, Daisy, I can't believe you just did that," Dale blurted as soon as the gag was out of his mouth.

"Neither can I," she answered, eyes darting all around the clearing, expecting Johnny to rise up at any moment. Her heart screamed that she needed to go to River. Was he even still alive? But she couldn't go to him until she was sure Johnny was no longer a threat.

"Can you do your legs?" she asked curtly, as soon as his were hands were free. "I'm going to check on Johnny."

"Wait," he called, but Daisy wasn't waiting.

She approached the spot she'd last seen the grass waving when Johnny went down, moving warily. What would she do, if he suddenly reared up right in front of her? She didn't know where the weapon had landed, but she thought it was over on the opposite side of the clearing. Her toe stubbed against a small rock and she leaned down and picked it up. Not much of a weapon, but at least it was slightly better than a cane toad.

Creeping toward the place she thought Johnny might be lying, she raised the rock above her head. The headlights caused crazy shadows in the grass, dark shapes that her imagination turned into a leaping specter. Her heart felt as if it were lodged permanently in her throat. One step forward. Two steps forward. A slight breeze tickled the branches on the trees to her left and she jumped at the rasping sound. It was only the leaves rubbing together, not the fiery breath of an irate man ready to pounce. Sally was still spouting curses in the background, but Daisy blocked her out, concentrating only on what was ahead.

A flattened area opened up in the grass ahead. It was hard to make out in all the dim shadows, but it looked to be the shape of a man sprawled on the ground. The shape didn't move, didn't make a sound. She studied it for many long seconds, but there was no change. Was he even breathing?

There was a sudden presence behind her, and she whirled around, ready to smash the rock down with force.

It was Dale, and she let out a sob of relief. He took her by the shoulders and moved her gently aside so he could peer down at the shape.

"I think he might be dead," she whispered.

"Give me that rock," he said, pointing at the makeshift weapon in her hand. He tossed it onto the feet of the man on the ground. It bounced off one of his shoes, but he didn't move, or react. Dale got gingerly down on his hands and knees and poked the man in the shoulder. Nothing. Not even a groan.

Daisy couldn't help the thought that bubbled to the surface. How ironic, if Sally had killed her own accomplice.

"I'm going to tie him up anyway, as a precaution," Dale said.

"Good idea," she agreed.

"I'm hoping he still has that sat phone on him, so I can call the cops."

That was an even better idea, but Daisy left him to it. She had something much more important on her mind.

River.

Ignoring Sally, who was still yelling at the top of her voice, Daisy raced over to where he lay, his back toward her. So still and unmoving. Daisy held her hands against her chest, suddenly terribly afraid to touch him. Because when she did, she'd find out for sure whether he was still alive.

"River," she sobbed. "Please be alive." Reaching out a tentative hand, she touched his arm. It was warm. She ran a hand down his rib cage. There was a slight rise and fall under her fingertips. He was breathing. She let out another sob, this one of relief.

She rolled him on his back so she could examine him. There was a lot of blood. It was everywhere, all over the front of his T-shirt. She located where are all the blood seemed to be coming from, a large wound on the right-hand side of his chest. Without a second's thought, she stripped off her own T-shirt and used it to cover the wound, applying pressure.

River groaned faintly.

Good. That was good. It meant he was still alive. But judging by all the blood on the ground, he might not stay that way very long.

"You need to call in a rescue helicopter," she shouted, lifting her gaze from River's prone body. "He's still alive.

Dale?" Where was he?

It was almost comical, the way his head popped up above the grass when she called his name.

"I'm on it," Dale replied, waving the magical sat phone above his head. He got to his feet and came to her.

As soon as he saw she was wearing only a bra, Dale removed his own shirt and handed it to her. At any other time, she would've enjoyed the view of all those rippling abs, but not tonight. Daisy blinked, then realized it was actually almost morning. The sky on the horizon was lightening imperceptibly.

"How is he?" Dale asked, at the same time his fingers were tapping out the emergency number for the police and ambulance.

"Not good," she admitted. "It looks like he's lost a lot of blood. We need an air ambulance ASAP."

Dale's handsome face caved into a grimace of worry. Then he began talking rapidly into the phone. She vaguely heard him request an immediate rescue helicopter from Cairns, then he gave directions to the old gold mine. Her attention was fixed on River, willing him to keep breathing.

Daisy had no idea how much time had passed before Dale returned and knelt beside her. "Robinson and King are on their way," he reported, offering her a bottle of water to wash her hands, and she scrubbed feverishly, hoping to get any residue from the poison off her skin. Dale continued, "But Dimbulah is an hour away, so..." He didn't need to finish; Daisy knew it was one of the cons of remote living. "Steve and Skylar are coming, too," he said. "They should be here in fifteen minutes. The helicopter will take a little longer, probably thirty minutes, they're scrambling it from Cairns right now."

Daisy groaned. That was too long. Would River live that long?

"I know," he said, wrapping an arm around her shoulder. "But if River is anything like his sister, he's a survivor. He'll make it through. He's tough, and he's got you in his corner fighting for him."

Daisy wasn't so sure, but she nodded because there was nothing else to say.

Dale stayed by her side, a steady presence for her to cling to, and she willed her brother to keep breathing, while continuing to apply pressure to stop the blood loss.

She felt Dale's sudden absence and looked up, blinking in the glare of the lights from Steve's truck. Steve and Skylar were here. She hadn't even heard a vehicle arrive. Dale gave them a highly abbreviated version of events. Skylar threw her arms around Dale and hugged him tight. She heard Steve say something about taking one of the ATVs to light up a clearing nearby, where the helicopter could land. Then Skylar was at her side, asking what she could do to help.

Daisy didn't know how to answer, so Skylar leaned an arm around Daisy, the same way she had with Dale, the physical presence lending Daisy some much-needed moral support.

The loud thwack of helicopter rotor blades announced that help was finally on the way. Soon, things began to happen at warp speed, everything blurring into a whirl of movement and snatches of conversation, as Daisy handed her brother over to the paramedics. She and Skylar stood back, with arms wrapped around each other, watching the paramedics work on River. Daisy was so grateful to the other woman for her support. Skylar hardly knew Daisy, and the other woman had never met her brother, but here she was holding her like she was one of the family.

One paramedic left her brother and went over to where Johnny lay on the ground. She wanted to scream at him to come back and help River. That man lying on the ground didn't deserve their help. But she managed to keep her thoughts to herself, and the paramedic was soon back by River's side. The grim turn of his mouth told Daisy all she needed to know about Johnny.

It seemed to take forever, but was probably less than fifteen minutes before air rescue loaded River into the helicopter. She wanted to go with him to hospital, but they shook their heads when she asked; there wasn't enough room.

Dale came up and wrapped her in his arms, and they watched from afar as the helicopter took off into the early-morning sky. Steve must've found Dale a spare shirt, because he was no longer naked from the waist up. Daisy was astounded when she realized the world around her was slowly coming to life. She could now see without the aid of the ATV's headlights. She leaned into Dale's chest and drew in a deep breath. It was the first time she'd felt completely safe since they'd left the lodge. All the adrenaline flooding around her body had slowed to a trickle. Without that hormone keeping her muscles working, she felt limp, like she might collapse at any second.

How was she ever going to explain all of this to the cops when they arrived? There were only two things she truly cared about right now. The fact that she and Dale had survived; that Dale still had his strong arms wrapped around her. And whether River would pull through.

CHAPTER TWENTY-ONE

Dale paced to and fro, wearing a path in the dusty gravel. Where the hell were Robinson and King? It felt like they'd been waiting an eternity for the cops to arrive, while they were left to sit here with Karri's murderer and a dead body. The rescue helicopter had been and gone, taking River with them, and now the flurry of activity had died it was as if they were in a horrible limbo. The clearing was in the shadow cast by the escarpment towering above them, but all too soon, they'd be baking in the full morning sun. It was going to be a long, hot morning.

Steve, Skylar, and Daisy were all perched on the fallen log where Johnny had so recently sat. All three of them were staring at Sally, who was staring belligerently back at them. Sally's eyes were red and swollen from the toad poison, but one paramedic had repeatedly flushed them with water to remove the toxin before they left, so she'd stopped screaming that they were burning. Even though rumor had it that the poison could be absorbed through mucous membranes, such as the eyes, Sally hadn't seemed to suffer any further effects.

Twice, she'd asked how Johnny was faring, and would he be okay once they got him to hospital. Everyone ignored her, but Dale was a little surprised by her questions. She clearly thought Johnny was still alive. The toad toxin must've really blinded her, if she hadn't been able to see that Johnny wasn't loaded into the rescue helicopter, along with River. That his body was in fact lying where he'd fallen, hidden from view by the long grass twenty yards or so away.

Robinson had called Dale on the sat phone from his vehicle and made it extremely clear that they needed to keep Sally secured and *unharmed* until they arrived. In other words, he probably shouldn't go up and kick her in the teeth, which is what he wanted to do. Robinson also mentioned that they'd take Sally Tsun straight into custody, to the Dimbulah lock-up, where two detectives would arrive from Cairns to interview her. And Dale could expect to see a forensics team and a raft of other officers pouring in from Cairns to secure the crime scene. This sounded like it was going to be bigger than *Ben-Hur*.

Dale wandered over to the log where everyone was sitting. "I think we're going to need to brace for impact. There's going to be a shitstorm of police and questions and media coming our way." Three pairs of eyes turned in his direction.

"We should decide what we're going to tell the guests. They're going to want some answers this morning," Skylar mused. "Perhaps we should call mum, she'll be the one in the firing line when they all wake up." Dale felt a stab of sympathy for his mother. He could imagine the conversation that'd taken place straight after his phone call this morning to Steve. Daniella would've been determined to come and see for herself. Steve told him he had to almost forcibly hold his mother back. But she finally agreed that someone needed to be there to look after the guests when they awoke, and to take any calls that might come in. She, Julie, Alek, and Bindi would keep it all together until the rest of them returned.

Steve looked up and nodded soberly. "You're right. I hope Daniella will be able to handle all of this."

"I hope Daniella will be able to handle all of this," Sally parroted, screwing her eyes up in distaste, and shooting Steve a sarcastic look. "Daniella this, Daniella that, she's all you care about. That and keeping the precious reputation of Stormcloud Station intact. You're all pathetic," she taunted.

"What did you say?" Steve stood and took a step toward his ex-employee, eyes glittering dangerously.

"Don't take the bait," Dale warned, putting a hand on Steve's chest to restrain him. "She's not worth it," he added. Why couldn't she sit quietly? If she kept this up, he was going to find it hard to keep her *unharmed*.

Steve's jaw worked as he tried to contain his rage. Finally, he let out a breath and said, "I'll be thrilled when she's locked up for good. Happy when this is all over." He let out a gust of air through pursed lips.

"Yeah, I'm sure you'll be happy. You can all go back to your sweet little lives. Secure in your isolation. None the wiser. None of you even guessed how much money we were swindling from you," Sally laughed haughtily.

Dale's hands tightened into fists at her innuendo. Then her words sunk in. What had she said?

But Steve beat him to it. "What do you mean?" he asked, stepping around Dale to stare at Sally. "What money?"

Sally laughed again, long and loud. It was almost as if a switch had been flipped inside the woman. They'd only ever seen *good* Sally before. Now they were seeing *bad* Sally. Dale didn't appreciate it one bit. Without conscious thought, he found himself drifting slowly in Sally's direction a few steps behind Steve. He wanted to hear Sally's answer as much as Steve did. But then Robinson's demand echoed in his mind.

"We need to wait until the cops get here. They'll take her formal statement," Dale said, catching up to Steve and laying a hand on his arm.

"I think we have the right to know," Skylar declared,

standing up with hands on hips. "If she wants to talk, then why would you stop her?" Her blue eyes flashed with a hard edge in the morning light. "I don't care about her formal statement. I want to hear why she killed our employee, our friend."

Skylar might be right. This was their chance to hear things straight from the horse's mouth, so to speak. To hear her confession firsthand, before the cops got here and shut down their questions.

Sally made his decision for him when she said, "You don't want to know. Not really. You're so wrapped up in your own insignificant lives. You don't give a shit about anyone else."

"That's not true," Skylar cried indignantly. She always was an idealist. Now Daisy was on her feet, and both women were closing in on Sally. It looked like he wasn't going to be able to stop their questions, so he may as well join in.

"It *is* true," Sally scoffed. "You're so self-centered, you didn't even notice I was skimming customer's credit cards."

Skylar gasped. "You were doing what?"

"Yeah, that's right," Sally said. "I was taking all the guest credit card details, right under your nose, and you never even knew. Karri was the only one who suspected anything. She was the smartest of the bunch, I'll give her that much. She overheard me talking to Johnny on the phone one night outside the staff quarters."

All four of them drifted closer, forming a semicircle around Sally where she sat on the ground. He was just as desperate to hear this woman's justification for her actions, but he was also prepared to get in the way if anyone became violent. The last thing they needed was an assault charge.

Sally continued, almost without drawing breath, seeming to need to get it all off her chest. "When she confronted me, I tried to bluff my way around it, telling her she'd misheard. But she knew. And I knew she knew. Then one day, she asked me for money."

"No, she didn't," Skylar breathed.

"Oh, yes, she did. Does it shock you to hear she was no angel, either?" Sally smirked at them all.

Yes, Dale was shocked. That didn't sound like Karri. Why hadn't she come to one of them and tell them what was going on?

As if Sally had read Dale's mind, she said. "Karri hinted she'd tell Daniella everything if I didn't pay her. I knew I was in trouble then."

"How long was this going on?" Steve asked, woodenly.

"At least a month," Sally admitted. "I caved in and gave her some money. Mainly because Johnny told me to, I didn't want to give the bitch anything. But then she still kept hinting that she'd tell Daniella." Sally paused and stared up at the sun, which was peeking over the top of the escarpment.

"Then what?" Steve prompted.

"Then, on the day of the big storm, I followed her out to the shed. I only wanted to talk to her, you know?" Sally stared at Steve, as if daring him to argue. "She was already sitting on the ATV. She said Wazza had forgotten to take the driver, or something like that, and she was going to run it out to him real quick."

Dale thought back to that day. He remembered Wazza saying he couldn't finish the fencing because he'd forgotten the pole driver. Karri would've seen it as soon as she walked into the shed. It'd be almost impossible to get the posts in deep enough without it.

"It was the pole driver," Dale said robotically.

Sally stared at him. "Whatever, I didn't care what she was doing. All I wanted to know was, did she have plans to rat me out to Daniella? So, I asked her point-blank if she'd told anyone what she knew."

"What did she say?" Daisy spoke for the first time. She was

leaning forward, watching Sally with morbid fascination.

Sally flicked Daisy a contemptuous glare. "I'd already paid her more money than she'd ever earn working her sorry ass off here, but she never promised she wouldn't tell. I wanted her to give me her word that I was safe. But she wouldn't. The little bitch laughed at me and said, *'Wouldn't I love to know,'* and then flipped me the bird."

Uh-oh, that didn't sound like the Karri he knew, but he was fast discovering that people weren't always what they seemed. Dale wondered what Karri had been planning to do with the money. They'd never find out now, he guessed.

"What did you do then?" Steve asked, a pained expression on his face, as if he didn't want to know the answer but couldn't stop himself from asking.

"She made me mad. I didn't trust the little bitch not to go tattling. I got angry. You know how they say, I saw red. That slut was going to ruin all mine and Johnny's hard work."

"And?" Dale prompted, when Sally lapsed into silence again.

"And, so, there was a hammer just lying there on the bench. I picked it up and hit her over the head. And she slumped over the handlebars. It was kinda easy. Like, almost too easy."

Shocked silence engulfed them all. Sally Tsun had just admitted she'd killed Karri. And she acted as if it was nothing. A rising tide of fury burned slowly up Dale's chest. How could this woman take a life—the life of someone so young, full of such promise—as if it was inconsequential? Because it wasn't. Karri had her entire life ahead of her, she should've been allowed to forge a career for herself, fall in love, get married, have that baby growing inside her. Wazza's baby. Not to mention how devastated her family were at losing their only daughter; their only sister; their hope for the future.

Dale glanced over at Daisy and saw the outrage and revolt written all over her face. Dale felt all of those things and more. He wanted to go up and shake the woman until she realized what she'd done. How could he not have seen what a deceptive, lying, calculated killer was behind those dark eyes?

"Did you check for a pulse? See if she was alive or dead?" Steve asked, voice deadpan. Dale wished he could feel half as coolheaded as his stepfather seemed to be; on the surface at least.

"No, I didn't need to. I could see she was dead. Her eyes were open and staring, you know? I was pretty sure she was dead." She looked up at the sky then, as if choosing her words. "I panicked a bit, then."

Surely, that had to be the understatement of the year. Dale would've been shitting his pants if he'd realized he'd killed someone.

"I needed to get rid of the body, and I remembered the creek was in full flood. So, I drove the ATV down there—it was easy, she was already on the bike, I had to push her to the rear a little, so I could drive it—and took it straight into the creek, with her still onboard. Then I ran all the way to the lodge, got changed into dry clothes, and no one else was the wiser to where I'd been, because all the guests were trapped inside by the rain and all the staff were madly running around securing things for the storm."

"How dare you!" Skylar yelled. "How dare you think you have the right to kill an innocent girl? For your own benefit." His sister's face was going a deep shade of crimson. "I trusted you. We trusted you. How could you do this to us?" Skylar raised clenched fists and took a step forward. Dale got ready to tackle his sister to the ground if she tried to attack Sally. But Steve was ahead of him, grasping Skylar by the wrist, holding her back. Dale let out a relived breath. It seemed Steve also understood they couldn't take out their rage on the woman in front of them, even if Skylar didn't.

"We all feel exactly the same way," he said softly. "But you need to calm down. Okay?"

Skylar stared at Sally, the hate palpable on her face. Dale didn't think he'd ever seen his sister this worked up before. Steve grabbed her hand and turned her to face him. "I know how you feel," he said, "Leave her, she's not worth it." Finally, his sister came to her senses, the hate bleeding away, to be replaced by white-faced acceptance.

There was so much more Dale needed to know, however. So many more questions, and they were running out of time; Robinson and King would be here soon. "What did you do once you returned to the lodge?" he asked. Apart from pretending that she hadn't killed someone, he thought darkly.

"I phoned Johnny, of course. He was already staying at the gold mine by that stage; he'd been here for weeks. He came up here in case I needed help. I brought food to him whenever I could get away. Stole it from right under your noses, and you never even knew," Sally snickered.

Dale suddenly understood where those steaks in the cool room had disappeared to. How much other food had Sally stolen without them knowing? Would they find the stolen ATV hidden somewhere nearby, as well?

"I told Johnny that Karri's death was his fault, so he needed to get me out of this mess."

"Why was it his fault?" Dale asked, wondering how she could possibly blame the girl's death on the other man.

"Because he was the one who told me to get rid of her in the first place." Sally spat the words like bullets at him. "He was the one who put the idea into my head. Johnny said she was a liability. A loose end that we couldn't afford to leave untied. That she'd ask for more money. Start blackmailing us, you know? I didn't believe him at first, but then when Karri got all cagey, refusing to promise she wouldn't tell anyone, well, I got worried."

It sounded as if Sally was trying to pass the buck. "But he wasn't the one with the hammer in his hand," Dale said quietly.

"He might not have had the hammer in his hand, but he was the one screaming at me inside my head. That's why he was staying at the gold mine. He was here to make sure that bitch didn't ruin our plans." Sally tried to get to her knees, but the rope binding stopped her. She pulled against the restraints agitatedly. "He told me to do it. He was going to do it if I didn't. It's his fault. I'm not a murderer, he is," she yelled. "Ask him. He's the one you need to arrest." She pulled so hard on the ropes that she toppled over onto her side in the dirt. "Let me go," she demanded. "I'm not the one you want. Let me go. Ask him. Ask Johnny." Drops of spittle flew from the woman's mouth. It was clear she thought Johnny was still alive, and he would take the fall for their crime.

Dale was shocked at her outburst. Until now, she'd sat so calm and serene. Now, she was a raving, screaming banshee. It dawned on Dale that she was a little unhinged. Perhaps had been right from the start. He realized he didn't know this woman at all. She'd worked here for over two years, he'd seen her nearly every day, spoken to her nearly every day since he returned from Montana, and yet, he'd never truly known who she was, or what she was capable of.

Sally continued to caterwaul, twisting her wrists so hard in the ropes she made her wrists bleed. He had half a mind to tell her Johnny was dead. That would shut her up. But something told him to hold his tongue. That information might be valuable leverage if used in the right way.

Dale dissected her words. Earlier tonight, he'd noticed the odd dynamic between the two; as if Johnny exerted a strange kind of control over Sally. It wasn't merely his physical violence toward her; it was more than that. He'd heard of battered-woman syndrome before, and how some women would do anything to please their man. Was Sally a victim of domestic violence? Had she been coerced into doing those things by Johnny? The truth would come out in the end. Dale couldn't feel sorry for her at the moment, however.

The sound of a vehicle drifted in from a distance.

"I'm not saying anything more." Sally said sullenly, lying still, as if it were dawning on her exactly how much trouble she was in.

Bit late for that, Dale thought, coldly. But they'd gotten everything they needed to know out of Sally, and it seemed they'd done it just in time, as the drone of the engine came closer. Then a four-wheel-drive police vehicle came barreling up the bush track. Senior Sergeant Robinson and his senior constable spilled out of the vehicle as soon as it came to a halt.

King made a beeline for Sally. He untied her feet and hoisted her up onto her feet while reading her rights, then he marched her straight into the back of the police paddy wagon. Robinson was taking no chances with his suspect. It was probably the biggest case they'd had around here for a while; perhaps forever. And Robinson wouldn't want anything to muck it up. Dale decided the cops didn't need to know that they'd conducted their own little family interrogation session.

Robinson cast them a searching look, as if he knew something had been afoot, but Dale merely smiled and turned away.

"Suspect is secure," King said, reappearing with his arms full of equipment. A roll of police tape, two pairs of gloves for him and Robinson, a camera and a whole stack of other items Dale didn't recognize.

"So nice of you guys to finally arrive," Skylar said, a snarky frown wrinkling her brow.

King lifted his head to glance at Skylar, and a strange look passed between the two of them. After a second, he swung his gaze away, but Skylar continued to stare at him. For a moment, Dale wondered if there was something going on between the good-looking cop and his sister. But no, that'd be impossible, Skylar hardly ever left the station, let alone had time for a relationship.

"Are we free to return home yet?" Skylar asked, and King locked gazes with her once more.

"Not yet, sorry," he said. "We need your preliminary statements first." When Skylar scowled at him, he hurriedly added, "It shouldn't take long, then you can go home to the lodge. We'll take formal statements when we've secured the site." King sounded so solemn, his handsome face almost lost in the shade beneath his dark-blue police hat. But his eyes softened as he said, "Actually, it's a good idea for all of you to try to get back to some form of normality in the next few days. But don't forget, we can arrange for counseling for anyone who needs it. You've all been through a traumatic time, don't try and get though it on your own. If you're struggling, let us know," King added. He glanced at them all, but his final gaze came to rest on Skylar. Was he singling her out for some reason? Dale narrowed his eyes as he watched the exchange. But perhaps King was right, Dale should keep an eye on his sister. Actually, he should keep an eye on all of his family, Daisy included. This would take a toll on everyone.

Two hours later and it was already mid-morning when they were finally allowed to leave the mine site. Robinson and King left right before them, handing the scene over to the Cairns cops who were pouring in, some arriving via helicopter and others in their police cruisers and four-wheel-drives. In that time, the cops had indeed discovered Stormcloud's missing ATV, concealed at the back of the tunnel Johnny had been using. They also found other items that belonged to the station; tools and stores of non perishable foods, most of which no one had noticed were even missing. Johnny—or perhaps it'd been Sally—had been having a great time, using Stormcloud as their own personal utility store and grocery market.

Daisy and Dale jumped in the rear seat of the truck with Steve and Skylar, leaving the ATVs where they were.

Dale hadn't let go of Daisy's hand for the whole ride back to the lodge. He'd had hold of it for most of the morning, in fact, apart from when they gave their separate statements. She seemed to need the human connection, almost as if she'd drift away from the earth if he let her go. There was a faraway look on her face, like this wasn't really happening. He could relate. It was taking a while for it all to sink in.

Daniella confronted them as they arrived at the front of the lodge, pulling Dale into a fierce hug before he was even halfway through the door. Julie stood right behind her, white-faced until her dad also appeared through the door and she did much the same, throwing her arms around him.

"Thank God you're okay. Tell me you're okay?" Daniella pleaded with Dale.

"I'm fine, mum," he said, returning her hug.

Then Daniella grabbed Skylar, embracing both of her children as if she might lose them at any second. It was an unusual show of affection. His mum must be experiencing a healthy dose of reality. But Dale would take whatever he could get, and so he returned her hug with enthusiasm. After a few moments, Daniella also tugged Steve and Julie into the group hug, wanting all of her family close.

"Jesus, I was so worried about you. All of you." She looked at each one of them pointedly, letting her gaze rest on Steve last of all.

As soon as his mother let him go, he found Daisy's hand again. Bindi stood near the bar, staring at them all as if they were ghosts, risen from the dead. Alek was close by her side, holding his ever-present clipboard against his chest like a shield. His long hair hung in his face, and he pushed it back with an irritated flick on his wrist. It was a sign of how agitated Alek must be, that his hair wasn't immaculately groomed and styled.

"Does this mean the police are releasing Warwick?" Daniella demanded of Steve.

"Yes, they are," Steve replied wearily.

"Good. Good," Daniella muttered, breaking away from the group and pacing across the floor. "But I can't believe it. Sally Tsun did it? She murdered Karri? And she was skimming our guest's credit cards? And overcharging them too, by the looks of it. Then pocketing the extra money." Daniella's words turned into a hiss of disgust as she glared out of the window. Dale decided if looks could kill, Sally would be dead a hundred times over. Daniella swiped a hand across her brow and pulled out a chair, sitting down heavily. "You need to tell me everything," she demanded.

Everyone sat, while Bindi handed out welcome glasses of water. Dale continued to hold Daisy's hand. It was a relief to sit down, and Dale drank two full glasses, not realizing how parched he was until this very second.

Then Dale began the tale, starting with the phone call Daisy received from River. Steve and Skylar added in bits and pieces, especially when it came to recounting Sally's confession. Daisy remained quiet throughout. Their story sounded fantastical to his own ears, even though he'd lived through the entire night.

Steve finally stopped speaking, and the room fell completely silent as everyone digested the story. Dale could hardly believe that Sally had spilled her guts so easily. But he was also grateful to the narcissistic woman's need to blurt out the truth, so they had some sort of closure. At least it would make the arriving detective's jobs that much easier, if she was happy to talk.

"I'd better get something prepared for dinner." Skylar said at last, standing up laboriously, breaking the somber mood. They were all totally and utterly shocked by the day's events. But they still had guests to look after, and Skylar was the first to remember her duties. The kitchen and her cooking were never far from her mind. It didn't really surprise Dale that she wouldn't shirk her responsibilities.

"I'll give you a hand." Julie stood and followed Skylar.

Daisy stirred beside Dale, tugging on his hand. "I'll go help, too," she said discreetly. "I need something to keep me busy," she admitted when he wouldn't let go of her hand.

Dale had kept her hand tight in his throughout the whole discussion. In some ways, she was the reason they had Sally in custody right now. Without her and her brother, they might never have caught Karri's killer. She must wonder how she fitted into all of this; much the same as he was. But she had extra problems to worry about. Like, how was River going to fare once the fallout from today's events came to light? River could be seen as a hero in some people's eyes. Yet, he was also a fugitive from the law. How was she ever going to reconcile the two? And would the police take his heroism into account when they looked at his other charges arising in Perth?

And then there was the gang—what were they called? The Black Kings—who wanted to partake in their own sort of vigilante justice on her bother. Would they still be after him, even if he went to jail?

"I'll come with you," he breathed. She needed him right now. Needed his support. And he needed to know she was safe. After all they'd been through in the past twenty-four hours, it'd be a while before he let her out of his sight again.

CHAPTER TWENTY-TWO

Daisy sat on the lowest step of the wooden platform, staring at the billabong. A mug of strong tea was cooling in her hands as she contemplated the evening vista before her. She would've preferred a glass of one of Dale's delicious red wines, but the tea would have to do. The sun was setting over the escarpment, streaking the sky with mauves and pinks, and the billabong reflected these colors back at her. A flock of little white corellas skimmed across the surface of the water, and alighted in a large river gum near the water's edge. The parrots chatted noisily to each other, carrying out their nighttime ritual, completely unaffected by everything that'd happened on the station today.

Daisy had to smile at their antics. It was an excellent lesson in perspective. She suddenly realized her human problems were merely that. Human problems and human dramas. But the rest of this vast country around her would go on, no matter what happened.

Daisy had escaped from the lodge. The Williams family and the rest of their staff were having another kitchen meeting. Wazza had arrived during the middle of dinner service, causing quite a stir. He was filling the rest of them in on all the details he'd been given upon his release from jail.

But Daisy couldn't face any more talk at the moment. She was all talked out. The guests had been fed, and Alek had set up an outdoor cinema on the grass off to the side of the billabong, where they could watch a movie beneath the stars. Daisy could see a corner of the large screen if she turned her head to the left, and she could hear the soundtrack, as well. But it was a minor distraction, easily tuned out. Normal activities would start again tomorrow, and life would return to normal on the station.

It was over. Whatever would be, would be. There was nothing more she could do to protect River now.

River was going to live. He'd been rushed into surgery at Cairns Hospital. Daisy had been in direct contact with his doctors, getting updated information every half an hour. Her mother and father were flying over from Perth to Cairns on the first available flight to be with River. Which was going to be interesting, because there was a cop stationed outside the door to River's hospital room. Ready to take him into custody as soon as he was recovered enough to be moved. River wouldn't be getting away this time. Her mother wouldn't appreciate that one bit, and Daisy was sure Evana would make her protestations known far and wide throughout the hospital. But River needed to stand up and account for himself. If he was truly innocent, as he claimed, then he would face the music, go through due process and come out a free man on the other side, like any other normal human being. And if he wasn't innocent... They'd all have to face the consequences then.

And they'd all have to face the consequences of River's gangland association. But they would do it together, because Daisy was going to make sure everyone was on the same page from now on. She wasn't going to do this on her own anymore. Her brain couldn't even comprehend what might happen next where The Black Kings were concerned. She'd sort that dangerous puzzle out later. River was safe from them, at least for the next few days, and that was all she cared about right now.

The times when she hadn't been on the phone to the doctor, she'd been on the phone to her mother, who'd remained fairly calm, considering the circumstances. Dale had arranged for a helicopter to fly her to Cairns in the morning, so she could be with her family.

She was leaving the station.

Her whole subterfuge with River was out in the open now. Everyone at Stormcloud knew that she'd been hiding out with her brother to escape the law. Some people were more accepting than others. Steve, Skylar, and Julie had listened to her explanation with thoughtful expressions. None of them said much, which put Daisy on edge; she'd rather know what they were thinking. Daniella, on the other hand, was more vocal, voicing her concerns to Dale that he needed to pay more attention to the types of people he invited to the station. Which angered Dale more than Daisy would've expected. He got right up into his mother's face and told her to back off, because no one was perfect.

But at least everyone knew. Afterwards, Skylar had come up and hugged her, saying, "I understand why you did it. Even though my boofhead brother drives me insane most of the time, I'd probably have done the same thing if I was in your shoes." Daisy was forever grateful for Skylar's acceptance. And Steve had given her a quick, reassuring pat on the shoulder in passing, on his way out to secure the chickens for the night. He hadn't said anything, but there was forgiveness in his touch. In a strange twist of fate, if it hadn't been for her and River, they may not have caught Sally in all her subterfuge.

Daisy had been avoiding Wazza all evening, avoiding the conversation she didn't want to have. Eventually, he'd find out that River was the other man Karri had been seeing; the one she'd left him for. Daisy felt sorry for Wazza, he was probably struggling to come to terms with the fact that he'd not only lost Karri, but the baby as well.

Daisy picked through the recesses of her mind. Of her heart. Trying to dissect the emotions and sensations she was feeling. For most of the day, she'd felt numb, slightly disassociated with everything that was going on. This was the first chance she had alone to really interpret what was going on inside her.

It was as if she'd used up all her emotions regarding River this morning, in that mad moment when she'd thought he might die. She was still worried about him, wanted to be by his side, but that desperate need to protect him at all costs had subsided. Once she found out he was going to live, it was like a surge of boiling lava of emotions had gouged through her, leaving her washed clean.

It was time River took care of himself.

River had taken up a large part of Daisy's world. Worrying about his welfare had been her constant companion over the past few months. Her brother had also filled most of the available room in her heart. And she'd been fine with that. Until she met Dale. Now her heart wanted to make room for more.

"Can I join you, or is this a private party?" Dale's deep voice sounded behind her.

"Only if you have red wine," she replied.

"As a matter of fact…" She turned to see him hold up an open bottle and two glasses.

She smiled, and he smiled back. There were those dimples. Those irresistible dimples. Her heart did a double-tap at the sight of him. He wasn't wearing his Akubra hat this evening, and his hair was left to curl enticingly over his ears. He handed her a glass and tipped a generous amount of ruby-red liquid into it. Taking a seat beside her, he did the same with his own glass.

"To a better day tomorrow," he said, tipping his glass toward hers. They clinked them together and took a large sip simultaneously. She rolled the wine on her tongue for a second, enjoying the deep tannins and plummy aftertaste, before letting the wine slide down her throat and warm her stomach.

"I've been meaning to ask," Dale said. "How come you enjoy red wine so much? Don't get me wrong, it's nice to have someone who appreciates it as much as I do, but..." he amended.

She laughed. "Not from my family, that's for sure. We don't have a wonderful cellar full of bottles like you do." She took another sip and turned to gaze out over the water. "It was one of the guys from my uni classes. I thought he was a pompous ass when I met him—actually, I still think he's a pompous ass." She laughed again. "But he was part of a small study group we started to help us all get through the assignments. Graham began bringing a bottle of red to our get-togethers, he said it helped him concentrate." Her mind drifted to those early days at uni, when she'd nearly been overwhelmed by everything. That study group had been the one thing that helped her get through, because she knew she wasn't alone. "The first time I tasted it, I loved it, even though he warned us all that it could take a long while to develop a palate for red wine. It was a Margaret River Shiraz, and I was amazed by the complex flavors. I started buying my own bottles, when I could afford them. Not the wine in a box, though, that stuff is mostly terrible. The rest of my family thought I was bonkers, because it's so much more expensive than beer or cider." Daisy raised her glass and considered the liquid through the dying rays of the sun. "Our study group turned into a wine appreciation group as well, and we've kept it going over the past three years."

"Here's to Graham, then." Dale raised his glass, and they clinked them again.

"Yes." It was funny to think about her life in Perth. It was as if that was a whole other world now. As if her life belonged here. Which it didn't. "Sorry I couldn't stay, I needed space to think," she said after she'd let the effect of the wine appreciate in her gut for a few seconds. "What did I miss out on? What else did Wazza have to say?"

"If I could've escaped, I would've, too," Dale said conspiratorially, leaning his shoulder gently against hers. The buzz of connection went down her arm and made her fingers tingle. "But Wazza did tell us some more interesting things about Sally and Johnny. And Steve talked to the senior sergeant this evening and got some more details on the crimes they'll be charged with."

"Tell me everything," she said, letting her gaze drift over the calm billabong.

"Like she said to us this morning, Sally and her boyfriend were definitely skimming the credit card details of some guests—not all of them, however, because she said that would be too obvious—she'd rigged the card machine so that whenever she swiped a guest's card it stole their details. She then handed the info over to Johnny, who'd wait weeks or months, before he used the cards. That way it was much harder to trace it back to where the details were first stolen from."

"Smart." Daisy dipped her head in acknowledgement.

"Yeah, it seemed as if they'd be running the scam for a while. Sally worked at the Pan-Pacific Hotel in Melbourne before she came here. It's why we hired her in first place, she came with such good references. But they think she was doing the same thing there." Dale snorted in contempt. "There are clues pointing to Johnny also being involved in identity theft. It sounded like he was hand-picking some of the richer guests from the list of skimmed credit cards and then stealing their identity. That person would often pay a lot of money to get their ID back."

"You mean he was blackmailing them?" Daisy asked. Did this couple's avarice know no bounds?

"Exactly." Dale nodded, running a hand through his hair. "It was only recently that Sally came up with the scam of charging the guests double the amount for their accommodation. Then she would syphon half the money off to her account. She figured those types of people were so rich, they never even looked twice at how much they were paying. But that's where she got it wrong. The police aren't sure yet, but they suspect Sally and Johnny were part of a much bigger crime syndicate. Perhaps being run out of Vietnam or Hong Kong. They'd been planning to move down to Brisbane soon, where the pickings are richer."

"Before Karri discovered what Sally was doing and blackmailed the blackmailers," Daisy said, having to keep the note of sarcasm out of her voice; she knew Dale wouldn't appreciate it.

"Yes." Dale gave a heavy sigh. "The Karri I thought I knew wouldn't do such a thing. But Robinson revealed that a large sum of cash was found hidden under her mattress when they searched her room on the day of her murder. What in hell was she going to do with that money?"

Daisy shrugged. She didn't know the girl very well. "Perhaps she already knew she was pregnant," Daisy mused. "Maybe she was keeping the money for her baby. For a better life."

"Perhaps. Although she'd have been more than welcome to stay here. Even after she had the baby. And I'm sure Wazza would've looked after her, he's a stand-up guy. He wouldn't have let her cope on her own. He's devastated to find out she was carrying his child."

"I'm sure Wazza is a stand-up guy, but maybe Karri couldn't see that. You know what kind of life they have over there in the community. The elders do everything they can to make it a good place to live, but there's still poverty and violence. Karri was probably used to having to fend for herself. If you hadn't offered her this opportunity for employment, where do you think she would have ended up?"

Dale shot her a look of surprise. The concept had clearly never occurred to him. But Daisy could empathize with Karri. While Daisy been brought up in relative luxury because of her father's status in the community, she still saw the way other indigenous people struggled to live their lives; struggled to integrate into society; struggled to stay true to their culture. She knew Karri would most likely have been scared to keep the baby because it'd mean the end of her employment here. In some ways, she didn't blame the poor girl for taking the money.

"I never really thought about that before," he admitted.

The sun had set; the stars appearing in the sky, and she turned to stare at the horizon. Daisy slapped at a mosquito buzzing around her head; they were the worst part of living in the tropics. She'd need to go inside soon, or get eaten alive.

"And maybe you're right about Karri believing she couldn't stay here," Dale admitted quietly. Daisy tipped her head and waited for him to elaborate. "Remember how I said that I thought there was something going on between Karri and my mum?"

Daisy merely nodded.

"I asked her tonight, and she admitted that she'd been wrong. Get this, she heard the rumor before from Alek—although why the hell Alek is telling her this kind of thing, I don't know—that Karri was seeing some bloke. This was about three months ago. At the time Alek thought it was someone on the station, although he couldn't prove it. Turns out Alek's little rumor-monger ears were half-right, because that was when she was sleeping with Wazza."

Daisy pursed her lips but said nothing. She thought she already knew where Dale was going with his story.

"Anyway, my mother jumped to the wrong conclusion, that it was me Karri was carrying out her clandestine affair with. She supposedly confronted Karri, who of course denied it. But my mother didn't believe her."

"She always has been a bit of an overprotective mother bear," Daisy said. "Why didn't she just come and ask you?"

"That's what I said. Once I got over falling off my stool in amazement that she could be that shallow," Dale said. "She gave me some lame excuse that she didn't want to upset me." Dale blew out a breath from between his teeth. "I mean, really? How could she have been considering sacking poor Karri over something she never did? Because of me?"

Daisy shrugged. She could see through to the truth, even if Dale couldn't. Daniella didn't think Karri was good enough for her son. Perhaps because she was black, and relatively poor. Who knew what went through Dale's mother's head? She had a lot of values and morals that Daisy didn't agree with. Daisy already knew Daniella didn't want her forming a relationship with Dale. And today's events had probably cemented those reasons more securely in the other woman's head. But Daisy no longer cared what Daniella thought.

"As long as you made your objections to you mother's interference obvious, there's probably not a lot more you can do about it."

"I certainly did that," Dale agreed. "I'm hoping after tonight, Daniella no longer feels she can meddle in my private life."

That was a good thing for Dale, and for any future partner

he might choose. *If only he'd choose me.* Where had that come from? There was no future for them. She needed a change of topic.

"So, was Johnny her boyfriend, or her boss?" Daisy asked, leading him away from the dangerous waters of thinking about him and her together.

While he shot her a puzzled look at her sudden switch in subject, he said, "Both, I think. She was really upset when Robinson told her Johnny was dead. She really flipped out."

"What an odd relationship," Daisy said softly. "A love-hate sort of thing."

"It was pretty sick, that's for sure. What she did for him, stealing, lying, manipulating and then finally killing. That's not genuine love, is it?"

"No, it's not," she agreed. Love needed to exist between two equals. Neither partner should have more power than the other. There should be trust and empathy. If she ever got married, there'd have to be mutual respect, as well as deep well of love to draw on. A little like what she and Dale shared. Actually, a lot like how she and Dale were when they were together. Sheesh, there she went again, thinking about her and Dale together. She wasn't allowed to fall in love with him.

She drew in a sharp breath. *Love.* That was such a complicated word. Dale was staring at her, almost as if he could read her mind. She flailed around for something to distract him. "What about the station? Your family? Is everything going to be all right now?"

His brown eyes were almost black in the failing light. So dark she couldn't read the emotion behind them as he continued to stare at her. Eventually, he said, "Julie is going to stay on for a while, to help. Until we can replace..." He couldn't bring himself to say Karri's name. "But yeah, otherwise things are going to stay pretty much the same.

Wazza was pretty shaken up by the whole experience, and he's going home to visit his family for a few weeks. Bookings have dropped off a little; not as much as you'd expect." Dale barked out an ironic laugh. "Mum seems to think the bookings will pick up quickly. It makes the place seen more dangerous, and people love the morbidity of it all, believe it or not."

That was pretty ironic. Daisy tipped her head backward and swallowed the last bit of red wine while staring up at the stars. "The sky is so clear here," she said. "Crystal clear. And the stars are like diamonds." She gave a chuckle at her own cliche. But it was true, the stars were so bright, so beautiful. Dale's shoulder brushed against hers, and she looked down to where his hand rested lightly on his knee, muscular forearms flexing slightly. Images of those arms wrapped around her waist assaulted her mind.

"Will you stay with me tonight?" His question took her by surprise.

She wanted to say no. It was going to be hard enough to leave him in the morning anyway, without having one more memory burned into her brain to haunt her. Because she had no idea if she'd ever see Dale again. They were an imperfect match. The odd couple who couldn't be together.

But then, she needed as many memories as possible, so she could hold them close to her heart, keep their precious moment together safe inside her.

She nodded and held out her hand to him. It was time to go inside and get away from the voracious mosquitoes. What better place to spend her last night at Stormcloud Station than in his bed? In his arms?

CHAPTER TWENTY-THREE

Dale watched Daisy climb into the helicopter. He ducked away as the rotor blades swung faster, hanging onto his hat and shielding his eyes from the dust whipped up by the down-draught. The helicopter lifted slowly off the ground, then once it was away from the trees and into clear skies, it tipped forward, accelerating up and away. A bright flash of silver against the blue. Two of the guests were also leaving this morning, and so Dale had arranged for Daisy to join the flight. It was the quickest way to travel out here.

Daisy was gone.

Of course, she had to go. She needed to be with her brother. And she was meeting her parents at Cairns hospital this morning. Family came first. And with Daisy, her brother was the single most important thing in her life right now.

Or at least, he had been. A few of the things Daisy had said to him last night made him ponder that statement.

Steve stood next to the two ATVs parked beneath the big river gum. He walked over and slapped him on the back. "Come on, mate, no moping allowed. There's still lots of work to be done."

Dale bristled at his words. He wasn't moping. Daisy had left, and that was the end. That heavy feeling in his chest would ease soon enough. Once he got his mind back on the jobs he had listed for today, he'd forget all about her.

He lifted his chin in Steve's direction, indicating he lead the way. Then he jumped into his ATV and followed Steve in his own vehicle up the gravel road, away from the helicopter landing pad and toward the main huddle of buildings. Even though Julie had joined the staff temporarily, until they could find a replacement for Karri, there was still a lot to be done. Jobs that'd been put off over the past few weeks because of the floods and then the murder investigation were all clamoring to be finished.

Cicadas buzzed in the branches above him. It was going to be devilishly hot today. They'd planned a horse trek this morning for the guests, while it was still relatively cool. The guests would take a break during the hottest part of the day, where they could either take a swim in the pool, or read a book in the comfort of their air-conditioned cabins, or indeed, take a nap. Then they had a picnic dinner next to the billabong and a spotlighting tour scheduled for later on.

There'd be no such luxuries as naps for Dale today. Even though he needed one after last night's activities. He was going to have to run on two hours' sleep. But it was worth it. Every precious second spent with Daisy had been worth it.

Without conscious effort, his mind drifted back to last night. As soon as his bedroom door shut behind them, they'd begun ripping off each other's clothes off like they were possessed. So desperate and hungry to have their arms wrapped around each other. Dale was no psychiatrist, but even he could figure out they were using sex as a form of release, a way to purge themselves of the hundreds of emotions they'd experienced over the past twenty-four hours. It was also an act of joy, of relief that they'd both survived.

He had luxuriated in the feeling of her coffee skin sliding against his, her taut stomach pressing into his own. He'd kissed her like she was the last woman on earth; and she'd returned his ardor like he was the last man. The first time they'd made love, they never made it to the bed. It was so quick and dirty; he had her up against the wall, barely remembering to put on the condom. Daisy had cried out so loud that Dale hoped Skylar couldn't hear them from her room down the other end of the hallway. But then, as he reached his own crescendo, he stopped caring.

The second time, they made it to his bed, and it was less rushed, though equally filled with passion. He'd stroked her cheek and stared into her eyes as she climaxed beneath him, is if he could see right in to her very soul.

Afterward, she had cried in his arms. It was an unusual feeling. Dale had never had a woman trust him enough to break down in front of him before. It was as if he held a fragile, vulnerable bird in his arms.

"I feel like I did everything wrong," she'd sobbed into his chest. "I feel like it's my fault River got shot. And now, after all we went through, he's probably still going to end up in jail."

That might not be such a bad thing, Dale had thought to himself, although he'd never dare say it out loud. From the little he knew about Daisy's brother, that boy had never taken responsibility for his own actions. It was time he grew up. Spending time in prison after he recovered from his gunshot wound would be a harsh reality check for the kid.

"I'm worried he won't survive in jail," she said, breaking into more sobs. It was a valid worry. It was true, indigenous people struggled when they were locked away. And the Australian justice system had a bad reputation for their lack of care when it came to Aboriginal people on the inside. Things were getting better, but it didn't mean River would find it easy.

"Perhaps he won't serve any time. I know he did wrong by

running away; obstructing justice, I think it's called. But maybe they'll find him innocent, or at the very least, let him go on a good-behavior bond." Dale said helpfully. Daisy nodded, but didn't seem to be mollified.

"My mother isn't helping," Daisy said through her sniffles. Dale knew she'd taken more than one phone call from her parents this afternoon, and had looked increasingly downcast after each one. "She's demanding to know how I let it all get this out of hand."

Surely, her mother wasn't trying to blame any of this on Daisy? Because if she was, Dale would have no problem marching over there and setting her straight. How could any mother put that much pressure on her own child? He caught himself on that thought and backtracked a little. Because he'd experienced something similar with his own mother. He suddenly felt more sympathy for Daisy; gleaned a little more understanding of why she was so desperate to protect her only sibling. From a deep, ingrained wish to please her parents.

"This is not your fault." Dale stroked her hair gently, but his voice had an edge of steel. She needed to let go of this guilt. He wasn't about to condone what she'd done, because technically, she'd been aiding and abetting a criminal. But she'd done what she had out of love, and a sense of duty. He respected her for that. She was one gritty, determined woman. "You did what you thought was right. And you can't let your mother or anyone else blame you for how it turned out."

Daisy stared at him, her large, green eyes wide as she pondered his words.

"Hmm," was her only reply. Dale hoped she took in what he said. It might not sink in right now, but later, when she had the chance to dissect what'd happened, she might see this was all just a horrible string of coincidences, and there was nothing she could've done to change the outcome.

Secretly, Dale wondered how much longer Daisy and her brother would've gotten away with their subterfuge. They didn't seem to have a coherent plan, and he thought the law would've caught up with them, eventually. That, or The Black Kings might have found them to dispense their own form of warped justice.

"I have to go back to Perth," she said in a small voice.

"I know," he replied. He desperately wanted her to stay, but there was no reason to keep her here. Her family, her culture, her study, all her friends were over there.

He brushed back her hair and stared into her face, tracing the familiar lines of her high eyebrows, her nose, the curve of her plump lips. He was going to miss her terribly. It'd hurt to let her go. A physical pain started beneath his breastbone at the mere thought of it.

Dale had never been in love. Not really. There'd been two or three girls in his teenage years. But the station had always taken all of his focus, and they hadn't understood his commitment, drifting away to become a fleeting memory soon enough. And whatever it was he'd felt for Violet, back in Montana, had only been puppy love. He knew that now, because he finally understood what true love was.

Because, last night at the mine, he'd finally discovered love. All night, he'd been urgently trying to protect Daisy, both from herself and from those two crazy maniacs. Then it hit him like a physical blow, in those few moments where Daisy had been fighting with Sally. What would he do if Daisy died? If she was no longer in this world? His heart had literally stopped beating as he watched her wrestle with the other woman, while he lay helpless and gagged on the dusty soil. He was in love with this feisty, damaged woman. And tonight had only cemented how deep his feelings went for her. The way she felt in his arms, it was extraordinary. It was a feeling of sincerity. Could she feel it, too?

If he told her he loved her, would she stay?

He couldn't do that to her. It wasn't fair. And if she rejected him, he'd hate to have to find out the hard way, that his love wasn't enough to keep her here. If it were true love, then you set the other person free. Didn't you? Because he only wanted her to be happy.

"Will you…" she hesitated.

"What," he prompted.

"Will you come and visit me?"

"Sure," he lied. Well, maybe it wasn't a lie. Maybe he would visit her. But he knew, even if they tried to make the long-distance thing work, it'd fail in the end.

She stared at him for so long he began to wonder exactly what it was she was thinking. "Maybe I…" She shook her head. "No, never mind." Then she reached up and kissed him. And whatever she'd been about to say was lost in the throes of passion.

There was a screech of tires and Dale looked up just in time to stop his ATV from crashing into the rear of Steve's vehicle as he pulled up outside the machinery shed. His mind had been so lost in thoughts of Daisy, he'd hardly noticed they were at the lodge. Time to get his head back into the game. He needed to get ten horses saddled and ready to go before the trek was due to leave in half an hour.

CHAPTER TWENTY-FOUR

Daisy placed her duffel bag on the end of the bed with a sigh. She reached up and massaged her neck, tipping her head from side to side to ease the stiff muscles, glad the long drive was over. It was hot in here, of course. But Daisy had a way to remedy that. She walked over and pushed the button to turn on the air conditioning. Standing in the cool breeze, she flapped her arms, luxuriating in the modern appliance. As she cooled down, she surveyed the bedroom. It looked nothing like the tiny little room she'd slept in six months ago.

Daisy was back at the run-down outstation she and River had shared, but the place had had a major facelift since then. They'd added two more sea containers to the main structure, one at each end. This bedroom was a whole new addition, and there was a modern bathroom attached at the other side of the building. The bedroom now contained a brand-new, queen-size bed—no more sagging mattress—a closet large enough to hang all her clothes, a bedside table, and even the luxury of a bedside lamp to read by at night.

She strolled out to take a better look at the main living area again. It was no longer dominated by scuffed and damaged Lino flooring. That'd been replaced with fresh floorboards, and although the kitchenette was still small, it now sported a brand-new gas stove top, a microwave, and a gleaming, stainless steel sink.

The best part about the whole renovation was the large block of storage batteries housed in a small shed out the side, and the brand-new solar panels on the roof. All generating enough electricity to run the air conditioning, refrigerators, and the lights. Even the backup generator had been replaced with a newer model. A large, covered patio had been erected out the front, a place to sit out of the fierce sun and enjoy a beer or eat a leisurely dinner. All the mod cons a girl could wish for.

It was all part of the contract she'd signed with Angel Gold Corp, a Queensland-based gold mining company, who were now paying her wage. They would provide her with adequate living facilities for the next three years of her project.

She was desperate for a cup of tea. And something to eat would be nice, as well. All the food supplies were still in the car, but she almost didn't have the energy to collect them. It was late afternoon; she needed to get something going for dinner soon. Daisy filled the kettle with water and switched it on, then leaned against the countertop while she waited for it to boil. The small round table with the mismatched chairs in the corner had been replaced by a large, rectangular, industrial-looking one, and four matching metal chairs.

Daisy was speared by a sudden pain in her chest. If she closed her eyes, she could imagine it clear as day, River sitting at that table, grinning at her.

She missed her brother.

The conversation she'd had with River two days after they'd captured Sally and Johnny replayed in her head.

River lay in his hospital bed, looking smaller somehow against the large expanse of white sheets. River had had surgery the day before and had pulled through better than expected. He was sitting up in bed, talking and beginning to eat, almost as if nothing had happened. Their parents had gone to have a meeting with River's doctor, to find out the exact extent of his injuries, but Daisy had stayed behind, hoping to have a private chat with her brother. She stood next to his bed and glanced toward the door, where a cop was standing right outside.

"What's going to happen to me now?" he'd asked in a low voice.

"I'm sorry, little bro, but it looks like the police are going to extradite you to Perth as soon as you're able to travel," she said, laying a comforting hand on his arm.

"I don't want to go to jail," he said in a whimper.

"I know." She rubbed his arm in a soothing motion. "Mum and dad will do everything in their power to make sure you don't. But the truth will come out eventually, and then you'll be a free man."

Then they'd have to overcome the problem of Ralphie and his gang. But perhaps their thirst for revenge would've died down by then. She had no idea how long a gang might hold a grudge for, but they'd have to deal with all that when they got home.

River stared out the window at the bright Cairns sunshine. His mouth twitched a little in a grimace.

Daisy continued, "Who knows, the cops might even throw your case out before it goes to trial, because you helped to capture a killer. Whatever happens, it shouldn't take too long to sort this all out, especially seeing as how you're innocent."

River made a noise that was something between a grunt and a moan, and he closed his eyes.

"River, what's wrong," she asked, leaning in to stare into his face. Did she need to call a doctor? Was he having a relapse?

When he finally opened his eyes, they were filled with

tears. "I'm not innocent," he said.

"What? What are you talking about?" The world seemed to go terribly still around her.

River hesitated, twisting the bedclothes into a ball between his fingers, until at last he spoke. "I was there at the beating. I didn't run away, like I told you. And I didn't try to stop them. I filmed it all. Ralphie told me what was coming, and he asked me to film it for him. I stood there and watched them beat a man to death and I didn't stop them." River sobbed loudly, and swiped a hand beneath his nose. "And I got it all on camera. Then I helped them rob Daniel of his drug money, and I took the cash Ralphie offered me. I'm such a dick. Can you ever forgive me?" He looked at her imploringly, tears streaking his face. She stared back into his familiar eyes as her chest constricted painfully.

He'd lied to her.

He hadn't been innocent after all.

She withdrew her hand from his arm.

She had a sudden, awful premonition. "What about The Black Kings? Are they still after you, too?"

He winced at her icy tone. "I made all that up." His voice was so quiet Daisy almost missed what he'd said.

"What?" she asked.

"Ralphie wasn't really coming after me. He was the one who encouraged me to post the video online in the first place. He wanted the world to know that no one should fuck with The Black Kings."

Daisy took a step away from her bother. Not only had he lied and deceived her, but he'd let her give up her life in Perth to see him safe. She couldn't believe he'd do this to her.

"So, you made up the story about Ralphie because…?" She waited for him to finish her sentence, but he merely stared at her, hazel eyes glazed and anxious. So she finished it for him. "As an added incentive to get me to help you get out of Perth.

Because you knew if it were just the police after you, that I wouldn't help. Is that correct?"

"Daisy, I—" He reached out a hand toward her and she slapped it away.

"Don't you dare." She backed away and then turned and fled out the door. He'd come clean with her only because he knew it'd all come out soon once the Perth cops got hold of him. Her faith in him was shattered beyond belief. River had always been selfish and needy, but never in a million years would she have believed him capable of this.

River had a minimum of a year to serve on his sentence, and even then, he'd only get out early on good behavior. The judge had decided not to take River's involvement in capturing Johnny and Sally into account to make his sentence more lenient because he'd said there was no relevance to the case River had to answer to in Perth. River had recovered from his gunshot wound, but the process had been a slow one, and now all he had to look forward to was a stay in prison.

She had refused to talk to him for many long months, but after the judge had handed down his sentence, she'd finally relented and gone to see him in jail. River had wept when he saw her, knowing without a word being spoken that she'd finally forgiven him. Forgiven, but not forgotten. The very idea that he could have been complicit in the act of beating someone to death sickened Daisy. This was no longer the brother she thought she knew. Daisy's heart ached as she thought of River locked away in jail, but he was getting what he deserved.

Suddenly, Daisy no longer wanted to be standing in this homestead alone. She needed people around her. One person, in particular.

It took less than five minutes to unpack the car and stow away the perishables. The rest of the unpacking could wait.

She should take the time to have a shower, change her clothes and fix her hair, as she'd been driving all day. It'd taken her five days this time, to drive from Perth to Cairns on her own, unlike her mad dash with River, where they'd shared the driving through the night and made it in a little over two-and-a-half days. But the urgent need to see Dale was overwhelming, and she ditched the idea of a shower.

Daisy hopped into her Subaru 4WD. This vehicle was such a pleasure to drive compared to the old Corolla. The gravel roads out here were a breeze to navigate in this car. No more getting stuck in flooding creeks for her. Angel Gold had also provided her with this lease car to make it easier for her to work in the area.

The drive from here to the lodge was around twenty minutes, and she tapped her fingers impatiently on the wheel all the way. With some trepidation, she tried to imagine the look on Dale's face when he first saw her. Would he be happy? Confused? Annoyed because she hadn't told him she was coming?

Daisy parked her vehicle right next to Dale's in the rear parking lot behind the lodge. Her heart went pitter-patter at the sight of his truck. Hopefully, it meant he was nearby somewhere. Not wanting to announce herself at the front door, in case the guests were already collecting in the dining room for dinner, she went through the rear, hoping Skylar would be in the kitchen.

Which she was. As soon as she caught sight of Daisy, she dropped what she was doing and ran around the large kitchen island bench. "You made it," she squealed, pulling Daisy into a bear hug. "It's so good to see you again."

"You too," Daisy agreed.

Skylar and her penchant for cooking with bush foods was one of the reasons Daisy had returned. It was part of her new vocation, to help more people understand bush foods and to even grow their own staples. Unbeknownst to Dale, Daisy had stayed in contact with Skylar, and they'd talked many times over the phone in the past few months. Daniella also knew about Daisy's plans to return, as she and Skylar needed Daniella's permission for the things they wanted to do on the station.

Dale would probably be more than angry that his mother and sister had kept that information from him. But Daisy hadn't wanted to raise his hopes. And she was uncertain how he was going to receive her. Because, while she and Skylar had talked most weeks on the phone, Dale had been glaringly absent. After his few hesitant conversations when she first returned to Perth, he'd stopped returning her calls. Skylar assured her that Dale missed her terribly, and this was just his perverted way of defending his own heart. But Daisy wasn't so sure. She hoped she hadn't misjudged his feelings for her, and yet… Dale had talked about how unhappy he was here when she first met him, about possibly leaving the station. She had this niggling doubt that perhaps he was planning on moving away. Maybe he'd kept his plans a secret, even from his sister. Please let her not have made a huge mistake by dropping everything and coming here.

"But I'm guessing it's not me you're here to see," Skylar said, with a cheeky wink. She held up a hand as Daisy protested. "He's up at the stables, feeding the horses and bedding them down for the night. And no, I haven't told him you're coming."

"Thank you." Daisy gave Skylar one last, quick hug, then ran out of the back door.

The horses were all lazily swishing their tails in the late-evening glow, waiting patiently for their hay bags to be hung over the fence in their yard. She could hear someone banging around in the feed store. Dale. Her gut clenched, and she almost turned around and fled back to the lodge. The thought of seeing Dale for the first time had her breaking out in a sweat, even in the already-balmy tropical evening. Shit, she should've taken the time to tidy herself up. Her hair was coming loose from its braid and her cotton blouse and linen shorts were rumpled from sitting in the car all day. What would he think when he saw her?

But it was too late to flee, because Dale emerged from the storeroom, a full haynet dangling in each hand. She drank in the sight of him. Shirt sleeves rolled up to his elbows, revealing his muscular forearms and strong hands carrying the hay. Jean-clad, long legs striding out, his Western riding boots clicking over the gravel. The Akubra hat hid his eyes for a second, until he looked up.

He caught sight of her, brown eyes dark against his tanned skin. She stood stunned, arrested like a startled rabbit in a set of headlights. She stared at him, and he stared back.

Then Dale smiled. A bright, full-fledged smile of joy.

Oh. There were those dimples. She missed them so much while she'd been on the other side of the continent.

Without conscious thought, her feet took her to Dale. He dropped the haynets and opened his arms wide and she landed against his chest, her arms wrapping around his neck. He kissed her. And she kissed him. Why had she ever been nervous about seeing him again? This was as natural as breathing. She'd dreamt about being held this tight against his body for the past six months, but no dreams could do this feeling justice. It was a hundred times better. A thousand times.

"What are you doing here?" he asked when their lips parted, and they finally came up for air.

"It's a long story," she whispered into his neck. "But I'm here to stay, if you want me to?"

He brushed a strand of hair away from her forehead as he gazed into her eyes. "Of course, I do." And she could see he meant it. He was truly happy to see her again. "Do you mean you're staying here, at the station?" Dale's confused look was comical. She stroked a hand down his cheek, enjoying the rough stubble beneath her fingertips. He hadn't shaved in a few days, but she didn't mind.

"No. I've got a job, working for a gold mining company. They've done up the old Back Paddock Outstation for me. So, I'm not too far away."

"Great, that's great." Then he shook his head, as if he couldn't quite believe what was happening.

She laughed, and said, "I've got a lot to tell you. So much has happened in the past six months. I had a bit of an epiphany when I returned to Perth." Which was an understatement. Those first few months after she'd gone home had been the lowest point in her life. She'd been miserable, missing Dale, worried about River, and unable to concentrate on her university degree. Environmental law no longer seemed to inspire her, and her grades had dropped. It was her mother who'd given her the idea to pivot. She told her to stop moaning about what was wrong with the world and find a way to make it right. To find her passion. At first, Daisy had taken that as permission to run to Dale, because he was her passion. But her mother had laid a hand on her arm and told her that a man shouldn't be everything to a woman. A woman needed more to be truly happy. And while she wanted to disagree, a small part of her knew her mother was correct; she would never be genuinely satisfied with her life if she gave everything up for a man.

Then she thought about her chats with Skylar, how she'd wanted to incorporate more bush foods into her cooking. And she also thought about her time spent at the community on Koongarra Station. Her cover story of being a consultant to help the community become more sustainable had been based partly on the truth. Her talks with some of the elders had planted a seed. Perhaps she could help them, after all.

So, after much discussion with her professors, she switched her degree from environmental law—which she still had another year to go—to sustainable development, with a major in agribusiness. With credits from her first degree, she would need to complete another two years. But she was happy with that. Her professional life seemed to be on track. The only part she wasn't happy with was it'd take another two years of being separated from Dale.

That was when lightning had struck. One of her new professors asked if he could introduce her to the CEO of Angel Gold. He was a colleague but also a personal friend, and he knew the mining company was looking to do some of the things that Daisy had been talking about implementing. A way for the mining company to give back to the communities, as well as a way to make themselves more sustainable in the long run, more environmentally friendly.

The company agreed to pay for her degree, if she would come on board and work as a consultant while studying at the same time. It wasn't unusual for a company to take on an intern, especially when they had a specific project in mind. The company also had a mine site near Cairns, and the cogs in Daisy's mind immediately began to turn. Could she do her study online? The answer had been yes.

A horse gave a loud whinny right next to Daisy's shoulder, startling her. She and Dale were still standing next to the horse yard, the forgotten haynets resting on the ground next to them. But the horses hadn't forgotten, and some were stamping impatiently, desperate for their dinner.

"Why don't you feed the horses first, and I'll tell you all about it later. I'll give you a hand," she added.

It was good to help Dale distribute the hay. And she was glad she remembered how to do it. He could hardly take his eyes off her, and he dropped one of the nets on the ground in his haste to tie it onto the fence. There were six more hay nets to hang up, and they worked quickly, in relative silence, until all the horses were fed and happy.

As soon as the last bag was hung, Dale scooped her up in his arms again. "Dinner service will be up soon, did you want to come and eat? Skylar is cooking kangaroo tonight."

Daisy's salivary glands worked overtime at the mention of Skylar's food. But she had an even more urgent need. And that was to get Dale naked as soon as possible.

"I'd rather check out your bedroom," she said with a come-hither smile. The look that Dale shot her, full of dark-eyed hunger, made the grin fade from her face. Replaced by a desire so strong it nearly bowled her over.

"You don't have to ask me twice," he growled, taking her by hand. They walked in the growing dusk around the side of the lodge. Daisy glimpsed the billabong, looking as serene and beautiful as she remembered, before Dale whisked her inside, through the family side entrance.

He led her down the hallway and into his bedroom. The door was hardly shut behind him, when her insistent fingers found the buttons on his shirt, undoing each one as quickly as she could, revealing all that wonderful male chest with a sprinkling of curls, then those hardened abs. Her hands wandered over his warm skin and a feeling of contentment, of coming home, settled over her.

Dale dropped his hat on the bedside table and lowered his head so he could nuzzle the soft skin of her neck.

"I missed you. I'm so glad you came back," he murmured. "I'm sorry I didn't call, but I—" She put a finger to his lips. There was no need for justification. She was here now, and he wanted her, and that was all that mattered.

"No," he said, pulling gently away from her finger. "I need to tell you something. I should've said this before you left, but I was an idiot. I fell in love with you. I'm still in love with you."

He'd said those magic words. Her whole move over here had been based on him saying those words. But it was still a shock. Her heart was beating so fast, she could possibly be having a heart attack.

She licked her suddenly dry lips. This was real. It was really happening.

"I fell in love with you, too," she whispered. How could she not? Her own real-life, courageous cowboy.

This would not be easy. His mother would be less than pleased, but at least she already knew about her plans for planting bush foods with Skylar. And unless she was a fool, she would've already put two and two together. Steve and Skylar would be fine with her, she already knew that. They'd go and face his family soon enough. But tonight, it was all about her and Dale. Reconnecting. Reigniting their love. Planning a life for the future. A bright future here in far north Queensland, with the man of her dreams.

* * *

Dale couldn't quite believe this was happening. She was really here. Really in his arms. He wanted to pinch himself, to make sure he wasn't dreaming. Because he had dreamed of Daisy every night after she left. But his dreams had never been this good.

On the surface, he'd done everything he was supposed to do. Worked hard, fulfilled his mother's every wish, showed interest in the running of the station. He was a fully functioning adult while he was in company. But at night when he was alone, he'd often take a bottle of red into the laundry and sit and think and drink and allow the melancholy to overtake him. There was a part of him missing. Only Daisy could fill that hole. Why had he let her go? The question rolled over and over and over in his head. He'd had no choice, really, but at least he could've said something. Let her know how he felt. Instead, he'd let her slip away. He talked to her over the phone, but the conversations had been stilted and painful. He just hadn't known what to say. And she'd made it clear her life was in Perth. So, what was the point of it all? Call him a coward, but he couldn't do it anymore. He hadn't stopped loving her, but perhaps he'd given up on a life with her in it.

Thank God she hadn't given up on him. Thank God she'd come back to him.

And now she said she loved him. It was the sweetest gift of all. His life had changed in the blink of an eye. For the better. He was a better man when she was around. His blood crashed through his veins. The heat of his desire and love boiling through him like lava. He loved her so much; he thought he might explode. And there was one way he could definitely prove that to her. By showing her with his body. By cherishing her, setting her aflame with his desire.

He picked her up in his arms and carried her to the bed. With tender fingers, he undid the buttons on her blouse, trailing kisses down her stomach.

Soon, they were both naked. He lay next to her on the bed, stroking her face, embedding every tiny detail of her features in his memory. The hair tie on her braid came loose, and he gently tugged the strands until her hair cascaded over her bare shoulders. Her hand touched his face, then trailed down his neck, across his chest and followed the contours of his back to his buttocks.

"Oh, God, I missed you. I missed this. I need you to make love to me," she groaned.

He could certainly do that. Levering himself up onto his elbows, he lay his body along hers. Oh, the feel of her skin against his was a certain kind of heaven.

A long while later, they lay together, propped up on his pillows. The room had grown dark, but the window let in enough light from the half-moon so he could clearly see her face. Earlier, he'd gotten up and opened the window, letting in a cooling breeze and the sounds of the night. Frogs singing down by the billabong, a night owl calling. The screech of a possum in the large river gum. He reveled in the afterglow of their love, feeling complete and whole once more.

It was a big move Daisy was making. It proved how brave and fearless she was. He couldn't believe he was lucky enough to have her in his arms. She'd told him how she'd switched her uni degree. It made sense. She'd always shown such interest in what Skylar was doing with her food. It was something she was passionate about. While at the same time, it was a way she could help her culture and stay connected to her people.

"What does your mother think of this? You and me, and I mean," he asked, absentmindedly stroking the sensitive area underneath her wrist.

Daisy made a sound halfway between a snort and a groan. "She's not happy, but she'll come around," she admitted, laying her head on his shoulder. "She doesn't get a choice, anyway. Because you are *my* choice."

"I'm glad you chose me," he said, and she gave him a smile so bright his heart might well have been trying to break out of his chest.

"What about your choice to change your degree and move over here? How did they take that news?" He could well imagine they weren't happy about that, either. And they probably blamed him for their daughter moving all the way across the country. It wasn't a good start. He hadn't met his future parents-in-law, and they probably already hated him.

"Actually, not as bad as you might think. My dad has always trusted me to make my own relationship decisions. It was only my mother who had other plans for me. My father is especially ecstatic about my new pathway. I guess in some way, I can thank my parents for my new vision. They always instilled in me the need to take responsibility for my life, as well as helping others from our community do the same. I watched my father for so many years getting involved in our culture, volunteering his time, helping when he could. I'd go with him every weekend and watch the local Aboriginal AFL team he coached. He could've made a lot more money by coaching one of the state teams—a few of them asked him to come on board—but he chose to work at the grassroots level, where he could be of most help. He was a great role model, but it took me a long while to realize it."

"I can see that in you," Dale said. "Your father should be proud, he's raised a daughter who's strong and undaunted, but who also wants to give back."

It was good that Daisy still maintained her independence. At one stage, he'd entertained the idea of asking her to come back and work at Stormcloud as a station hand. But deep in his gut, he knew that'd never work. She'd come to resent it here. She was the sort of woman who needed to determine her own future.

"Thank you," she replied simply. "It's taken a while for me to come to accept that, for me to stop blaming myself for everything that went wrong with River. But I'm getting there," she admitted. "I still have hopes that one day, when River gets out of jail, we, as a family, can help him sort his life out."

"You're a brilliant sister, and you'll be a wonderful mentor, if he lets you."

"I hope so," she answered quietly, as if she still didn't quite believe it. "What about you? Are you going to stay on the station?" That's right, he had tossed around the idea of leaving the station. He'd been unhappy and unsettled after he returned from Montana, not sure where his path truly lay. And right after Daisy left, he wanted to leave, too. Couldn't face being reminded of them together every time he walked into his bedroom, every time he took guests to the gold mine, every time he walked down to the billabong. But after he'd helped his mother and Steve pick up the pieces and keep the Stormcloud Station's reputation intact, he'd seen things in a different light. He loved it here, this place was in his heart. Even without Daisy, this was where he was meant to be.

He'd take over the running of the station one day, but that was a long way in the future. For now, he was happy to learn alongside Steve and his mother. Help them build this into their dream of being the best eco-resort in the whole of Australia. Because it was his dream, too. And now Daisy was here to share it with him. Life was perfect.

"Yes, I'm staying. I think this would be a great place to bring up kids, don't you?"

"Whoa there, cowboy," she giggled, reaching around and grabbing him by the waist, levering herself into his lap. "Even though I admit we would make beautiful babies together, I'm a long way off having a family, yet."

That didn't matter. The fact that she had even admitted she wanted a family with him was enough.

"But I wouldn't mind if you kissed me again." She captured his mouth, and he pulled her down into the bedclothes with him, lost in a tangle of limbs and hips and mouths.

Life was perfect just the way it was. He had Stormcloud. And he had Daisy. What more could a man want?

Also by Suzanne Cass
NEW
Stargazer Ranch Mystery Romance Series
Combustion: Prequel Novella
Wildfire
Firelight
Snowbound: A Christmas Novella
Snowfall
Cloudburst

Island Bound Series
Books can be read as stand-alone
Bound by Truth
Bound by Silence
Bound by the Stars

Colors of the Earth Series
Books can be read as stand-alone
Shadows in the Dust
Shadows in Deep Blue
Shadows of Red Earth

Romantic Suspense
Single Title
Island Redemption
Glass Clouds
Chasing Bullets

Love in the Mountains Novella Series
Books can be read as stand-alone
Rain on a Tin Roof
Lost and Found
Rescue his Heart

Please Leave a Review
The greatest gift you could ever give an author is to leave a review.

About the Author

Suzanne Cass is an Australian author who writes rural romance and romantic suspense abounding with passion and danger.

Her debut novel, Island Redemption, won the Romance Writers of Australia Emerald Award in 2016. Suzanne was also a finalist in the 2019 Romance Writers of Australia RUBY award.

She had always had a fascination with the tough resilience of people who live in our amazing red-dirt outback country. When not writing about the characters that inhabit her head, Suzanne can be found roaming the Perth beaches with her border collie, or encouraging from the sidelines as her two sons play sport.

Stay in touch via my website

www.suzannecass.com

Or